RETINA BLUES

RANDALL MAC

Cheers Brent —
I hope you finish it —
and enjoy it.

Randall .

Copyright

To the memory of
John Fraser
and
Ron Sutherland

With thanks to Will Vandyck, Andrew Fraser, and Sioned for being Sioned.

One
Cathedral Town

It was raining blue steel. The kind of rain that instantly put him in Cathedral Town. Marble sized globes of tequila tinged condensation depth-charged from the icy pipes and spars that formed the sky 300 floors above. The air tasted thick, wet, and salty. Rich with the sweat of millions. Who take what they need then breathe it back to congeal in the works of stressed out recycle bins, to return to earth as today's summer shower.

He stepped to the side allowing the others to pour from the cab. The pounding of the rain on his head and shoulders competing with the dull ache of last night's whisky. The old woman's oversized bag battling with his leg as she passed. She muttered something inaudible against the background din. Standing still amidst a sea of jostling strangers he pinpointed his location, C.C. Street. Been some weeks since his last visit. The gut reaction was always the same; mouth closed, breathe through your nose, till it didn't taste so bad.

He was pretty close to where he wanted to be. This was as far as the rail cabs would go. Four blocks from the central zone where the core maze used to be. From here he was on foot. Vehicles prohibited by the street sprawl and the accumulated debris and garbage of eighteen million people who nobody or any Company in particular was responsible for, or publicly acknowledged relations with.

He had heard them called denizens of the damned. *If* Cathedral Town was to be graced with any recognition, other than as the sad remnants of failed utopia, the afterbirth of a dream state society, it could still stand tall as the largest community on earth. Disowned by governments, immune to market forces, mocking to the world of inflation and real estate, eighteen million people of multi racial backgrounds from all walks of life lived on top of each other as a single entity. Each shared a common understanding, that at some point they had all chosen to stay.

He reckoned he would find his target just a couple of blocks inside the core. Forty five minutes or so on foot. Pulling up his collar, running wet fingers through his hair he moved off through the anonymous crowd of bedraggled humanity. His contacts adjusted fractionally towards the red as he moved inwards from the traffic. The light being squeezed by the encroaching walls. Like the depths of some vast tropical forest, natural daylight rarely reaching the floor.

'Well.. yuh know..... can't say its good to be back. Though, I am glad to be.. *here*, if you get my meaning.' She spoke slowly. A southern accent without a drawl. Her voice edged with the familiar calmness that he always found so attractive; that complimented her ruthless nature, that gave her that unpredictable edge in tense crucial moments. The question was rhetorical. Of course he understood.

A long pause later she asked   'Is it still so..o damned hot.. still smell like a skunk's ass?'

'Yeah.'

'Least *I* don't need an umbrella. So who is this guy. Another lonely heart?'

'No – hundred per cent dealer. Calls himself Stef. Stef the chef. Considered himself a bit of a mixer, couple of years back. Was in with some serious Companies, including Detroit. Blacker belonged to Detroit. They'll have his download.'

'And Mr chef's gonna get it for us.'

'Yeah.'

'Ain't Detroit gonna get curious?'

'That's why Vortex hired us. Just another private contract. No Company involvement. They won't give it a second glance. Anyway Blacker's long dead and if Stef's half as good as Vortex said he is, Detroit won't even know he's got it.'

'Icy!'

The street scene lessened the further in he went. The chaos of resident Cath's, hawkers and buyers thinning to something almost resembling a crowd. He strode onwards, splashing through the potholed ground cover, plotting as straight a route as possible through the random array of permanent stalls, mostly created from ripped out vehicles long since abandoned. Indifferent to the stares of un-enchanting buskers and hologram images selling the God of your choice.

This outer rim of the core had evolved laisser-faire with unembarrassed displays of excessive hedonistic wealth fused with lowlife existences permanently on the sell, hawking anything and everything associated with their salvation or infliction, depending on how they viewed it. Money exclusively occupied the upper levels where custom built pirate proof domains assimilated entire floors.

He crossed what had once been a pocket park set in the paw of a 270 floor sphinx sculptured from black glass and metal. Entering another narrow street, taller than it was long, the subtle intensification of refracted light from the increasing numbers of illuminated emblems, each advertising their version of the very essence of life itself, confirmed he was approaching the core. Two blocks later he had reached his mark.

'Is this it? Mr chef's abode.'

'Yeah.. the truck,' he replied gesturing unnecessarily towards a red reinforced plastic articulated trailer embodied in the envelope of a nearby building. 'With all that spaghetti on its roof the truck's probably a booster, a private generator feeding off spillage from the maze.'

'How we gonna do it? One in the side, one in the back - like last time?' she said in her easy manner.

He frowned slightly in reply. The humour if intended was a bit close to the bone for his liking. As if she was testing, looking for a small hint of guilt. He knew there was none. What had happened, had happened, and that was that. It could just as easily have been him. But all the same, it bothered him. 'The trailer's got a door, let's go knock on it.'

Stef was playing with himself in a bath of strawberry flavoured vitamin water when the room lights flashed in sequence indicating that someone was within three metres of the trailer. Before he could switch on the monitor that someone was banging on the door.

The man on the screen was tall, rough shaven with short cropped military style light brown hair and looked like he had a largish frame. He wore an oversized heavy raincoat of dull lilac which reached to the top of soft lace up boots. The I.D. link on the monitor flashed - NO TRACE - telling Stef that the man was neither an ex-client nor an enlisted member of any of the main Companies. Stef pressed the intercom 'What can I do you for?'

'I want to buy....' The man spoke slowly leaving the words trailing.

'What *exactly* do you want to buy?'

'Something for the weekend', the man replied holding out a wad of street cred still used in Cathedral Town but worthless elsewhere. 'O'Neil said you were the man to see.'

With a slow heavy clunk, electronically released bolts slipped and the door opened. A reddish looking man wrapped in a toga smelling of something similar to strawberries said 'Better come in then.'

Once inside the bolts slid back into place. He sensed his lenses shift several degrees compensating for the sudden brightness of light. The inside of the trailer was pretty much as he'd expected, consisting mainly of electronic equipment with a small living quarter, and surprisingly, a large old fashioned free standing bath.

'So what can I do you for?' Stef repeated smiling.

'They call me Claymore - I kill people for money. You are Stefano Leo Mumby.'

'Oops,' said a voice in a southern accent that only Claymore could hear. A long silence ensued. Stef's face frozen on the echo of his own name. The man in the long coat spoke again. 'And guess what.........yeah... I came all the way here...to this toxic hole..just..to..visit..*you*.'

'Wha..what do you want.' Again the suffocating silence gripped Stef.

'A life,' said the man, smiling thinly.

'I'm paid up..I paid all of it..last month. I paid it all man..I don't owe nothing! Look check...just check!'

'It doesn't have to be yours.'

'Check with the Slav..just check that's all.....what?' Suddenly aware it was his own voice he was hearing, Stef forced his mind into focus. 'What..how much do you want?'

'Told you. I want a life. A particular life. The life of Chas Blacker.'

'Who's Chas Blacker?'

The man had moved from the door and was now standing side on casually studying a small antique oriental box containing several state of the art translucent discs that lay on a chain hung metal table. The kind of disc capable of containing whole networks or enough knowledge to establish and run a country.

'Icy,' said a silent voice.

'Chas Blacker is dead.. I think.' said the man. 'Dead or not, he is, was, an ex-employee of Detroit. I understand that you are familiar with Detroit.'

'Ah! Your looking for a download!' Stef let out a faintly audible sigh and felt himself relax slightly.

'It's very important that I get it,' said the man, still looking at the discs.

'I'm....not with Detroit...'

The man turned facing him. Stef felt the need to continue '.......anymore.' They don't owe me any favours. They don't trade that kind of stuff..and it... it's not accessible.' He felt himself swallow knowing that the truth was written all over his face. That it was standing right there in front of him.

'Break his legs,' she said silently.

The man put down the box taking his other hand from his pocket. He put a small half moon shaped metal object next to it and ran his palm over its smooth surface. With a hesitant clicking sound it expanded lengthways forming a full flat circle without changing in depth. He touched it again and it opened like an accordion displaying a number of discs similar to those in the oriental box.

'Elixir...state of the Art. Untraceable. Worth more than you'll trade in a year..or so.' The man knew he didn't have to say it, but said it anyway. 'Yours. They said if you played with one you could tell. Feel free.'

Stef said nothing. Glad for the moment; feeling that he might actually have some say in what was happening here. He took the third disc from its slot and placed it into a short range home-veg that probably went little further than the light switch. He then took it out, put it back, and asked if it was appropriate to make a call. To a friend. The man smiled no.

Stef then took it out again and put it into something that seemed to appear from the wall. Hitting a panel the wall lit up. 'Sweet Jesus.. iced up enough to fuck with a battleship.......well a little one.'

'Oh they'll fuck with a big one. If that's what you're good at.'

Stef played with what seemed to be the spectrum and some, his face relaxing the more he did. Eventually, releasing it again he inserted it into what Claymore took to be his main spirit of life, and well.....just beamed. 'Guess they'll do. So who the hell *is* Chas Blacker? Must have been some kind of guy.'

'Had his moments. I need to share them. Can you do it?'

'Where'd you get this? I'd, eh, need to check em properly.'

'You've lost track of the conversation here..Stefano... they're yours, not a payment - a bonus. All you gotta do is....what you do.'

They just sat there for a while.

'Nobody sane rips off Detroit. Do you have any idea wha... what your asking?'

'They'll never know. My acquaintance with Blacker will be short..and unobtrusive. And *absolutely* confidential.'

'And afterwards?'

'Afterwards...nothing. I'm gone. No trace to you. You came recommended. You stay that way.'

'Stef swallowed again. Sat there. Thought about nothing. After a while he said 'Ok. Lets do it!'

*****

Irritation comes in many forms. To some it requires the consistent repetition of some minor personal hatred. To others, the confident undisputable assertion of a particularly disagreeable point of view. To the fat man in the undersized expensive suit, it was simply - people. That is.. everybody and anybody.

'Look at me again and my friend here will sit on your face,' he porked at the fifteen year old kid.

'You little fuck,' added his similarly dressed even fatter friend, bitterly twisting his lips, like he was talking to someone who had just killed his entire family.

The kid called Yoyo sat squashed between them in the packed train cab like an undernourished sausage in a giant bun. For most of the journey he'd been immune to his surroundings. His head lost to whatever virtual world his Zoneboy had taken him. The alarm tightener in the belt of his khaki jeans set to silently alert him to his arrival at Cathedral Town stop 168. He considered *his* time to be unequivocally valuable. Ten hour shifts on the dead meat farm forcing 8 oz burgers into 7.5 oz. boxes for the next guy on the line to do whatever was required of the next guy on the line, had punched the message home.

Yet - the stranger's words audible over his head set, spoken at point blank range, the hot breath and hint of spit at his ear, the incomprehensible mean intent of whatever was happening... this however, definitely demanded his *real time* attention.

He glanced sideways in each direction taking in the sheer bulk of the grossly fat men double parked on either side of him. Their words repeating themselves in disbelief in his head. He could only reason that his head movements must have reflected the content of his programme, giving the appearance of loitering in the fat man's direction. Scary.. but ridiculous. They must have known that he was blind to them when packin'.

He looked around the overloaded cab. No-one else had noticed or was paying any interest. The moment lingered before he realised that his middle finger pointing straight in the air, had on his behalf, given the only reasonable reply under the circumstances.

He switched his Zoneboy back on. He felt the fat man who had first spoken slide his arm gently around his shoulder and heard him whisper in his ear.

'Cathedral Town 168 terminus stop' recited the rail cab. The doors slid open and the passengers shuffled their way into the rain. They closed again when the motion detectors registered the last one had exited. The cab lay silent. It had twenty minutes to recharge before its return journey. It was empty now, save for a youth dressed in khaki trousers, a hushed, comfortable peaceful expression on his sleeping face, his neck broken.

*****

Three hours passed. Little had been said, Stef intent on the shifting patterns of the wall. Focusing in on threads, enlarging them, refocusing. Weaving a delicate tactical trail on the edge of each new spectrum created. He'd used one of his own discs, opting for their tested security. The singularly simple penalty claimed by Detroit on hackers, especially ex-employees, all too clear in his head.

Eventually the colours passed, replaced by columns of codes. Each was represented by a series of geometric patterns requiring definition before the code themselves could be challenged. Stef smiled and relaxed almost completely. He'd been here before. The patterns were different now as most probably were the codes but the principles were the same. To any outsider good enough, even with enough weight of ice to get this far, there was no where else to go. An infinite wall of shifting geometry. Stef locked a second disc and engaged the geometry with a translucent overlay of random colour which seemed to hover for an instant before imitating the shape of the forms below. Slowly the colours changed to a straight spectrum of orange and yellows forming irregular blocks. Ripples of light giving the impression of an overall pinkish tint. With all the grace and passion of a sinking passenger liner the colour vanished beneath the pink glow, which itself then shrank darkening to red enveloping a singular geometric shape below. 'Bingo,' grinned Stef. 'No matter how many times they change its form - Detroit's ice always recognises itself.'

'How much longer?' asked the man.

'Almost in. I've defined the main arterial route from a few billion mimics...now I just.....superimpose and relax its code. These are individually iced up hard enough to get lost forever in the same thoughts that I'm introducing now,' - *FREEDOM* - the wall flashed. 'Ok, lets find your Blacker!'

Stef was talking freely, feeling good. 'We're invisible for now. Where do you want Blacker?'

Claymore took out a small metallic disc from his pocket and tossed it to him. It was of simple format capable only of straight copying and downloading. Stef ran it through his own lie detector checking that there was nothing to leave with Detroit linking it to him, or messing with anything he didn't know about. He then loaded, started to download Chas Blacker, and sat back.

'So what do you want with our friend here?' said Stef with a new confidence edged with cheek.

The man remained silent.

'Once he's in, could tox him up a bit for you? Free like. Got some real good gear. Can negate anything you didn't like about the geezer. Stick in some bonus script. Got a whole library here. Replace some of those nasty irritating little habits with some real delights.. conversation stoppers,' Stef said, smiling slightly wickedly.

'That what you did for Detroit?' asked the man.

'Ask him about memory depth enhancement. Can they do it straight from a construct?' she said with an easy inquisitive tone.

'For Detroit.. sure, sometimes. They used basic root reproduction programmes for their military. Virgin clones. Uploading minimalist mood free nodal prog's with a content capability of specific function limitation. Below legally recognised sentient life levels. Real scary mothers if you ever happen to meet one. Eat, sleep and perform. Don't last long though as can't programme the root survival instinct which lies in impenetrable parts of the subconscious. Real fast in terms of reaction time but always get killed doing something basically stupid or get confused and start blowing away their own team. Tricky stuff and way *not* cost effective. That was Detroit ..recently though. Private jobs. The old and rich with their personal favourites trotting by their sides. That is young, tanned, gorgeous, happy and..obedient little favourites. Personal fads too. You don't want to be paranoid about being paranoid. Wipe it. No difference from a standard nose job really. Feeling timid..hey, just add a little bit of this guy or that guy. Your friends will be impressed and you get what you want. What you deserve for a change. And if you don't like it....take it back out. Yeah there's definitely a market. Some real works of art walking around out there thanks to Stef the chef.'

'What about memory depth enhancement from a construct?' said the man.

'The memory can be sharpened, or programme aided enhanced making assumptions but won't be hundred per cent real, not from a construct. Detailed memories are stored too deep in the subconscious to enable a clear download in the first place and with a construct you got nothing extra to work from. Can't go deeper, probe laterally or provoke stronger images. The construct is all that's left. That what you want for your man?'

'Nope, just the original slate.'

'I still think we should break his legs,' she said softly.

'All done, ready to go,' said Stef holding the disc in his outstretched hand.

'I don't need to talk with Blacker or to interact with him in any way. He doesn't have to know that I, or he exist.'

'Ah .. you want to wear him,' smiled Stef slowly nodding.

'I don't want the man, just who he was.'

'Sure, that can be fixed. But you know that you wont be able to upload to D.N.A.'

'But I *will* be able to use it in the *maze*, right?' replied the man with a harder emphasis.

'Sure, in the maze you'll *be Blacker*. Real life version of the icons they used in virtual reality set-ups in the last century.'

'Icy. Be glad to leave. Authenticia assholes,' she hissed. 'Ask him what's so wrong with flesh. Ask him why he stayed.....what's so fuck'n' great about Cathedral Town anyway.'

Stef handed him the finished disc.

'Ask him..then break his fuck'n' legs.'

'Guess Cathedral Town's the place to be for business then,' said the man, concluding both conversations as he picked up the half moon disc container, placing the discs on the table and turning the box over in his hand.

'It's the place to be full stop,' enthused Stef. 'Cathedral Town, affectionately known as Cath's to residents; synonymous with *anything you desire* syndrome. The guaranteed good life up for grabs to everyone and anyone. All you need is a little bit of cash and the will to believe. In return you can live out the life of your dreams.'

'Bullshit! Was the government's answer to society being eaten from the inside by the *abuse* of Authenticia. Yesterday's promise...today's goddam apology,' she hissed.

'Ok...' said Stef as if he had heard.   'Authenticia created its own problems. So it screwed up family life and got itself nicknamed doomsday drug. Natural progression if you ask me. Extended family replaced by nuclear family replaced by Authenticia family. Could choose *who* the hell you wanted to live with for a change,' he said laughing. Now we have an autonomous city state around what was the nucleus of Authenticia technology, influence, and all the wealth that spun from it. Ok... so the government dumped on us - but this is *still* where it's *at*. This... is the one place on the planet that *anything* can be bought. And the price...none of this money up front shit.' Rarely monetary. Good old fashioned barter. Here.. *buyers themselves* can be bought and.....it's here Companies do the *real* business. If you ask me...every new idea worth a damn comes outa Cathedral Town.'

While Stef rattled on the man ran his thumbprint over the bottom of the smooth casing releasing a lower section which rotated outwards from itself. He inserted the disc and let the case virus checker do its thing. When the blue pulse indicated it was clean he removed the anti remote security band, which looked like a 20th century watch, from his wrist. He partially slid a thin flexible glass plate the width of his thumb nail from the side of the case and placed it over the sensor spot beneath the band. The case glowed stating that it was talking directly to the chip lodged in the neuro channels of his brain. Again he ran his thumbprint over the case.

Stef had stopped talking. Just sat there smiling. 'How's that?'

Claymore felt nothing, which in itself felt strange. He knew that he now held the entire life.. memories, visions real and imaginary, mannerisms, beliefs, likes and dislikes, love, hates, fragments of bleached dreams, fantasies, lies, unspoken truths and.. fears of another human being. Every detail of every remembered part. Even his death.

Stef watched him leave on the monitor while slipping his new spoils into the safe slot which emerged from the trailers roof. Later he'd corrupt them to read like regular discs to anyone with a casual interest. He switched on the hot plate fixed beneath the bath and started scheming. *These*.. he thought smiling, would renew the badly needed edge back into his life.

Outside of the air conditioned trailer the air tasted as sweet as it had four hours earlier. Leaving the street a couple of blocks later Claymore emerged into Plaza St Mandela, once the envy of café societies throughout the world. Designed to re-enact the passion of the bullring. Multi-tiered levels thirty floors high of open verandas set in a circle three hundred metres across, enabling users to view the entire Plaza and the spectacle below. Five fountains each created twenty metre three dimensional coloured graphic reconstructions of past masters. The walls of the highest floors dressed in downward angled mirror encased the setting in an iridescent glow, claimed by Cath's to be visible from the moon.

Many of the sprawling tables and bastardised remnants of multicoloured canopies were still there, but most of the upper galleries appeared unused or had been enclosed to form shelters. The legendary unhurried atmosphere below replaced by new images akin to a medieval army at camp the night before battle. Groups of excited buyers and residents exchanging laughs and stories amidst discussions around more serious matters. Bonfires and barbecues being lit beneath temporary tents and tarpaulins in preparation for evening barter. Boxes and crates of just about every thing illegal in the outside world being hurriedly opened. A collage of living obituaries for those who get off on second hand dreams. Old heads for sale, exchanged, copied or upgraded to suit all tastes. Some pleasant, some not so. Portable holo-ad systems being set up and tested. No major deals would take place here however. Plaza St Mandela was still for the tourist. The real business took place away from competitive eyes, accessed by invitation or appointment through the hive of clubs run by local colours.

He sat in one of the few remaining cafés. Ran his finger down the menu scanner built into the bar and ordered a straight whisky. The entire café, tables, stools, were carved from a huge singular piece of dark coloured substance, soft and metallic in texture. It appeared to move from intense shadow through a spectrum of colour. Hints of yellows, blues and greens. Living off the brightness of its environment. On close inspection it resembled an oil slick caught by the sun. Above the entrance steps where a name would be expected a sign flashed 'SIT'.

'You're not in a hurry to leave then?' she asked.

'Might as well eat. See if there's anything worth picking up in the night market,' he thought in response as a waiter appeared with his drink.

'Bourbon.... always preferred the smell to the taste,' she said.

Looking down into the glass he remembered those thin lips, her coy dry smile, the same each time she said it. A hundred times in the past. Usually just before she drank enough to make any sane person vomit at the thought. He saw her image. Slim, slender bone structure, proud cheekbones, with short pure blonde hair. Hint of curls. Picture of innocence - except for the word BITCH cut roughly with a blade down the right hand side of her face, interwoven with a delicate vertical line of Celtic script; and the hard lines around her eyes.

He remembered the way she used to tip her glass slightly, roll it, floating it under her nose before downing the first. Seemed like another lifetime. A window to the past. Not something current ..real ..now. Like nothing had changed. Frozen like nothing ever changed. He snapped back in. It'd change soon alright. He'd sort it second this job was done. *Everyone...* would get it back together.. as best as could be expected. He'd be alone again with the living. Call it obligation. Was more than that - but screw it! Just let it run its course. 'I'll drink one for you,' he said downing the short fat glass.

'Just get me to Vortex. I'll drink for myself! she snapped at him with pace. He caught the waiters glance. Ordered a straight shot anyway and began vacantly scanning the Plaza, kindling thoughts of food.

'You see...what I see?' she said drawing the words out.

He focused on his line of vision. 'Where?'

'Beside the balloons...the lemon balloons.'

Then he saw it. Back of a bald head way bigger than most, sprouting from what must be a huge frame behind the food stall canopy which concealed it. And another....face, caught through the shifting heave of the crowd, obesely blotched, swollen like a mutated overripe orange, about to burst as it shoved something edible into its hole. Small red pig like eyes. Staring straight at him.

'Get around ..don't they,' she whispered.

'Coincidence?'

'If not.....they must have been on the cab. Check it.'

She switched focus and re-ran her memory of the cab journey. Looking into the spaces between and around his vision span, as only a construct can do. 'Nothing.' She concentrated on those getting on and off, just out of his normal angle of vision. 'Definitely not in our cab. Could have been in the next carriage.' She retracted again watching the heads and silhouettes appear as it curved around bends in the road. No sign. Lastly she sharpened his peripheral vision as he had turned to pinpoint his location in C.C. Street, taking in all three carriages. Saw the last of the passengers dispersing into the crowd till the cab was empty. The only person remaining was a sleeping youth wearing khaki trousers, engrossed in a cheap head set. 'Negative...but they're sure as hell here.'

The face stopped chewing, mouth still open; slapped his other half on the shoulder and together began to plod heavily towards the café. People seemed to instinctively make way for the advancing wall of fat.

'Well ain't that a pretty sight,' she said in a tone of amused disgust. 'God help the mother who raised *them*.'

'There not brothers. The bigger one's cloned. Construct ..downloaded from the other. The smaller one's got a name and a serious paranoia disorder. Convinced himself that the world hated him cause he was the ugliest thing on two legs. So.. got himself cloned, but had it doctored to be bigger, more repulsive and stupider than he is.'

'Guess he feels sexy just hav'n it around.'

'Yeah ..and they're both psychotic.'

They were standing in front of him, blocking out the light. Grinning.. sort of. 'Made us then. Huh,' rasped the smaller.

'Not that we didn't want you to,' added the larger.

'Don't matter,' continued the smaller.

Claymore sat unmoved through the short silence which followed until the smaller said 'SO!!...'

'So what.' Claymore replied.

'So your after our mark ....again!'

'Your mark', he laughed gently and heard her breathe.. 'the big boy's fingering something heavy in his pocket, and I don't think it's his dick.' Claymore lent as far back as the stool would allow increasing his sphere of vision of the two. His right hand in his coat pocket, his left hand lying flat on the bar.

The larger read the gesture and grinned more openly, enjoying the exchange.

'Vortex gave it to us,' said the smaller, red eyes peering down at him.

'So why bother me?' replied Claymore.

'Cause..he gave you a little extra ..Huh,' looking towards the larger who removed his hand from his pocket.

Claymore closed his hands into a loose fist. His pocketed right hand empty. The sensor pads in the fingers of his left activating the sonic dealer located in the plate beneath the skin of his palm. No need to point. His utterance of the command would burst every blood vessel, blow apart every head within ten metres. Except his of course. The toners in his chip saw to that. Too bad though for the couple at the next table. Which was why being caught in possession carried a mandatory five years.

'But what could you want with a dead Blacker?' continued the smaller, his twin having produced a bottle of strawberry mineral water from his pocket.

'Icy.'

'As always,' he continued,   'Vortex has his own game plan. Has his own team on it too. Gives you a little..us a little...spreads his bets. If *they* get to her first - nobody gets paid. Thought you might like to share.'

'Oh you mean like ..*last time!'* her voice floated across his retina. He knew the anger was there though absent from her tone. He looked back at the fat man. Directly into his eyes. Saw him standing there in the flamenco club, saturated in his own sweat. The sickest look he'd ever seen on a man's face. Smug satisfaction where there should have been at least some shared understanding if not remorse. He had thought about shooting him right there but the gun in his hand was empty. The gun which he had just emptied into the face of Savannah - the woman who's life he now carried in his head.

He'd had a bad feeling about that day ever since. Agreeing to her as a partner had been stupid. Sleeping with her even stupider. She was both smart and attractive but her logic had a bitter surreal twist to it. Ruthless with a smile. Like her face. He'd asked about the blade marks once. Self inflicted, she'd said. A message that read *if she did that to herself what wouldn't she do to me!* Partners and getting involved were two things he just never did.

They had entered the club separately on his suggestion. One in the front and one through the side. The deal was simple. Straight trade. Vortex's credits were good, and he knew the goods were clean. Should have been straight in and out. He'd approached the bar where a pony tailed Latino youth sat surrounded by twelve or so fellow gang members. All were dressed in redundant military electronic camouflage web. Thousands of tiny individual discs capable of re-creating their exact environment as they moved through it rendering   them   technically   invisible.   The   gangs reprogrammed and used them to wear their colours. Claymore had identified them by the flowing orange and yellow stripes which had once been the national flag of Catalonia.

It was strictly Claymore's deal. The fat men were already there as agreed. They were backup, that was all. Nothing was required of them, just a presence. Crossing the floor he instructed his chip to cut out all background noise focusing on low voices and whispers. The passion of the flamenco guitarist and mono tone of the vocalist vanished. His head filled with the sounds of conversations, but somehow couldn't expel the rhythmic tapping of the dancer's shoes as she stomped out a Soleares. A single thought - *you carry flamenco in your soul* - flashed in his head. He'd once heard that said of the 'duende'; how the gypsy clans touched their audience. But then he didn't know what duende was. Must be remnants of some historic sentient interface with the chip geared at making it more efficient.

He shook with the leader. Handed his case in exchange for a thin Perspex wallet which he inserted into the mother holder provided by Vortex. Acknowledged the reading and walked away. Three steps later his head erupted with noise. Turning, he saw the dual coloured coats of the gang members replaced by flashing graphically explicit obscenities, and heard the unmistakable giggles of the fat men. Saw the scrambler in the smaller one's left hand, a large hand cannon in his other. The bigger one's hands were also full. The seconds froze as the gang punched digits trying to switch their humiliation off. Then someone saw the fat man's scrambler held high, gun pointing at the floor. Then everyone was shooting at everyone else. He'd emptied all but a few of his own rounds when he realised that no-one save the fat men, Savannah and himself were left standing. The sight of the destroyed bar and entangled bloodied bodies not marrying sensibly with the enforced silence in his head. Then boomed the crack of some private joke amidst more giggles.

The silence stood till a gang member, slumped motionless over a table, lunged himself behind Savannah firing once into the small of her back as his forearm around her throat pulled her into him as a shield. His machine pistol lifting from beneath her arm erupting at Claymore.

Instinctively he had raised his gun, sighted at the youth's head and squeezed. The angle had been tight with only an inch or so of his head visible behind hers. The shot had been good, counter balancing the sideward kick of the gun by a shift of weight in his wrist. The youth's volley impacted in his thigh - Claymore's heavy calibre shell passed through her eye tearing at the side of her scalp before lodging itself in the centre of the youths head, detonating and lifting them both off their feet.

She had lived long enough to make the hospital run and through most of the night. Time of her death officially recorded as 6.43 a.m. Saturday June 21 2097. In her few moments of consciousness he had agreed. Almost without hesitation. An obligation written as a gentleman's oath. A last right of partnership cast in penitence. A call from Vortex was all it took. The hospital psi bank did the rest.

Vortex had laughed. Having worked with Claymore for years he well knew his views on partnerships. That he had never had nor needed one. Now this. Vortex instructed the hospital to download her persona into Claymore's chip, and told her that he would fund uploading it later to a new D.N.A. cloned Savannah.

For Savannah, there was however a price. She had Claymore's agreement to carry her, but Vortex's agreement was dependent on her being carried until at least the next job was complete. When Claymore had asked him why, he'd laughed and said 'She's a pro... two pro's for the price of one.' They both knew that to be bull, and that carrying her one second longer than was absolutely necessary would most definitely be resented by Claymore. Vortex, he guessed, had embarked on one of the favourite games of those bored with absolute power, a game of no real consequence other than fulfilling his personal amusement at pissing someone else off.

Now, as he sat in a café in Plaza St Mandela, with the same fat man standing in front of him, offering him the same deal, with *her* laced remarks constantly fuck'n' with his head, he realised that in fact that was exactly how he felt. Truly pissed off.

'So.. wanna share a little ..Huh?' repeated the smaller.

'Thanks.. but no thanks.. had my share of *sharing* lately.'

'Well that's just too bad. Don't be steppin' on our toes then ..Huh.'

'You won't like it if we step on yours,' added the larger turning slowly to follow his partner through the stalls.

Claymore sat for a while before ordering another straight shot for the road. The appeal of food and the night market had passed.

An hour later he weaved his way back through alleys and streets the likes of every other in Cathedral Town. It was now, as darkness fell and the shadows consumed the ground that he clearly saw the resemblance. Like walking through a colossal cathedral of dark, gloomy, narrow aisles and neon stained glass walls. The criss cross struts and spars high above, once used for entrapping holo images to rival the stars, forming their own version of the decorative fan vaults typical of any 14th century masterpiece. And yet every bit the epitaph to a bygone age.

He had never much taken to the hyped lure of Authenticia, or the psi-tech which evolved from it. Preferring the secure truth of the real thing. One life...to be lived here and now. But as he passed through the stalls to the chants of the hawkers, the voice of Savannah and dormant living memories of another embedded in his head, the words of Luke echoed from his youth ...'the Lord entered the temple and threw out the sellers and buyers saying .. "you have made my house a den of thieves." He could feel it - Cathedral Town - its purpose, mood, its sense of place, much more than was inherent in the cold metal and glass of its architecture - a pulse deep beyond the shrivelled facade, a presence akin to the very substance of religion itself.

Like it or not, he was part of it. No longer just passing through. Employed by those who owned and had built empires from it. Dependent upon it to do his job. So what! He had got what he came for. To get paid all he had to do was use it - to find the woman called *Sands*.

Two
Ice on the battlefield

Pain.. pain.. pain.. subtle, cold....numbing, intoxicating her senses.. demanding her full attention.. her system shocked into impenetrable blackness... eyes shut.. open.. can't tell... can't feel where it hurts.. head pounding with thunder....resounding truth.. way deeper than deep sh...

Images adrift in a black eternal void, her mind desperately competing, pulsing where there should be physical agony, reaching out to test the pain, protecting her, casting shadows, distractions....a girl child.. green overalls decorated with pretty hand drawn flowers spelling out her name *S A N D S*... large darkly dressed men... smart bars living amidst riveted steel plates.. the smell of burnt custard... oversized bunches of noisy metal keys... a woman, her mother.. smiling.. and a boy.. older, twice her height.. happy times...

More recent memories, clearer, chip enhanced eighty per cent recall... Faro, her Lieutenant, friend, occasional lover, shirt off and grinning drunkenly at a Tapas girl trying to pick up a live frog with her lips to keep the rest of her clothes on....

Her, Sands MX 2645, lined up with Sloth, Kimmo, Gastro, like on parade, but matt grey combat jackets open, T-shirts below, handguns visible, tucked in short holsters to the left and right.. stone faced in front of twenty or so *filth elite*, scavenge unit of deserters, mercenaries, ex-dealers with nowhere left to hide.. telling them 'let her go', *her* being Vasos their comrade at knife point against the bar.. a sea of faces laughing back at them, exaggerated hand movements saying 'get lost'.. swift flick of a blade by Kimmo.. one dying elite.. click of anti mother "F" compact flame units dropped from beneath Sloth and Gastro's jackets.. no talk.. knife released.. Vasos walking out... Sands feeling good..

Shock wave.. bursting through, devouring the other images.. one hundred per cent recall, no chip enhancement.. *a three minute old memory*.. the sound of his combat jacket imploding.. Faro's hazel coloured dead eyes staring down at her ripped body.. her eyes following his stare.. below her knees - gone.. most of her right side - gone.. left hand, lower arm fused with her jacket.. laser wound to her chest.. alive.. not for long.

Sensation of splashing light... silent movement sweeping over, through her... burning behind her retina.. black fading to grey, graduated.. lines.. squares.. colder still.. cold as ancient ice... brittle noise.. blue glare.. blue without colour..

*****

The Star Buster had strangled its engines pulling its massive bulk to a halt above the event co-ordinate and announced itself as her saviour with seconds to spare. Decades too late for most of the unit. The event itself was pretty much over before it started. A verbal fracas between two junior communications officers on opposing sides. Rumoured to be over which Company had the best zero tolerance air strike support. Unknown to them, neither Company had any available, leaving the ground troops involved exposed to artillery units loosing strife shells and ricocheting laser fire off low altitude hard light projections. Both units were virtually wiped out in the exchange.

Four weeks later, she rested aboard the medical cruiser HONEY WAGON. They had reconnected her neural chip earlier that morning, having checked it for damage, or infestation from exposure to virus beacons during the event. She activated the memory enhancer, at first focusing further back to familiar memories to regain the feel of it. She moved forward and thought of the event. Her last true memory, chip enhanced, threw itself at her..Faro's bemused gaze..her smoking congealed – mess. Her mind recoiled in shock, then slowly, matching the rhythm of her heavy breathing deliberately risked a second look. By the time she stared for the sixth time she began to accept that she was looking at herself. Suddenly it felt real good to be alive.

What she saw next was accompanied by an odd sense of anxious curiosity. Her mind was vacant but the chip had remained active, recording the event through the limited aperture of her open fixed unconscious eyes. She watched as if viewing a scene from an old film or sharing someone else's chip projected experience. Shadow engulfed her plane of vision as the gigantic bulk of a ship blotted out the morning sky turning day into night. The chip introduced an element of infra-red. The ships bays opened spilling life preserving beams of heavy light across those whose mortality readings registered *dim* or *erratic* but *alive*. She felt her own memory gratefully acknowledge the penetrating cold defending her from death amidst a confusing palette of colour. Witnessed backup drones drift deftly down. Physically winced as drones moving amongst the dead and frozen living, snapped off entangled brittle limbs as the light retracted and gravity beams hauled in their catch...all while the mother ships guns roared in silent fury.

For the past few weeks she had been kept in a sedated state of dreamless hibernation. The regrowth process, set in motion immediately on her delivery to Honey Wagon had by now began to form recognisable shapes. On awakening, the nurse had informed her of the progress. A soothing voice. The strong suggestion of a smiling unconcerned face. Unasked questions answered through the darkness. Paralysis. Blindness. Inability to utter the slightest sound. Again the reassuring presence saying that this was intentional and necessary for the time being. Explaining, as if he could hear her scream '..*then why wake me..?*' that the medication dulling her consciousness would react disagreeably with the next stage in the process. That for this stage she would spend her time crossed over to a grade A leisure programme compliments of the Company. To consider it as a paid vacation at the end of which she would awaken looking every bit as good as before. Rested. Feeling brand new. He then said 'Oh about five to seven months.' She imagined the pressure of a hand on her shoulder as he added 'You are very lucky to be alive...and to belong to Company Vortex.'

They of course were absolutely right. The next six months had proven an enjoyable rest. She wasn't restricted to a Company programme as she had expected but was enabled full access across the Authenticia system. Once engaged, she got the answers to every question she had been dying to ask. Took up scuba diving and underwater studies. Made some new acquaintances. Time passed. For a rare interlude in her life she found plenty of time to think. She was also kept fully informed on each stage of her healing process, but with each update came the same vision. *Her bruised torso suspended in slow spin vacuum, battered and burnt by neutronic lasers actively bastardising each newly formed cell. Sculpting her new cellular structure to the desired pattern. The ultimate pastiche work of art.* And with each vision came an unbearable itch to move in flesh and blood again.

Her hunger for life, and too much time, forced her to look at herself anew. They had told her that there had been few survivors. That many of those who had were also under repair. Faro, they said to her amazement and delight was still alive. Snatched unconscious, seconds after his final heart beat. His brain had however suffered a degree of irreparable damage from oxygen starvation during the long seconds between his body death and the arrival of the ship. The degree of damage was as yet unknown.

If his life could be salvaged and his body repaired the Company would endeavour to do it. She knew this to be true. It was the honouring of this level of responsibility evident in previous Company actions that ensured a similar degree of loyalty, sometimes fanaticism to the Company from many troops. What aggrieved her was the price. Arguably, *any* price for stealing a trooper from death and reconstructing them to a perfect state could be regarded as reasonable. The Company therefore considered their deal to be particularly generous. Her repair would cost her a seven year tour. One year's tour for each required months regrowth from injuries sustained through combat in pursuit of Company interests. The tour was on full pay and standard conditions. For those already signed up for another seven years or more, regrowth would in effect be free. For others it simply meant more of the same. For the Company it ensured both loyalty, and, as legally they were Company property until the tour was up, a continued source of experienced troops.

She had already been Company assigned for nine years. Currently in the fourth year of a second five year contract. She had however recently decided that enough was enough. That at the end of her remaining ten months she would look elsewhere for a means to pay the rent. It was the LoTech incident the previous spring which had forged the decision.

*****

LoTech was a Mars colony thirty years in the making. It was originally established as a religious retreat located beyond the outmost edge of the colony string. Funded by a consortium of Companies of which Company Vortex was a minor player, its goal was advertised as the pursuit of the unification of all religious orders by provision of a haven for those who wished to repent the failures of mankind and start afresh. The true, and hidden agenda, earmarked LoTech as a stepping stone to large scale terraformation of Mars. Shares in, and responsibility for a colony, no matter how small, opened doors for legal rights of ownership of vast areas of the planet.

As the years passed, the long term nature of the investment, the uncertainty of direction, and other more pressing in house Company concerns drove all but Company Vortex and the pilgrims themselves to lose interest. Over thirty years Vortex established full ownership of what became known as LoTech Zone. The original colony had grown to relatively vast proportions and acquired city status. In total there were some seventy four colonies on the planet. Of these, seventy one were little more than encampments, directly associated with mineral extraction or high risk military tests. The other two were religious spin offs from LoTech. The city in contrast had amassed vast areas of belt zone equating to almost the size of earth. Within these, development other than that sanctioned by *Vortex Mars* was prevented.

COMMITMENT ONE on Vortex Mars People's Charter was the guarantee of 'A POLLUTION FREE LIFE'. This backed by the promise of continued financial injection drew colonists by the hundred thousand. For several years the Company recouped most of its investment from transportation fees, over which it had monopoly, and new citizenship fees, which the Company openly admitted were outrageously expensive but when compared to the opportunity to start afresh were negligible.

The city bubbles grew in number and size spreading across the red desert like some monstrous organic growth. Grand natural valleys were enclosed, customised climates created; alpine valleys, fjords, tropical rainforests. Sporadic bubbles expanded horizontally and joined the main flow. Then the spaces between began to fill. Soon for a thousand miles in every direction the red landscape was in the minority. An expanse of broad highways lead from pockets of giant commercial buildings designed as crudely elegant mountains of sand blasted red rock and etched glass as a mark of respect to their host environment, mingling with green flowing parks, townships and cropped fields interrupted by crystal clear rivers. LoTech was no longer a risk environment for the disillusioned and desperate but an idyllic land of plenty, free from pollution, overcrowding, crime, and the petty Company wars or events, which plagued Earth. Vortex had his gold mine. The problems came when he tried to mine it.

The city's sprawl had become organised. New voices emerged gathering support and strength, questioning the power and wealth of Company Vortex. Local business groups had acquired influence in the city, and established wealth from mining interests and deals with Vortex adversaries beyond the belt zone. The seeds for future rival Companies were being sown. They challenged the legal rights of ownership of areas of the belt zone close to the city; stirred moral debate as to the right of ownership of the air that people needed just to live. They provoked a general atmosphere of social discontent. All this of course amounted to little less than a slight irritation to the absolute power of Company Vortex.

Over time however, through persistent networking and manipulation of the media the message began to take hold. Suddenly, as if overnight, it was no longer greedy business and spin off militant groups who were leading the march. The populace themselves were clearly no longer satisfied with their recently found sanctuary. They expressed resentment to the restrictions imposed by the Vortex monopoly and to the huge scale of its expansion plan. They had come to regard the LoTech belt as belonging to them. They objected to their inability to benefit directly from the vast wealth its development would surely create; began to crave the power to shape their own existence, to carve their name in heritage. A new generation had arrived. A generation which demanded *independence*.

Vortex representatives were expelled from the city, their ships were declined landing paths and the legality of claims to land ownership and assets within the belt aggressively challenged. Through the aid of hungry competitors a military network was swiftly established. Defence grids were assembled, and everything which could fly or be built within the nine months period of talks was armed to the hilt. The LoTech knew that alone their cause would be fruitless. Their real hope lay in the promises of allied Companies with ready-made fleets and long standing conflict of interests with Vortex. Promises which proved short lived and paper thin.

The full extent of Vortex conviction became apparent when its fleet assembled off Orion's Belt. Three battleships and twelve cruisers formed the core surrounded by an array of troop carriers and specialist ships. Their flanks enclosed by over sixty destroyers. In rising to the challenge Company Vortex had not only increased the size of its own military fleet, by the armament of commercial liners for use as troop carriers, but had rented several smaller fleets. Some of whom had publicly sworn to stand by LoTech. Two hundred and fifty ships in all stood at ease. Twice the size of the fleet of the LoTech alliance. The alliance also missed the presence of their main space defence, three pocket battleships promised by Company Senate, Company Vortex's main adversary. It was suggested by some that these were withheld in exchange for Vortex agreement to non-intervention in Company Senate's ocean reclamation programme. Time would reveal this not only to be true, but that the ships, dry docked throughout the event, had in fact been in no state for combat at the time of their assignment to the LoTech force. By the time the fleet reached Mars its opposition had shrunk to a few die hard fanatics, mainly of religious cults honouring oaths to the original generation of settlers.

The LoTech event which followed was short and brutal. Sands was in the second wave of attack ships to slice through the defence grids and roll directly over the city itself. She saw little strapped in deploy position within row on row of 500 fellow marines, but heard the flight lieutenant remark on air that the bubbles popped like plastic toys. She knew that when a bubble ruptured, anyone inside who was not suited up would suffer an excruciating death in the low gravity atmosphere. On the green light she tumbled from a hatch, her personal grav unit kicking in, slowing her to a fast controlled pace, which would jolt to a cushioned halt as she approached the ground, her hard light defence shield vanishing below her feet the second of impact.

Their brief was to segregate and secure a sector of the city. Other units had the same brief for other sectors. Once the city was secure the sector containing the command centre would be split into smaller sectors and taken. The aim was to win decisively with minimum damage to Vortex's thirty year investment.

Vortex relied almost entirely on the success of his ground troops. His warships, capable of inflicting serious damage to his investment kept at safe distance. The fighting was fierce; the LoTechs heavily armed and penned in. They had superiority of numbers but against well organised professional troops stood no chance.

Where the opposition was heaviest *ghetto blasters* were deployed. Effectively, a compact and not too stable version of a star-ship engine, driven hard by programmed armoured carriers into the centre of the hot spot. Once activated, gravity waves bulged outwards until trapped and squeezed by an enclosing wall of light, the resultant force pulling, pushing, tearing apart everything in its dense chaotic reach. Reducing buildings to rubble and dust within minutes. Of the carriers themselves nothing remained. The troops then moved rapidly through the levelled streets hitting the next sector before it could organise.

She was in the fourth sector. One of the more densely populated commercial quadrants. Here they expected the fighting to be hand to hand. Too much expensive infrastructure to simply blow away. She and Kimmo were crouched behind a burning public transit train when the Sergeant barked the order to pull back. Within minutes all units had retreated to the periphery coordinate and the area of bubble sealed. The ground shook and the remaining bubble structure overhead creaked as the heavy destroyer slowly displaced the sky. Six ghetto blasters trundled past.

She exchanged puzzled glances with Faro milliseconds before the destroyers guns dominated everything.

Sector 4 had been confirmed as LoTech central command. For thirty minutes the destroyer's guns spat death amongst the carnage being reaped by the ghetto blasters. On leaving four weeks later, she saw from the air that an area of two kilometres diameter had been levelled. Three hundred floor high buildings packed together, interconnected on many levels, densely built to maximise expensive air space of the largest bubble span of the city - erased along with everyone in them. Erased to end an event that was already over - to make a point. Never to be forgotten. The entire incident left a bitter taste. She knew little of the reasons behind the event nor whether the Company's cause was just or not. In previous events facing other Company forces, following orders had always been enough. In the weeks which followed, policing the shattered remnants of the city, watching LoTech citizens reseal their environment, repair the structure that had filled them with pride enough to excite them to war, the full impact of what had taken place, of what they, she, had done, was all too clear. The reality of the Company lesson was there in every face, behind the fearful eyes of children staring at the suited up aliens, prisoners in their own land.

*****

Slipping on her inner body armour, she matched his stare with narrow focused smoky blue eyes. His facial posture, the piercing depth of his look, never faltered. A look that registered ownership. That said 'I can do anything I please with you.. to you'. But a look which also disclosed a great deal of interest, almost as if demanding something more. With their eyes locked, she continued dressing until fully dressed, then stood to attention.

Her tunic bore no insignia, was dark blue, free flowing with matching straight legged boot length trousers. The off-tour boots bore the feel and resemblance of soft leather, laser scanned and cut to a custom fit. Her inner body armour was standard issue consisting of two wafer thin layers of Peruvian liquid cloth, resistant to small projectile fire at medium range, feather light and worn always, whether on or off combat duty.

At ease,' ordered the duty Sergeant standing three paces from the man with the wintry stare and civilian suit.

She relaxed her stance, her eyes remaining fixed on the civilian who had been waiting for her as she emerged naked from the vacuum. There was a long silence as he continued to stare at her. Then in a soft assured voice he said 'Strip.' Her eyes flashed in surprise then switched to the direction of the Sergeant for guidance.

'Are you deaf....strip!' shouted the Sergeant.

She did as ordered, removing the clothes she had just put on, and for the second time, stood naked in front of them.

'Attention,' said the civilian softly. This time she obeyed his order.

He ran his eyes slowly over her. Mid-twenties.. slim.. medium height.. hint of feminine muscle.. short cropped bright blonde hair, darker eyebrows.. a perfectly proportioned face and overall classic beauty.

After some time he unfixed his stare and smiled, a pencil thin smile of approval.

She had been aware of his presence once before, during the later stage of her rebuild. Her last two weeks had been in full consciousness. Acclimatising to increasing levels of gravity. Test after test. Stimulation of nerve ends; provoking expected reactions to instructions from her brain. Repeating them until the reaction times surpassed excellent. His voice was that of a stranger amongst the familiar voices outside the vacuum. Authoritative, high ranking, by the nervous stilted way the doctors replied to seemingly simple questions. He had complimented her appearance and asked if she had been physically improved in any way other than the standard Company implants. They said she had not. Mostly they responded to his questions by 'Sir' - then someone called him Vortex.

Vortex, in person! She had once wondered if he was in fact real or simply a fictitious Company front. Now he stood in front of her, the most powerful man in the world. Staring at her through surgically black pigmented eyes, rumoured to enable telepathy. A face chiselled from winter fog, and skin which seemed to lick at the light. The softly spoken words uttered from the cold slit in his face carrying the unmistakable aura of power.

He had nodded to the Sergeant who ordered her to dress. When she stood fully clothed, Vortex spoke again 'MX 2645 Sands - and how are we this morning?' After the short silence which followed he said 'I trust that you are feeling greatly improved since your *death*. The good doctor was kind enough to show me the footage.' After a short time he smiled again adding 'Delighted to have made your acquaintance.' He then left without having introduced himself.

That afternoon, the Sergeant who she came to know as Sergeant AX 6539 Vidal, saluted her and informed her that she now held the rank of Lieutenant. On the order of Vortex.

Well...vacation over. What to do? she thought. Having toyed with the idea of leaving the Company for some time, the sick taste of the LoTech Event had provoked a decision. Faro's dead eyes had sealed it.

Yet again....she felt great. More finely tuned than she had ever felt in her life. Full combat fitness returned and up for it. Whatever *it* was. And *Lieutenant*...that was a much better game, and carried considerably more privileges. And deep down she knew she thrived living on the edge. Anyway - the choice was no longer hers to make. She *owed* them seven years - seven years she'd give them.

Three
Pachinko

His target ...the silence before the origin of time. From before the downfall of noise. His ballad ...the nerve endings of all life. The flesh roaring in blindfolded whispers milliseconds behind. A blazon streak torn to and fro between the blue and red; between red giant and quark .....from ARMAGEDDON to GENESIS.

Jinx felt as if he was being tugged and gently pushed along. He was definitely the centre of attraction, and felt very alone. He knew that he was neither chip linked nor asleep. He was wide awake.. and in control. What wasn't clear... was *he* directing, or being directed?

It was as if he was liquid. Some kind of estranged fluid mental energy. Raw. Absolute yet.. not appreciated. A bewildered energy demanding to be free. To be understood.

This was the second time since *the change* that he had entered. The first time he had just sort of... hung there. Aware that he could make *something* happen but too afraid to find out what. This time he had tempered his fear, and decided to flow with it, to allow it to guide him and see where it took him.

He sensed that it was intelligent; but not the kind of intelligence that thinks. More the kind that likes to watch, soak it all up, then allow itself to be harnessed. Taking pleasure from the sharing.

It gradually unfolded itself, leaving him unclear as to exactly *when* it had dawned on him that he did not control it, nor it him, but that he was part of it. He had let it capture him, had looked deep inside of it and had known it for what it was. *His soul*.....but not his alone.

It was a union: a graceful mergence of every living thought past and present; every mood, compassion, idea, dream envisaged and those as yet unthought, waiting to be found or remembered. It was everywhere. It was every essence of life from now and from before. All part of the one stone, the building block of life. Engraved with the passions and virtues of flesh and non flesh alike, sharing a sense of purpose....the desire to exist. He knew it to be the sublime life force of the universe.

The rhythm chilled his mind as language distilled by eternity poured through him; his target revealed...*the silence before the origin of time.* Hurling him backwards to the moment before the beginning of the universe - and back still. To the final hour of the unthinkable crime.

There he would stop, to bear witness. Then it would tear its way home, towards vacuum, where once again it would become the chatter of newly born stars.

Witness! It hit him and stopped his breath. There was everything but the expected silence. He stood within the universe of pre creation.. *and it was screaming.. dying....in fast forward.*

His view was of stars, thousands of millions of stars. White dwarfs fizzling out their last dying breath.. red giants incinerating entire planetary systems.. super novas by the millions illuminating billions of lifeless crystal black dwarfs.

Lances of light shot towards vibrant stars from crafts which left the instant they appeared, sometimes with others in pursuit. The light passed through, spliced into four and encircled each captive in a delicate web, mimicking its form. Darkness. Sudden brilliance burnt his eyes as a star erupted through its grip, the stars rate of energy consumption increased a billion fold. Its longevity of life reduced from a thousand million years to a few months.

Excited webs retracted in victory; spiral folds of fragile silken energy re-focused forming secondary lances, then tore into the heart of patiently trembling neighbouring stars. A singular umbilical length remained. Seconds..... an unimaginable surge of insane energy... tumbling, ricocheting as a bulging chaotic wall of raw anger crashing through the live connecting threads into its captured sister, forming another cannibal web of a thousand times greater magnitude. The process repeating itself from star to star intent... until the inevitable strategic destruction of the cluster.

From death came more death, came light, came expectation, came.... fuel for the chain as the first victim's eventual total energy transfer to its companion, and onwards to its companions neighbour, burst the sky in super nova deftly timed to create a black hole. In turn - sucked relentlessly towards a puncture wider than the milky way into the supremely black mis-place rimmed in dizzy light from a wreath of weeping stars. The gateway to the universe.. his universe.... over which he stood. A witness to the ultimate Armageddon.

He stared for what felt like forever. He collapsed his mind. Again *the flesh roared in blindfolded milliseconds behind him* as he was thrown into the universe from which he had emerged. Roller-coasting...into its massless void of pre-destiny; silver slithers of black lace; sheets of light in the shadowless void of a silence smoother than vodka, echoed in multiple stereo; running a trillion questions coated with head-fuck; fragmented by bullet expectation; crucifixion jealous of its own beauty. Solitude before time. *Then it erupted* - an infinite wall of biting white hot, equal but opposite radiation...a shock wave charging forward, hitting emptiness, pushing against - nothing. Racing itself. Forging elements to cool 300 millennium later as the chilled atomic soup of creation.

Simple patterns gently pushed and pulled themselves into increasingly complex cycles, to repeat for infinity. The collapse of dull lifeless nebular mass gave birth to the stars; a thousand million stars, illuminating the dust of ring nebula evolving into planetary systems. Divine galactic paintings, spiralling, receding from each other at ever increasing rates. Each with it own stellar clusters of kites of knotted white luminous crosses; bulging bright centres amidst celestial graffiti of exploding supernova and neutron stars. A multitude of comets reflected across his eyes; gleaming chariots riding the millions of years of black serenity between. His presence, reminding him of the salamander lizard fabled to live in fire while around it the world evolved, changing unrecognizably.

He saw galaxies born, live and die; watched the atoms from dying stars absorb the ultraviolet to repaint the canvas in their own signature colours. A final statement of who they were.

He spun onwards - four thousand million years to a sun that was his place of birth. The milky way he recognised as home, and his planet shrouded in whispers of cloud. He revelled in the ice rings of Saturn and witnessed the Aurora Borealis through Jovian eyes; its beauty created from particles erupting from Io's volcanoes, to stretch thousands of miles across Jupiter's poles, invisible from earth, whose atmosphere absorbed its ultraviolet wavelengths.

Jinx had ridden the life force of the cosmos. Borne witness to the ultimate sin...the erasure of a universe to enable the birth of his own. He had stood in awe and wonder as worlds unfolded before him. Had understood that *he* was less than a speck, a blink of light that would fade and pass unnoticed, but throughout he had felt its warm pulse flow through him.

It had began with a whisper. Now it raged with the urgency of solar wind. It was part of, but separate to, the physical energy that was busy conjuring the stars and planets around him. It was subliminal...alive...and hungry to share.

Four
Comrades - not

Sands sat side saddle on the stationary bike looking down from Peak Pass at the black valley below, its grass skin peeled back. Massive scarlet scraper loaders with wheels she knew to be eight metres high, and orange and scarlet striped shifters crawled like worker ants some five hundred metres below, stripping its priceless soil for off-world needs.

Ten months had passed since her first brief encounter with Vortex. Everything that had seemed so important then: the LoTech event; her half year's regrowth; her forced decision to dedicate seven more years to the Company - it all seemed so simple in comparison to whatever the hell she was going to do now.

She stood and stretched for a moment taking in one last view of the panorama, *mother Earth on her way to the stars*, then signalled the bike to start. She straddled its 5000cc engine thumbing the pad which instructed Marie's bike suit, on loan with the bike, to retract its body armour and helmet. She preferred the unrestricted freedom of the fatigues and sunglasses. Shifting the drive into manual she increased the revs to share its strength, then shot off towards the pass. She increased her speed until the bike's verbal warnings reinforced its flashing danger signals and entered the tunnel approaching 200kmph leaving it on the opposite side of the road, slipping neatly between the giant wheels of a slogging 500 ton lifter, leaning low in approach to the long sweeping curve to the lower valley. Enjoying the quality of the new road built and paid for by Terraform Vortex.

Soon the mountains shrank into low rolling hills, some two hundred miles from Marie's. Fifty miles fast road until she hit the one hundred mile belt of soft-town residences, commuter traffic and enforced speed restrictions. She thumbed Marie's coded sequence into the bikes jurisdiction panel enabling her chip to interface with the bikes signal. She instructed the chip to delete her view of the excavated hill slopes and flashing gaps of rolling landscape. The micro film screen slid into place across her military grade wrap-round Raybans. The road was still there, but now snaked its way through a forest of shadow. She focused her mind on Corfu island, east coast, then as an after thought refocused to Yosemite Park where she had spent some good times some years back - and instructed INSERT. The grey landscape was instantly replaced by rugged mountain terrain of lush greens, sharp browns and a sky of enriched blue. Matching her memory flash to archived images of the area, the chip superimposed them on the path of the road. New traffic appeared and disappeared at speed. Real and simulated vehicles all looked the same. The only way to tell for sure was to hit one. Illegal but fun.

She pulled the throttle harder switching road sides to take corners at a speed which took the tyre traction adjusters manufacturers advertisement *"no-one lives forever - unless they've got a tractor"* beyond the test. She re-focused switching into night, the shifting view ahead reducing to headlamp distance, red tail lights rushing towards her. Her vision became a swirl of competing colour; red beams, diffused yellow spots, staggered bright white glare. The exhilaration, her heart racing at a pace she'd grown to crave, become addicted to - tore into her mind, casting it back to butt heads with the depth of her real dilemma.

Its main defence shields buckled and its outer hull breached, the armoured personnel carrier had swivelled on its tracks and sped towards the protective guns of the grounded mothership wedged in the next valley. The Senate heavyweight class tank, switching its energy to its rear guns, pulsed one burst of fire into their projected path before enabling the lumbering spin which would bring it in pursuit.

Sands had listened through scrambled static to the Captain and gunner officers panicked debate. Heard the command to fire as the missile shot from the carrier's front mountings heading in the direction of the mothership and away from the Senate tank. Watched the external view depicted on the screens as the missile disappeared over the hill, the larger and more heavily armed tank appearing in clear view and decreasing range behind them. Felt the engines reverse and the carrier spin on its tracks again as the Captain ordered all remaining power to the damaged front shield and front guns. Long seconds passed as the distance narrowed then the seats rocked as the front guns erupted beams of destruction. The left guns fired early and wide, the under and over guns fired straight at the advancing tank forcing it to deviate to its left. As the enemy tank's own guns fired back she felt the carrier accelerate forward to meet it guns blazing in what must have appeared to the heavily shielded attacker to be a final suicide run.

The exchange had lasted a few seconds only, the carrier's shields completely gone, the attackers still strong and energised to the front, when a single fully charged shot from the missile which emerged fast from the right delivered its one and only payload. The unprotected rear of the Senate tank erupted in light then dissolved.

She and her fellow marines had not played a direct part in it; had not conceived the plan or influenced it in any way. Yet she knew that the manoeuvre had saved their lives and felt both responsible, and proud to have been there. She knew that every marine in the hull felt he same.

Now as she danced her path through a Yosemite valley swathed in darkness, her mind's eye saw those same comrades, friends, staring at her screaming - TRAITOR!

The roaring of the bike's engine again filled her head. Her glasses flashed *heavy traffic* ahead. She slowed, switched to normal vision and cruised in the outer lane aware of the police slow signs projected overhead. The ride through soft-town was slow and dull. Her head cleared.

She joined the sweep into the interchange which would give her access to the grids. She could cover the next fifty miles faster at ground level, but early access to grid level 4 would allow priority passage through downtown and would be less painful in the end. Once she hit the serious downtown traffic she'd have some fun with Marie's personalised grid-hack which like the police, enabled a straight route through. The kick wasn't just out manoeuvring police cruisers, whose main job was to intercept grid violators. That is, if they weren't dealing with accidents or maniac fuckups from a higher level grid freeze dropping its load on the grid below. The real kick was seeing the ashen faces of city suits as they hit the panic button as she suddenly and illegally changed grid and arrived in *their space*.

Marie's was four blocks away now. She had seized the day, cleared a passage through a lot of mental shit. Time, she now knew, would clear the rest. She entered the short fifty metres of the cul-de-sac and thumbed the entry code for Marie's apartment. The outer bronzed metal doors slid back screeching against the concrete floor. The inner door to the lift was already open as the bike skidded to a halt before rolling onto the revolving platform.

The last couple of hours had put things in the frame. There had been no startling revelations. She now saw that things had pretty much been resolved and had remained only to be recognised. Traitor she was. But traitor to what? To the Company which had taken care of her for its own ends? To Vortex the man, who she had the *honour* of meeting half a dozen times and who was directly responsible for her current situation? To comrades who she had believed in and who had believed in her. Mostly dead. Faro.. would have understood.. except he too was dead, regardless of their bullshit. She had seen his eyes. The others; comrades, friends, sure.... once. Now it was up to them. Time moved on. As the lift turned the bike full circle on approach to Marie's floor, she saw in the cracked blackened remains of the wall mirror the woman she had so recently come to know. No longer MX 2645 Sands - now just plain Sands. Mid-twenties.. slim.. medium height.. fit.. hint of muscle.. short cropped bright blonde hair which she had let grow a half inch since the army crew cut. She smiled below smoky blue eyes feeling....reborn, and thought *fuck em all.*

Five

Cybertramp

Cold condensation streaked windows, black unlit street beyond..occasional headlight reflection..... 'I'm sitting in this frig'n café, it's two o'clock in the morning, it's raining outside and looks as frozen as my insides feel, *....sound of the floor being swept..lino, brown ragged holes catching crumbs..broken dusty fan.....* and I'm listening to you telling me that your grandmother was screwing Elvis, your grandfather was President of the United States and you..after a glorious career at Westpoint spent two years in Nam and *......bacon flavoured air..warmth..cosy..no inquisitive eyes...* are considered by everyone who matters..to be a frig'n war hero!' *..their third mug of coffee..Formica tables.....*

'Well – oui.'

'And all this took place in what..two frig'n hours!' *....fat grubby proprietor..hot steam..continual rubbing of hands on filthy apron..nicotine stained fingers..South American Indian hat....*

'Et non monsieur' *..hot beans, roasted tortilla chips, mugs of smokin' tea..truckers, 'long-haul' talk..back lit..patterned oily smoke...* 'I did not say that my grandmother was screwing Elvis, I said my grandmother *was* Elvis.' *...music, local station, radio static interrupted, "black magic woman..got your spell on me babe"..painting of faded Christ on the cross.....*

'Girl, you've gotta get your head out of that shit. Jesus. Listen girl, that Authenticia shit ain't for real. I mean..your real girl, that cool marine you live with, she's real - that other shit, it ain't. It's ok for a meet like this, but you don't *belong* in there.'

'Qui, but sometimes it is....preferable. ...*occasional passing train, whole place shakes..timeless day or night.....*

'On the subject of a meet - where the frig is Johnstone, he's always late...and deals the shitiest smack in town.'

.....her sensation of hangover tiredness..long day.. 'It is two in the morning Cleo.'

'If it wasn't on tick I'd tell him to shove it.'

'Pardon - this Johnstone, he deals smack on tic.'

'No girl, he has a friend who needs a favour..you know, so, I do this friend a favour, whenever...but I get mine upfront.

...bored..arrive soon.....please.....

'He'll be here though. Never met a cleanser..seemed real interested.'

The door opened and he entered alone. Lean and tall. A good looking pot marked black face, sharp intelligent eyes. He shook the rain from a raven coloured ankle length coat. She noticed the rough stitching where it's hood had been ripped off. He seemed to regain his breath looking first to Cleo then at her. He briskly eyed her over, then leaning down picked up a piece of toast. Cleo had shut up.

'You must be mademoiselle cleanser.' He gestured the toast in the air, 'Johnstone,' he said.

'Good morning.'

'You mind?' he said flicking his head suggesting that she slid over so he could sit.

She moved her coffee and slid onto the inside seat facing Cleo.

'I do not spy on people..or find people who do not wish to be found,' she said with a clean French accent, lighting up another cigarette.

'Cleo says you can find just about anybody. Can get into everything. Cleo is known to ...exaggerate.'

She raised her chin, blowing smoke at the ceiling. 'I can open most doors', she replied without looking at him. 'What is it that you wish me to do for you?'

'Gotta meet a man my man,' interrupted Cleo, his hand slipping beneath Johnstone's as he got up to leave. As Cleo pocketed the encrypted package which would buy him a few good days, she smiled realising that she was the favour.

'Relax. I am not looking for a person. Just some information. You have any problem with information?'

'None.'

'Good. There is a Corporation called AXIS; was a Company called AXIS. They were bought over day before yesterday. I have a client who would like to know why. That is all.'

'I would require them to be more specific.'

'That's it. That's all there is. And..it was a small_Company. Get everything you can. The answer *will* be there. No-one expects you to recognise it.'

'The fee is 10,000. It will take me two days.'

'Good.'

She stubbed her half smoked cigarette out in a pile of similar length butts. Said goodbye and left.

She removed the headset having instructed Loki to smoke her exit route. He had simulated her continued presence, slipping deeper and deeper through multiple layers of System Federal, skirting the edge of prohibited zones, eventually fading to zero in a later dimension. She had remained there, but invisible, having slid into overlap with Johnstone's trace for some time after Loki had exited her space. Anyone retracing Loki's path in search of a secondary exit would find none as it had not yet been created. Only someone smart enough to recheck the time band some minutes after its fade would detect her real exit. She had made a similar move on entrance, emerging from a null area between two prohibited zones. A precaution she always took when meeting clients.

With Cleo, she had allowed herself a more personal relationship over the last year, but had still retained a professional distance ensuring that he had no idea of how to contact her other than within the system. His only hint to her true ID was that she used her own persona as graphics for meets. His comment on 'her marine' had however triggered her to run a security check on her way out. She had been running them since Sands went A.W.O.L. Sands had said it wasn't necessary as those looking for her wouldn't want too much attention. And that it was partly personal. She ran them anyway. As before, it was clean. No-one asking loud questions.

*****

The late evening view across the city rooftops always held her captive. The kaleidoscope of light that was Cathedral Town. She'd stare and wonder for hours. Each twinkling light was a tangle of stories, an intricate web of family life, or solitary existence. Each dark space between, a life absent for the moment, but sure to return. Eighteen million of them. A meshed mass of turbulent energy held in singular focus. Like the reflection on a pond, the complex chaos of life hidden beneath.

She was alone in the penthouse, level 294 of a nondescript block in sector 81. It was part of a much larger habitat gutted by fire three years earlier, with twenty or so floors below. The owners had simply moved on, the works of refurbishment being beyond economic repair. Her wing which overhung the main structure had been shielded by the building's inner upper buttresses and was pretty much intact. Marie and two friends had enclosed it, and set up bypasses from the energy and purification system. After some time her friends had moved on leaving her alone with the view.

Marie was French. From Cleron in the Jura hills. A pleasant quiet little town built around the Chateau which guarded an arched stone bridge over a small river. Smooth and passive in the summer. Rocky caves of white frothing water in the winter.

At the age of eleven with the death of her elderly parents she had moved east to the coast to live with her uncle Roland, her fathers younger brother. He had a colourful and spacious house in the flat part of the valley at the end of the road, below the distant spires. Her years there had been good. Warm memories of searching for *the fish*. Of long wooded walks skirting the beach and always ending up at the spot where the river met the sea. Tuscan weather. Refreshing rain.

At nineteen years old she was petite; jet black hair cut in a bowl. Slim, soft and well rounded, turning many stares as she walked the passeggiata with small fast steps, her head held straight, chin high, down the streets of Florence. Engulfed in the warm illumination of a Mediterranean evening.

She dressed in simple short summer slips. A cigarette her only accessory; held between two straight fingers. She'd snap the petrol lighter shut and always blow the smoke straight ahead. Her skin was light olive. Her eyes deepest brown, and seemed to add direction to the smoke. As she spoke she'd flick her head towards you with an attractive subtle bounce to her fringe.

She had endless male attention. Had enjoyed more than her fair share of attractive men, both in and out of bed. But never quite found the magic spark. Often she'd sense a calculated routine that left her cold. The predator glint, predictable cool smiles that overplayed the moment, the slow ritual of lighting up as they worked out their next line, or a momentary flaw in their act caught up in a sudden belief that they had cracked it. That they were on to a good time. She had too often sat in a cafe her drink barely touched; listening in her head to her own thoughts drowning out the background pursuit of some horny, tanned, young man entertaining her with stories of Roman nights. Through a haze of fresh smoke.

Marie loved music. Carried it in her head. Passionate light renaissance with bursts of drama. When she wasn't floating somewhere within it, she'd search for rhythm wherever she was. Her pleasure lay in its creative innocence. Immune to the arrogance of the real world. The way she remembered the kingfishers of her river Loue. She studied composition and history of music at Florence Accademia Conservatorio. It was there that she became drawn to the language of sculpture, poetry, and creative cyberspace.

At 20 she hit big time. Changed continents. Moved to Chicago to work with Senate Authenticia, a first tier division of Company Senate. Promises of fastrack initiation, access to the cutting edge of technology, silver lined remarks, subtle hints of illegal research, even the invitation of danger....dreams of sculpting four dimensional poetry.

Marie told the flat's sound system to relay a favourite mellow wave at her resonant relaxation frequency. Combined with the evening view, that ought to loosen her up. She'd become accustomed to the need after a meet with the likes of Johnstone.

The passive waves brought reflection. Authenticia had ravaged the fundamental principles of social thinking, sending tremors through every culture around the globe. And she had played a significant part in it. There since its birth; the marriage of chip enhanced cerebral interface and multi dimensional holographics. Expressed as jacked in parallel reality or free standing interactive illusion. Kiss goodbye to the mundane. Live out the dream.

She had played a legal technical design role in evolving a technically illegal state of the art system. Access to the inner depths of the primal system at her disposal; the entire commercial and military resources of the second biggest Company on the planet to play with. Security non existent in a system constantly eating itself - she had learned fast, utilised it and learned more. Passing some of it on, sharing with teams of hundreds like her.

It took three years before the global system created parallel environ's realer than real, *'VR on acid'* as Cleo had remarked, custom made to whatever you got a hit on. Took another three before the collapse of the social system and the destruction of traditional family life. Twelve months later a leisure based society that increasingly couldn't finance itself caused the crash of the international stock market - the world finally paid heed to the whimpers of Federal. Authenticia was outlawed. Retained, was the cost saving Federal penitentiary system, privately run state homes for the elderly, and the institutionalised 51 band social and business international communication circle -System Federal. The public outcry was global. Three months later Cathedral Town was granted independence. Given its desired status as a solution to the problem.

The flat's sounds jarred her conscious with gentle reminder waves, like the steady pumping of brakes. Almost time to go. Qui..Authenticia had its day and she had played a big part in it, she thought. Had witnessed its birth, nurtured it through infancy, revelled in its adulthood. And like many others she had refused to accept its demean. For Marie it wasn't escapism, or sex, or even just the fun. It was its absolutism. It was the *opportunity* to create whatever she wanted. Black and white or a turbulence of living colour; but always customised to the individual's liking. The perfect medium for her art.

She could sculpt her poems, hang them in music and light. She'd busk, but not for credits; she would watch their response through seemingly impartial eyes, and revel in their pleasure. Safe, that all who stopped to look would value them and wonder each in their own unique way. To the aggressive mind; to touch the pool of air, its particle thin sheens of petal flavoured glass within the dripping beat of the drum, would bring a moments passive escape; to the timid, a straight hit of passion. The better the sculpture the more subtle, more provocative the response. The pleasure they gave was always evident. So she clung to it.

Her latter days as a cleanser, identifying patterns evolved from the primal set up, the system that set up the system, opening and closing invisible doors wider than space itself, tying in the loops which provided the pretence of spatial dimension, now enabled her access throughout the maze and its shadows, and to her stage. Her talents came well paid. Two tours a month was enough to keep her living well and leave her free to pursue her art.

'Moi, hooked..non!' she had told Sands who didn't seem to understand the finer points to life in the underworld of the maze. 'Toxic head, Non! Techno junky, causing viruses, loosing new AI's..Non, Non! It is my stage - *free* technology and an audience who want to play.' She knew it to be true. She knew of too many other sad souls, *cybertramps* like her, but who were too caught up to know the difference. Who spent as little time on the outside as their bodily functions permitted. And then, there were the less experienced who had to piggy back their way around, scrounging entries here and there; some who had got so far in they couldn't get out, or were consumed by the shadows.

But she had bitten. Not a habit. More of a potent pact with pleasure. Pleasure of the freedom within a system with which she had become par excellence in its use. A freedom which she also recognised and affectionately envied in Sands attitude to *real* life. A truly *free spirit*. Regarding her own use - she would just have to be careful, that was it.

*****

Loki and Thor beamed as always on her arrival. They looked nothing like Norse Gods of mischief and war. They looked exactly what they were....her fairy companions. Her friends. As a child she had imagined them. As an adult she had made them real. She returned their whispered delight in kind. Loki perched his tiny frame on the tip of her shoulder. She twirled her fingers playfully at his belly and he became a ball of blue, bright silver black light. Squealing in impish glee. Thor hovered by her ear. Scents of Yellow and bronze.

With a broad smile she briefed them through an intimate code of gestures and fast flowing grinning French. They'd get Johnstone's stuff on the way out, first she had to make a short prison run to pass on some news that ought to make someone laugh again. She liked that kind of run. Too many clients were looking for the other side of the coin.

Shadowing...prying. She refused to find people who had intentionally got themselves lost. Sometimes she'd get well paid for just getting private dicks in and out undetected. But always insisted on knowing why. Refused as many jobs as she took. Was rarely lied to. The fear of being left there, stranded, their exit routes tied, through the necessity of camouflage, to their entrance circuit, tended to reduce the temptation for deceit. Users with few exceptions, were well focused on the knowledge that once their neuro-paths were jacked and their mind ceased to function on the outside, virtual death meant real - permanent death. And that it usually came impolite and painful. An invisible circuit could emerge them anywhere; as an isolated entity in a 10 star pleasure camp or in the prohibited layers run from Cathedral Town, or even in the folds of the shadows at the mercy of rogue AI's.

This job was simple and to her liking. Straight business espionage. A one off. Straight fee. Thor and Loki glowed like adrenalin. They lived for anything that could be loosely passed off as fun.

They dropped the goods at the Federal Penitentiary. Job done, they rode piggy back on the trace of an unaware tourist, then switched to another and another, emerging from a prohibited layer on the edge of the shadows to move directly on the target Corporation.

The target appeared dull, a dark star amongst a spectrum of glowing beacons to nebula furnaces pulsing to be discovered. Magnets for those with invites or at the least, honourable intentions. It was clearly closed for business. But not deaf. *New* ice everywhere. Expensive ice.

Elaborate protection for a node this small suggested a probable gateway to another level. Large Corporations spanned a multitude of levels. *Flowering* provided easy access for clients but crucially provided the Corporations with shadow space between branches. Essential for future expansion, but could also host invisible ice as guardian to each node preventing total infestation from any singular attack. It was there that the unorthodox brands of ice thrived. Evolved from the primal system, consuming contaminated ice loosed from Company or Corporation conflict, and general system fallout. Creating its own worlds and its own shadows. Impenetrable, unless by invitation. Known as *Shadowlands*.

'Corporation..gateway..whatever it is...its setup pattern is well post primal, plus new ice...isolated in its shell..can't get in..' she whispered.

'Need an active system..but it's shut,' frowned Thor, his head lopped to the side.

'Let's soften it, muddy its security a little,' enlightened Loki.

Smiling, she did exactly that, instructing her own primal viruses to enact backtrack loops softening the interaction between the old and new. 'Qui..there it is....pre ice activity... but only what *was,* nothing current.....good enough for now.' Pre buyout noise, tons of it, going in and out.

Five hours of searching later... '*Wrong kind of noise*..timed patterns...then silent gaps, nothing... until another batch and..answers to unasked questions?' she thought aloud. 'This is *not* a gateway. It's a singular line of information looped in and out, randomly spread to read like a full vertical horizontal exchange.'

'Source it,' recommended Loki.

It was a satellite..and familiar...the same source Leo had used to contact *Johnstone.*

Accessing the satellite was no problem as it was freeriding on the original system. She melted down to primal and ran it invisible anyway. She had once learned painfully of the foolhardiness of assuming an easy entrance was an easy take. First impressions were not always as they seemed. Nothing.... a void...a box number. And a message...THANK YOU MADEMOISELLE CLEANSER. YOUR FEE HAS BEEN REGISTERED TO YOUR ACCOUNT AS AGREED. She stared at the black words for a long long moment. A billboard - target, created specifically for her. The Corporation itself had never existed. But she *was* employed. Whatever that meant. And 10,000 up for openers... had to be good. She jacked out and the silent minutes passed uninterrupted. Then as if pulling itself into focus it hit her. The subtleties of *her test*; whoever he was, he knew the maze, understood *cybertramps*, could have done what he had asked of her himself. His interest had been purely one of security. Hers.

She thought of Johnstone's pot marked face and wondered who he really was. She could hear Sands' bike revving in the elevator as she once again took in the evening view of the city and poured herself a large brandy to warm the dirty ice of his eyes.

Six
Cold Rage

Jinx was back. Standing on the rim of creation - as he now knew it. He had watched the implosion of their cosmos, the transfer of its mass and energy to give birth to his own universe and as a speck within it - his galaxy and his world.

He had shot....from a face full of stars expanding beyond an imagined horizon, through the gaping tear in space to a ripple-less black decaying cosmos, timeless relative to his own. Of infinite volume; now almost empty of mass.

He saw that the process of de-plenishment had ceased fractionally short of completion. Sporadic distant flecks of light illuminated vast gusts of anti matter shields enclosing a few isolated areas, behind which the surviving races rested. The race that had released its weapons of purity, in the ultimate selfless act of religious healing, insisting on its universe dying without dignity or grace, had long since perished by their own actions.

Jinx had cruised the dragon paths of the Akasha, the life force of the cosmos. It had taken him beyond its horizons through the child to the mother universe. As he sped, frozen moments had grasped for his attention. Isolated fragrances, milestones of significance to many had stopped him like a solid wall of faith.

He had sensed great sadness; ripples from the past woven through time and space. Sadness tinged with rage: but the rage was not theirs. It belonged to a *new* race. He felt its presence close enough to touch. Envisaged it as invisible eyes spread across the heavens. They too had borne witness - but the destruction was not the cause of their anger. He sensed - indifference.

A cold mind. Of vast intelligence. It seemed to know him, but could not reach out to him. It was as if there was a bridge – that could be crossed from his side alone. He tasted values steeped in self-righteousness, and arrogance of the scale prescribed only to a powerful lord or to the wrong kind of god.

As it began to fade he instinctively reached for the flow. In a blink, time ceased, frozen, as a relative million years of endurance and razor sharp culture glistened as reflection in the multitude of minds which confronted him. He read overkill to the Nth degree; tasted black blood from the veins of the dying civilisations which had preceded them - and stared into the eyes of a predator.

Repeatedly they tried to touch him, but in vain. Their frustration grew louder, now clearly evident as the source of anger. They were isolated; part of the overall flow but as distinctly apart as the mother and baby universe; a separate tier in the hierarchy. They could watch but could not enter. Then recognition dawned - Shadowlands!

His mind reeled in shock - as the full implication of what *he* had done hit him. It had been nine years since he had completed the task for Vortex. Nine years, including the war, since the arrival of Jake. Only recently did a smouldering curiosity force him to explore for himself, after his traumatic initial experience. *Now* he understood why Vortex was so keen to find the marine – Sands.

Seven
Meet Jake

Gun metal charisma. Small dark tinted windows. Fat new black tyres. Shiny chrome bumpers, matching hubs and headlamps. Four short stubby old fashioned looking aerials. *Ambassador*....immaculate..polished beyond perfection. His one material possession..his sole love..his talisman.

It was late afternoon, on a dry, angry hot southern summers day. Near the main road at the centre of a small town, on the edge of a bigger town, appended to a city that once had a name..which he had forgotten.

She knew that they couldn't see in. That those who stared were just perusing 'PRAISE THE LORD' stencilled in bold black text across the top of the front windscreen. He'd parked the small car angled in a gap half its length, its ass protruding outwards into the road forcing inner lane traffic to stop and pull out before passing. Surrounded by crowds of bustling *happy shoppers* as she'd once called those who shopped on credit. It was more compact than small. Plenty of room though the fur lined roof was low. The leather seats as comfortable as any couch she'd ever sat on. The built in air conditioning adding that final touch of decadence.

'So what's it like being fucked by a God?' he merrily inquired, letting go of her wrists and sliding back onto the seat.

'Demonic, utterly demonic.. that's what its like,' regaining her breath as she brought her knees back down and absently re-arranged her skirt.

'Good..we'll do it again in a minute.....or two.'

They lay there for a while, across each other, listening to the sound of the air chill.

He called her *Sop*. Said he preferred it. That obscure birth names contaminated the innocence of the soul. In truth her real name just had too many letters to bother with. Stretching down she pulled a packet of pre-rolled weed from the top of her short length cowboy boot. 'So what makes you *so sure* your a God anyway?' She lit up.. 'And not just another stoned out *I'm gonna save the world* religious nut.'

He smiled, a light ghost of a smile. 'Hah..h'.. the smile became a laugh..a truly honest laugh fitting one who had absolute conviction in what they were about to say without really knowing the words which would follow. 'An angel.. came to me. As I was sitting on the hill above Ardmore, in Ireland, and asked me for my forgiveness. I said.."*sure thing*", and then it fucked off. Before it left it flashed a thought, or epitaph even, before my conscious. "*I am human and nothing human is foreign to me*". I felt like I knew the man, Virgil that is, as if I *was* him. But the thought was a momentary, almost incidental passing fragrance on the face of something far more important. A farewell and an introduction... of sorts.. to something. Fuck knows what.'

'A dream?'

'No. Real.. *very* real. Since then there have been many other... others. I have experienced multitudinous visions, been on jaunts all over the planet and further, wandered casually through catastrophic events of *cosmic* proportion. Drawn there.. by some irresistible force of ....focused untamed energy. Dreams too. But even they were real.'

'You mean that they se..eemed real?' she teased.

'Wasn't like dreaming. This was *happening* somewhere else. It wasn't all physical. Some, most of it was conceptual. Ideas hanging in the air, ripe for picking, or to be left to fizzle away.'

'So can you take me with you on one of these wild trips?' she laughed, her eyes wide in jest through chilled smoke.

'Hah.. h..not yet. For the moment, I am ..but a witness. Shackled to paths which lead to echoes of events of *another's choosing*.' His hand moved inside her T shirt tracing the outline of the gaily patterned mandala printed by Huek, monk of The Order Of The Jake. Its symbolic diagram of the universe depicted as a temple. Enclosed on three sides by an exaggerated J; the fourth side of the square sealed by the shadow of a transcendental city. 'It is the *dragon paths* that guide my travels.'

'Don't see how that makes you a God hon. You can't remember who you are or where your from and most the time you can't remember what you did yesterday. Surely if you were a God you would at least remember your name!'

'Yeah..there is that. At first there *were* doubts. Then I grew to understand. I am drawn, through the eyes of another, into a chaos.. crashing waves of newly born lucid thoughts, ambitions, dreams belonging to a infinity of living souls. I feel their pain. I foresee as they cannot, the cause and effect of their seemingly inconsequential actions. Their lives are bared before me. I know that the power to shape all of this is mine. I can sense beyond any doubt that it was once mine to indulge... but cannot reach out and take it! Something changed from whatever was before. Smashed the tablet leaving me - a castaway. '

'Sounds serious.' She smiled, amused by his sense of drama. 'It *will* be.' Accepting the joint he asked 'So what kind of God would *you* like me to be?'

'Well lets see.....what's important.. is knowing that those you love will always be looked after.'

'Yuk...h.ha.'

'Well if you're gonna be a God, you'll have to be a *responsible* god. Can't be off pissing it up all the time when there's a world to run.'

'Responsible...h.ha. I thought at first..that I may be the Antichrist, given that I don't exactly fit the goody goody typecast. But then, as a God I don't have to conform to the traditional stuff..do I. Good, bad, values, ethics, morals.. all that. To me.. religion is the luxury of *shutting the door* to responsibility. At least for the punters. All people really want is some peace of mind. I'll give them that. I will *consume* responsibility. They will never have to worry their little heads about a thing. A people's God. A *have fun or get your ass kicked* type of God.'

'Sounds great.. but don't you need a jump start. I mean what's gonna turn them on to you hon. You being stuck here with us mere mortals an all.'

'My religion will be the unveiling of a uniform madness shared by billions ..*or selfishly devoured in silent solitude..*' he added whispering aloud, shadows of meaning he sensed as central to his current dilemma passing abstractly out with his reach. 'My followers..a new flavour of devout anarchist.' He stopped abruptly, jolted by the roach burning his finger. Stubbing the end into one of the twin spanking clean chrome ashtrays he beamed a smug satisfied grin.. 'To answer your question.. soon I will have in my possession that which has so far been out of reach. And ..I will be divine again!'

*****

'So where is this Jake geyser...we've been here twenty minutes..time is money. Five more then tell him where to find us.' Tight fitting Brown suit over a slight to medium frame.

'He'll be here..said they'd be back for six' replied Huek monk of The Order Of The Jake.

'Gone six. Is this his flat.. thought you said he was a roller. He'd better have the money and not be wastin' our time..'

'He shares the flat with Gav, but Gav's been in Singapore since April. Want some tea?' replied Huek.

Brown suit's eyes found the teapot perched awkwardly, things growing out of it, definitely not edible, amongst a pile of stained china cups and chipped saucers.

'Pass..I'll just use your toilet making his way across the room. He shut the lockless toilet door... lid was down..lifted it ..full of shit, piss and multi coloured wipes..put the lid back down and pissed in the sink.. re-entered the room 'Your toilet doesn't work Huek.'

'Yeah. Gav broke it..'

'Gav's in Singapore since April..he said looking directly at Huek... this is August.'

'Yeah, bastard broke it,'replied Huek.

'You said "they"..who's "they?"' asked the other one, dressed in a similarly cut suit in garish green.

'Oh, Gav's woman...they go everywhere together. Jake's good to her,' replied Huek monk of The Order Of The Jake.

'Yeah... what's she like?'..asked the brown suit, exchanging mocking glances with his partner as he imitated Huek's slow childish manner of speech.

'She's sweet.... skinny.. pretty with skinny legs,' replied Huek.

'Skinny means no tits ..right.'

Huek shrugged and continued to knead his fingers behind the cat's ear.

The brown suit looked around focusing on individual items of furniture. An old beat up table, some rickety, badly repaired wooden chairs. Torn and thread worn rugs of differing styles partially covering wine stained rough wood-wormed floorboards, piles of discarded rubbish and beer cartons. An amused sneer grew bigger and bigger as he worked his way around the room until he met two vertical slit green eyes staring right back at him. It was the most beautiful, cleanest looking cat he'd ever seen. Gleamed in the debris of its owners lifestyle. He stared into its eyes for a long moment...' So what do they do..Jake and Gav's misses?'

Huek smiled down at the panther continuing to stroke beneath its neck. 'She's a learner, goes to Dough School so she can be a cook on the big boats and travel a lot. Jake's God.'

The magnetic band chimed as the door slid open. The panther lifted itself into a sitting position letting out a deep throated welcoming growl that got everyone's attention. The man in the doorway was medium built and pushing mid 30's. He was dressed in tight fitting brown synthetic jeans rolled mid way below his knees above lace up military boots. The jeans were held up by elastic braces over a plain white T shirt. No jacket. There was a slim and attractive young woman by his side.

From his slouched position in the armchair furthest from the door the green suit said 'Our heavenly father I presume.'

Jake glanced inquiringly at Huek who shrugged 'They can get the package you want..its waiting at The Snowdrift club but they'd like to be paid for it now..I thought they could wait as...' Jake lifted his hand indicating that he understood then turned to the one who had spoken.   'If it's at Snowdrift let's go get it.'

'Yip' answered the brown suit.

*****

Snowdrift was downtown lower circular. Ground city of the triple tiered bulk of megalopolis vertigo. City on city. Twenty minutes or so in Praise the Lord. Jake suggested Sop stayed in the flat as this was business and wouldn't take long. The cat seemed keen to come along for the ride. Jake passed it to Sop in response to brown suit's lack of enthusiasm to sharing the ride with a half size cyber genic panther. Huek pointed out that it was real. The cat pissed on the floor as if to prove the point.

They drove in silence save for the smooth purring of a perfectly tuned Ambassador engine. Along blazing neon avenues. Through haunting back streets mute in shadow, intermittent beams of fused light mingling with sheens of pink and orange illumination from the grid above and traffic pipes of higher grids.

'Neat lining,' remarked green suit fingering the furred roof.   'Comfy little love nest..eh! Nice looking ..Gav's woman.' Jake stroked the keypad on the right dash 'SNOWDRIFT'. Music, Gorecki's Tranquillisimo filled the space.

The Snowdrift club as expected turned out to be another hole in the wall. Chinese beer, smoke, cheap suits. Few curious stares. What *was* interesting to brown and green suit though was the three others making space for themselves at the corner bar. Resembled monks, kind of, dressed like Huek, shaved heads, loose charcoal tunics tied at the waist by cord. Loose trousers, same cloth, same colour. Coincidence - had to be. At their feet sat a full sized black panther.

Brown suit eyeballed the barman for beer. Green suit disappeared to some distant table returning a few minutes later. Jake gestured *outside* and he and green suit left for the side door to the service alley. Green suit laughed shaking his head 'Why the drama, this ain't heavy...just a plain history of who's who. Could get you her detailed military background..but you ain't paying for that...right.' Casually checking the three other monks were still at the bar.

'Who says I'm paying for anything,' replied Jake, gently shutting the door. The first blow broke green suits nose. The second sent him reeling feet in the air falling backwards over something firm and black. As the moment's glazed stupor retreated his heart froze, head filled with a chilling deep throated low rumble, back of his neck wet with the breath of something non-human, large heavy paws pressing down on his back.

Jake lit up, spoke quietly 'Should you ever find yourself passing the time face down in a puddle, on a hot summers night, around the back of somewhere that you now know you shouldn't have gone, and feeling stupid about saying something that you now know you shouldn't have said... you will also know, that there is something absolutely surreal about looking up to find your entire field of vision filled by a pair of well worn, steel framed army boots standing motionless six inches from your face.'

He drew the smoke deep then slowly let it out. 'When you do sense the motion you'll find that you can't decide which came first ...the cracking noise or the pain.'

Huek spoke from behind him, the club door ajar..brown suit hemmed in at the bar in silent conversation with three hard looking monks sipping beer. 'What was it..the car or the girl.....both?'

'Neither really.' Jake drew in on the smoke 'All violence is gratuitous..if you need a reason you're looking for an excuse. Before you know it you'll be running round town leaving thorny imprints on the foreheads of any bastard who doesn't believe in your particular point of view.' He leaned down picking up the package. 'Pay the other one at the bar'.

'What is it anyway?' asked Huek nodding at the disc.

'Records, life history of the woman I told you about. The one who appears in my visions.. she's real enough. She is called Sands...... scruffy.. gorgeous..raised on death row like a factory kitten that grew into a panther.. veteran marine refreshed from forty percent body weight on the ice fields of combat...has something that everybody wants and intends to keep it, or maybe sell it to the highest bidder. So say the visions. With this... he smiled tapping the package... maybe *we* can get to her first.'

'Can't we bid?'

Jake laughed. 'Our funds don't stretch that far. What she has is *very* valuable.'

'What does she have?'

'I don't know....but it belongs to me.'

Eight
Ah dare ya

The fish were the succulent sunken boats of gourmet dreams. Yet.... puffed up, theatrical colours, pouting lips stealing food from mouths beneath the dry stupendous eyes of their only possible friends.... their imagined subtle flavours and soft flesh were lost to him.

'Glowlanders. Indigenous to the pipes between the city and the falls. The glass is frozen photo genetic light cells shooting particle spread lasers off plates located deep within the water. The images are millisecond delay. Damned impressive for water at laboratory black conditions. The fish of course don't even know that there is a world out here.' The voice was well bred and mature with a friendly hyper edge.

Claymore looked for him as a reflection in the wall, but the glass was too pure. It was unusual for any of Vortex's hired minions to speak unless pre-instructed to express a specific point of information. Bursts of sociable nothingness were most definitely not par for the course.

As he turned to face the man he recognised it in the stare. B.L.D (blind); a youthful millennium societies' answer to alcohol induced crime. A hybrid organic mind virus designed to attack the impulse for those who craved the drug. What it left was a confused sense of longing; a pained look locked in memory of lost love, pushing against a relentless unforgiving idea of revulsion.

The man's eyes were fixed on Claymore's silver flask. Its motion frozen in individual frames....its scent rich with fever, laced with the passion of hungry rivets blasting into gleaming new steel..its so so familiar demanding after taste... each drop of golden liquid a surreal torrent from swollen winter falls.

'J.D.......B.L.D..' Claymore reflected with indifferent disgust. 'Born to be enemies...with so much in common.'

He rolled the flask sealed, slipping it into its pouch beneath his coat. He preferred its antiquated bashed tin appeal to the sleek tech versions which held 100 times in suspended volume. He looked beyond the doorman as their glass bubble rode upwards in the tube through yet another tier of finned fluorescent witnesses into a pool of noisy naked bathers thrashing zestfully amongst some life-like looking dolphins, turtles and other large unknowns. It slowed momentarily as if preparing to leap, disengaged from the tube and shot out and upwards at what seemed like a rapidly numbing desperate bid to leave the earth's atmosphere. A street perspective appearing and dissolving into an infinite city panorama in a blink. A few seconds later it braked to a perfectly cushioned stop at level 225 where the door vanished and a corporate carpet of graphite and steel emerged.

Stepping out he thumbed his ribbed mute orange invitation card. An arrow pointing left materialised on the wall directly in front.

Ten minutes of emotionless grey walls later the card flashed green. The words WAIT punched themselves into the air a metre from his face. A marine dressed in dark blue fatigues stepped through the wall. 'Señor Claymore.'

On the other side a second marine joined them. They marched with de ja vu for a full five minutes through echoless door less corridors, then stepped into a person sized dumb waiter which dropped several floors at the mercy of gravity, arriving with an intended jolt some four meters below their floor. Two further marines armed with light machine pistols stood over their point of arrival exchanging non conversational remarks with their Spanish comrade before allowing them to ascend to floor level where Claymore was asked to relinquish his pass.

Escorted across a cone shaped hall, a fourth marine palmed an entry code and lead them through a short narrow corridor with a partial view across a huge room full of busy personnel. The room was set at a plane of 70 degrees from the floor on which they stood. When they stopped, their relative ground plane adjusted itself to match. He knew that he must either now be 70 degrees off plane with the rest of the world, or the rest of the building had been all along. Either way his equilibrium felt right.

'Icy. If getting in is so much fun - getting out in a hurry must be a real crack up,' said Savannah.

'Your first visit?' Claymore asked with genuine surprise.

'Yes ..never took much work from Vortex. Had his own people for what I do..did best.'

YOU HAVE CLEARANCE FOR GRADE THREE ARMAMENT ... flashed in front of his face. The arrow indicated forward. Pillars and walls slid apart creating their own maze; giant dominos collapsing in ordered patterns, presenting stacks upon rows of weaponry; mainly small arms that any crazed psychopath would have creamed his pants over. Wall to wall standard Company assault rifles; lighter graphite compacts; attachments for every possible need; body armour; smart suits; jealousy mines wired to blow on detection of non-Company wavelengths; anti tank / personnel projectiles, nicknamed TRUMPS, so state of the art that they were always kept in reserve in combat; ammunition of every shape and calibre. Everything from bringing down a man, to a company of men, to a very large building. Stretching as far as the eye could see.

'What the fuck's grade two?' Savannah chuckled.

'Something you can drive away in I guess,' he answered absently scanning the corridors and shelves.

'Lookin' for anything in particular..or we just on a shop?' It was the first real excitement he'd heard in her voice since the day she died.

'Bit of both. He's ok for me to stock up now and again. One of the big advantages of being regular on the pay role.'

'Pick up a PK25. I love the sound of those babies..and a Monsoon..you ever used one of those - practically eats whatever you point it at..used one once at a meet with some German shi..'

'I'm looking for something particular. But scan for point 95 clips........and your PK25,' he cut in.

'The clips are back two corridors third row to the left. What in particular?'

'Oh. A blast from the past. Nicknamed 'AH DARE YA' by an old friend..Cherco.

'What the he..ll is that?'

'AK100..standard marine issue off-world hand gun come assault rifle depending on what attachments you use. On tour they're fully chip integrated.. which is what I want.'

'You want to interface! 50mm image projected from the sight directly to your retina...target cross with lock on zoom..practically impossible to miss. But.....if you wanna link up, your chip has to be customised. Needs a personal secure link. Your chip ain't got that capability......unless there're doors here that I can't feel?'

'Lots of them. Inactive since a long time, but operational.'

'You're carrying me around in a *military* grade chip.'

'Yeah...'

'Vortex?'

'No.....before that.'

'Senate... I thought they took those things out?'

'Not always. Only if it can hurt them.'

'Well looks like you get to play after all,' she said, then threw in, 'On the wall.. second row to the right.'

'As always.. your know your toys,' he replied, his eyes catching the AKs.

'Never had the fun of using one.. not havin' been military. You never felt the need before. So why now?'

'Cause she's got one.'

'She got you worr..ied, this little girl!' she inquired in a sarcastically mocking tone.

'Not any more than usual,' was his curt response, adding 'She's combat. Ex Vortex ground forces, and I hear she's got attitude...ain't just gonna throw her hands in the air.'

'So you're not gonna have time to miss. You realise ..if you'd had one of these babies - i'd still be walkin' around.'

Ignoring her ice he said 'And she had some real close, unit buddies. Can't assume she'll be alone.' The room spun as he spoke. *HIS* image - through another's eyes..Savannah's eyes.. rushed across his mind. They were back in the club - he saw himself lift his gun, point it at her, then the room was churning over, the floor coming up fast. *Her* memory - her death.

'Did you do that?' he asked driven aback. It was the first time she had reached him..touched his mind like that.

'Ha ha ..like it?'

'Didn't know you could project visuals.' The words BITCH tattooed vertically in Celtic script spread across his mind, then focused forming an attractive sculptured profile; sharp blue eyes turned to look him in the eye. And smiled coldly.

He released it from the rack; another slid forward to fill the gap. For a hand gun of such lethal force its envelope was a compact 0.3 metres from the barrel to grip. Empty, it felt too light to be real. As he injected the last of its three ammunition clips the weight began to feel satisfyingly familiar. The fourth clip was the heaviest. It housed the mind chip glazed by scores of reflectors, immersed in mercury speckled with random fluid chains of virus intrusion detectors, to ensure a private relationship with its user. The friendship he would establish with it would, if he wished, override any need for the trigger mechanism enabling him to fire directly by mental command.

'Lord's juice...link me up to this babe...I just gotta shoot some! Now I know that feelin' my daddy used to talk about.. when he cashed in the insurance money to buy his first and only Mitchigan 20 gauge. Everyone else was goi'n for the latest fashions in overkill but he..went out and got himself a polished chrome and wood single chamber true shot. Elite craftsmanship. He said it was all to do with the power of belief. Like the sheer beauty of the gun would will the deer to run towards the shot.'

Claymore flicked on the boost, the power indicator pulsed two beets against his palm. He could feel her pleasure licking his mind as she continued. 'With one of these babies you could practically talk the shots to the deer.'

'Maybe later...I don't want any surprise interruptions while on the job.' Carrying her was one thing, he thought, but he sure as hell wasn't hookin' her up to any AK100.

He lifted a loose butt and main barrel sliding and locking them into position. The weight felt complete now. The familiar sanctuary of sitting down with a fresh bottle and an old drinking buddy. He ran a causal half stroke over its length, absently pushing the weightless shoulder piece into his body, and pressed his cheek and eye against its manual sensor. The sight ejected into place - and with it a razor edged memory. He was focusing across a torn edge of mango swamp, over the sun baked earth of Kerala some twelve years back.....cocooned in pounding silence. The view through the sight had slammed into his face, isolating the mute shouts of distant troops, rendering him deaf to the discussion taking place immediately in front of him.

The troops three hundred yards ahead numbered around four hundred and stood mainly in unorganised groups with an air of casual indifference. Uninterested in the thump of single shots at three minute intervals.

The line of civilians zig zagged between corrugated roofed farm sheds and outbuildings disappearing behind the end houses of the village, hiding their number. Troops at staggered intervals pulled out the men. The women and children were herded into compact groups and told to sit. Selected men were pushed aside and motioned to walk to the village banyan tree, through the burnt out church. None came out the other side.

Until recently the officer and two Sergeants facing him had most probably been civilians with regular jobs and family lives. Today their thoughts and actions flowed from years of prejudice, fear, loathing and reprisal.

To his rear was a unit of forty men of which he was second in command. Fully equipped Company Senate troops wearing Federal peace colours over their tunics. They stood and lay positioned in a rapid compound enclosed by smart wire; their two warrior armoured personnel carriers having entrenched themselves amidst the collapsed ruins of a five hundred year old Portuguese fort. Orders - SECURE THE

PASS. ENGAGE ONLY IF ATTEMPT MADE TO BREACH PASS.

Cherco, his commanding officer, stood to his left. Both were in direct chip link to the troops fifty metres behind. The direct comm link was open between Cherco and Claymore alone. He could feel the edge build as Cherco repeatedly asked central command for permission to open fire only to be repeatedly denied. He knew the man; knew that he believed absolutely in loyalty to one's chain of command. Knew that twenty years of active tour had forged the belief in that loyalty, and knew his guts were twisting like his own.

The men behind them waited. Watched and waited. Their orders were clear. Their hard hitting "ground troops rip the wings off - warriors eat the heart" strategy, should Cherco give the order, burned in their minds.

The enemy officer standing in his shadow openly fidgeted, his body language reeking of contempt, searching for distraction. Repeatedly scratching a piece of flint against the rifle held lazily across his arms. His lethargic expression a hellish reflection of Cherco's frustration.

Cherco finally spoke. 'In my head.. I will count to ten by which time your men will have ceased their murder and will have started to leave the village..or my men will open fire.'

The zip smile briefly left the officers face. He started to speak as a crease slowly returned. 'Your orders are t...'

'Eight...six........two........'

The numbers hit zero. Cherco's eyes flashed at Claymore who replied aloud 'Live for the moment...' and put 5 AK shells into the still grinning enemy officers chest.

'..or live with it for the rest of your life.' testified Cherco and ordered his men to attack. The last words the dead officer had uttered were 'Ah dare ya!'

It was Claymore's first, and strongest memory of having broken the rules. One which would set the cast for much of his later years.

Claymore disconnected the butt and rifle barrel extension placing them back on the weapons rack. 'No use for them these days,' he said to Savannah.

'Yeah, good ol' Cherco,' she put in sarcastically, as if reading his mood. 'Wonder what he'd think if he could see us now?' It was Cherco who had introduced them some time after the war. Having heard that Claymore was living on the fringe, after leaving the Company. That he was looking for a partner. He had introduced her as an "anything goes kind of girl," and had definitely been proven right. Later, Claymore did little work with her as her background angle turned out all assassination and payback. Her reputation however, had opened doors. They were allowed access to the more seedy side of the seedier side of business where he would never normally have been tolerated. Previous targets accepted him on a professional basis as long as he was with her. She had proven useful in a partnership which cut both ways. Lately however the blade had a single edge, and it was rapidly becoming uncomfortably sharp.

He tucked the AK100 into his coat making a mental note to get a slip holster custom made. Emptied a smoke canister case and refilled it with standard pre-loaded clips, then walked back through the hall.

The two marines were waiting where they had left him. They escorted him back through the long frigid corridors. One corridor was alive with personnel respectfully undertaking routine maintenance to a sentient sentry gun located behind a stripped grey wall. The last time Claymore had seen a gun that size it was attached to a warrior tank.

He realised he was smiling. That was what he liked about shopping at Vortex's - that no one asked any questions. No need to sign. He could just turn up, take what he wanted and leave. Everything about Vortex was pretty much the same.

Nine
Dragons in the making

Jake slipped the key and entered silently. She was asleep as he had left her. Her head and shoulders covered by the none too clean bed sheet, the rest of her back and legs exposed to the air. The way she always ended up sleeping. Safe but cool. He pulled a beer from the fridge and crashed gently in the one comfortable chair of the flat. Its springs and layers of throws folding under and around him, as if demanding a smile of comfort.

He sat for a while till she stirred, pulling his thoughts back from nowhere.

'Is it late?' she asked sleepily. 'Did your Snowdrift deal go well?'

'Yeah sure. We met a king..and stole his queen..swopped her for two shiny black stallion's and a diamond tear shed from a dragons eye. Hah..h.' He was smiling.

'I need a drink of water,' lifting the sheet from her head. He held up the can of beer, she nodded and he lay down beside her as she drank. He finished it and they made love. Then she slept.

After some time he moved from the bed into his study; a small dimly lit secondary room, windows taped over in dark plastic bags, the centrally placed wooden desk piled high with recently acquired books. Mainly science mixed with philosophy and politics. His depth of scientific knowledge touched him with a quaint sense of amusement. Whatever he read he recognised as having already known and forgotten, placed aside redundant in the greater plan of things. He cleared a space between the books and candles, knocking the spent beer cans to the floor. Connected his portable console, headset, and crossed over.

For a while he floated in mainstream, collecting his thoughts, then homed into his receiver pad '..a warm up..let's see who wants to talk..' he silently decided. He ran the system checks ensuring that all calls had been politely and adequately answered introducing The Order Of The Jake in the fashion he expected; that those who had expressed more than a fleeting interest had been directed along the correct path towards righteousness, inspiration and most of all.. shared wealth. And that those less convinced were logged for a complimentary return visit by Jake in person.

The first potential converts appeared as Roby and June. Permanent residents of the Hotel Deluxe Mexico City. Jake hit search targeting *data only* for the address. Information flashed across his vision. Number of residents, membership policy, Company involvement. Second level establishment.. home to the rich, but not exclusive. Little Company intrusion, 90% financed by residents..30,751 members, more than half of which were permanent guests. His mind's eye saw them cocooned in their life pods, their daily bodily needs attended to by a skeleton nursing staff. He smiled at the absence of Company intrusion allowing him to target *Roby and June* in a manner he had been unable to do for Sands. Personal details materialised before him....89 and 94 years old..good health, projected technology assisted lifespan of 40 years..stress free psychic profiles..healthy bank accounts....content, stable individuals with a good future ahead. So what did they want from The Order Of The Jake?

June was serving for match point when he arrived unannounced. Roby was decked out in the sun, newspaper over his face. She shouted in triumphant delight as her final ace snatched the game. Jake smiled shyly standing in full view. He wore the garments of the Order but had otherwise chosen to look exactly as he appeared in reality. The only difference between himself and the other guests was his absence of a shadow. The tell tale sign that he was not a guest but an uninvited visitor, operating in isolation from the secure incubation of their world.

She recognised the difference and quietly said 'Roby.. we have a visitor.' Roby drew the paper from his face, donned a pair of cheap looking sunglasses and looked up at her and then at Jake.

'I am of the monastic Order Of The Jake. I am Jake. How can I can be of assistance?'

'Oh!' replied Roby 'Can I get you anything..a drink?'

'Got any Chinese beer?'

'Sure.'

'We were being inquisitive really,' offered June in the silence while Roby attracted the waiter. 'I.. we didn't expect you to call so quickly..and certainly not in person. I hope we hav'n't inconvenienced you?'

'Think nothing of it. It is my pleasure,' smiled Jake in return. 'I would be delighted to help you in any way I can.'

The drinks arrived courtesy of a short ordinary looking brunette waitress. She stooped and whispered something into June's ear who gesturing lightly with her hand said 'Really....he is welcome.'

It was Roby who opened the discussion 'It's not that we are in need of religion. We are both atheists. Our lives...here...have been extended and hopefully will continue as such for some considerable time. When the time comes for one of us to go, we have decided to leave together. In the meantime we intend to enjoy ourselves to the full. Outside..

June was confined to a chair, and I was nearing my end. Here we have our bodies back..' he gestured with his hands looking down at himself, 'Twenty five years old if a day.'

'You were a little skinnier' laughed June.

'Ha ha..maybe..but then you were a little fatter. In here.. it is like a holiday cruise that never ends. After a while you really can't tell the difference between what is now and what was before.'

'We are very happy. It's just that we have a longing to belong to something.. bigger, something that everyone shares in..in your world and ours. As Roby said..we never were much of believers.'

'This is my world' replied Jake. 'I live across both realms of existence.'

'We are looking for something that *we* can believe in.' added June. 'Some kind of ...'

'Reassurance,' interrupted Jake.

She stared into her glass for a moment then continued 'Yes ...I suppose so..something to remind us that we are.. ...alive.... still human.'

Jake nodded. 'The Order Of The Jake is a young order. Little more than an infant. We are different things to different people. For some we are *salvation*, and I....an entity with whom they can share their deepest sorrows...to whom they bare their souls...a God created in *their* likeness.. one who talks back. To others the order is little more than a source of comfort, and I a faceless friend, a concierge. If what you seek is a greater purpose than mere survival... I can fulfil that purpose.'

June and Roby looked to each other and June slowly nodded.

Jake continued 'Daily our numbers grow, and with them our resources, thanks to the generous donations of apostils.

My brothers and sisters toil endlessly within the realm of the physical world, movers and shakers, as they say, while I ...travel. Soon we will be millions.

Since the dawn of civilisation, from the flock like movement of Neolithic man from nomadic plains to worship at the shrines of the first village settlements, then from village shrine to citadel and city, the pattern has prevailed. The physical and social evolution of urban form has always been parallel, *forged*, by a new dominant religious order.

Today I lay the mark for a magnitude of social reform unequalled in history. The seeds of its success lie at the heart of the very urban order to which we bear witness. *The denouncement of Cathedral Town*. Eighteen million people banished, albeit at their own choice, from the union of so called free society. Their strength of conviction provide the foundations from which we will rise. From which we will create a new spatial order beyond mere physical definition.'

'Sharing directly in the daily lives of others, and involvement in the fulfilment of a vision such as yours would certainly be a welcome addition to our lives. It may well go some way towards what we are looking for,' responded Roby, '..and the donations.. what sum would be considered generous?'

'All donations are considered to be generous. Donate only what you can afford. A gift which reflects your level of expectation of the order is fair. Should you choose to join us or not..the order will always exist for you,' replied Jake.

He left fading slowly from view. A faint hollow radiance remained for a while, the sole indication of where he had gone, a warm reminder of where they longed to be.

His beer had gone flat on his return. Huek had let himself in and was sitting on the fridge reading. 'You were a while. Mexico city..interesting?' asked Huek.

'Met with some new disciples..drank some beer..watched some tennis.'

'Did you use the package from Snowdrift?'

'Not yet...tomorrow....i'll visit the *Federal Prison For Terminal Inmates*.....around dawn.'

Ten
Bonsai warriors

'**W**hen do we get this bitch? I thought these hovercrafts were supposed to be quiet! We should look up some more of her army pals...*squeeze* them a bit...some fuck must know where she's gone.'

'Done them all. She wasn't too popular on leaving,' replied the smaller. They had taken up two seats each and left one between them.

'And who *is* Claymore? What's he doing in *our* game?' griped the larger.

'Sad fuck with a guilt drive,' came the mumbled reply through a mouthful of airline freebies. 'Shot his bitch in the head...now he carries her download around like a penance. Vortex says he's it..*state of the art bad ass,*' he continued, stuffing another ham and peanut butter sandwich into his mouth, still staring unashamedly at the legs of the young woman sitting opposite. 'And it ain't our game. The game belongs to Vortex. He chooses who plays. And he *always* uses more than one player.'

'He paid us upfront...right?' asked the larger.

'Stop worrying. Vortex always sees us alright. Likes our personal touch. Got you this little trip ..didn't he. Get to see the Sumo..don't you. Any idea how difficult it is to get into these exhibitions. And *we*, bro...are travelling first class..ain't *we*. With as much free eats and drinks as we can swallow,' he said, still staring at the uncomfortable young woman. 'All we need now is a little pussy.' The remark caught her eyes and he let out a throaty laugh with an edge of mucus, and displayed a smile of plaque coated yellow-green teeth.

'I'd like to enter. Think he could fix that?' continued the larger.

The smaller laughed again. 'He can fix anything. But he wouldn't. Sumo is about honour and tradition. No clones allowed. House rules. Anyway..you'd just embarrass us both. Takes more than those doctored slanty eyes to be a Sumo.' Cramming in another hunk of sandwich he leaned forward a metre from her face. 'If you don't mind me sayin'...you look like a right stuck up little bitch', and smiled a mouthful of chewed food. '....If you like I could show you who's boss.'

'No thank you,' she said ever so politely.

'Huhh,' he laughed in a low sneer.

'As if you've ever had a woman you hav'nt had to pay for,' she added in an embarrassed rush, her neck and face going red, and lifted her magazine blocking his view.

He exploded with laughter spitting food over the floor and almost choked. When he'd calmed himself, he sat back, closed his eyes and quietly said 'Now to *enjoy* the rest of the journey.'

She was his. Her voice, her face, her gestures...*every* detail of her ....no stockings ....shapely thinish legs, similar thickness all the way up ...short skirt...kept tugging it down ...lightly tanned skin ....scruffy old expensive shoes ....glazed pink lipstick, this morning's ....light blue and white checked shirt, cotton .... shiny brown leather brief case with brass buttons ....low focus thin rimmed gold glasses ..clean long brownie-blonde hair....and that rosy sensitivity.

She sat quietly, not stirring behind the magazine as the minutes passed. He knew she had to be thinking about him.

How cute, how unique he really was. How she just had to find the courage. Then she did.

She dropped the magazine sharply on her lap. Her redness was gone, replaced by a much more professional look, like he expected she'd use in the board room, or around the boss.

'This what you want?' she asked without emotion as she pushed her hand beneath her legs and pulled her pants down, slipping them over her shoes...then slid forward on the seat inching her skirt up. He sat and stared as she unbuttoned her shirt letting him see the thin blue bra. *All for him* ...then he realised that the others were staring too. He pressed the switch which introduced the privacy curtain around her seat and his, and pushed the larger's leering head out as it appeared through the join. She slipped forward onto her knees and placed both hand on his thighs. He took her head in his hands...felt the soft crush of her hair... smelt it...touched her cool smooth skin....and pushed her head down.

By the time they reached the far side of Michigan he had enjoyed thirty minutes of utter pleasure. He opened his eyes and flicked off the programme. She was still sitting there, magazine held high. *Must have read the fuck'n' thing four times by now,* he thought with a wet smirk. The larger was asleep and wheezing like a half strangled pig. He leaned forward till his nose was touching her magazine and using his finger pulled it down just enough so that they could see the line of each others eyes. 'Have a good trip.....I sure as hell did?'

He sat back and kept talking to the back of the mag.
'Picked me up a little something in Cathedral Town. Kind off a new version of Zoneboy Authenticia. I don't think it's very legal..though i've no idea why that would be! You see... it records everything it sees and hears around it, then uses that

to create its own scenarios. It recorded your little tantrum earlier. You just *have* to see what it came up with. Remarkable really...I didn't think you'd have it in you.' He leaned over and slipped the Authenticia disc into her breast pocket, an amused chilling look across his face. 'Plays on any Zoneboy. Enjoy!'

The hovercraft rolled into the dock as silent as a migraine in quadraphonic. They ignored the over polite hostess and moseyed on down the terminal. A solemn looking oriental female met them, a hand held projection reading 'Vortex' illuminated the space directly above her. They shared the ride with a Japanese business woman and her very non-business partner, neither of whom admitted to speaking anything other than whatever language they were speaking. Both smiled politely as they left the car.

As they entered the grand hall the walls around them shrank into a perfumery of western opulence. Hats that people *had* died for. Sickly monied outfits for which the cut was the label. In contrast was the shy half inquisitive looks from passers by and occasional courteous short bows from Japanese couples and groups of businessmen mistaking them for contestants.

A less discrete look would have removed the *in awe* expressions. Drugs, alcohol, obesity....engraved in fuck you attitudes. The smaller was still wearing his specs. The screen lenses slid back and custom made refractors took the sting of the daylight bulbs from his dried out red eyes. First stop had to be food. Of the best quality, and served by those who gave off an aura of having been born for that singular purpose. Dispensed with a genuine enthusiastic smile and a glint which pleaded with you to want more. They ate with their fingers. Sushi on 20oz steaks with steaks on top.

The business woman they had shared the car ride with appeared again, handing the larger two front row seat reservations and apologising in perfect English for having somehow ended up with all four tickets. Her appearance had altered slightly. Her Divano jacket of fine sheets of artificial cloth laced with metal strands was now protracted, having dropped the interfaced sheets of material to form a contour flattering evening gown of pre programmed style and colour. It's stiffness flowing to allure an imaginary shift in the breeze. They accepted the reservations without comment.

Introductions were beginning at the far end of the hall. The Sumo entering for their traditional rights of enlightenment. The first two contestants were already warming up with repeated squats and breathing exercises to clear their minds.

Eating their way across the floor they set off on a direct line towards the contestant ring. In their way stood a piece of multi dimensional artwork within an empty radius of four metres surrounding it. The sculpture dominated its space. First impression suggested that it sat randomly without acknowledgement, unannounced, lonely almost, amidst the thrall of activity engaged in the hall. It was delicately placed on top of a simple heavy stone, white with speckled grey. The stone lay on a bed of clean dry silver gravel. In all it was a metre high and wide.

As it attracted the eye it seemed to sharpen with ambition, enticing an interest without overstating its cause. Its artistic focus blurred and like a magnet threw aside all other challenges to draw them in. Two or so more steps and it became their host, the room vanishing as their minds and vision took a step into the unknown.

The sounds of the crowd were gradually replaced, fading into echoes of seasons past; scents of wet moss lined rocks and the softness of falling cherry blossom within the roar of a fresh water fall, more distant falls whispering in the background; an overpowering sense of sorrow, healthy cleansing sadness laced with jade; tales of valour and friendship carried in the silent beat of a butterfly's wings and the sense of deer watching from the forest. Wild geese departing overhead.

He tried to throw it off. His flabby face whipping from left to right visibly amplifying his need. His larger twin stood still by his side.

'Great fuckin' rhythm bro,' laughed the larger. 'This reminds me of that gal in Texas..you know...the one who liked me...cool man...*good* vibes.'

'She..was a guy, fuckhead..and an ugly one.'

'Yeah...Yeah..you were just jealous,' snarled the larger.

'Lets get out of this freakshow it's making me itch.' They idled to the side, the peaceful buff fading into reality.

He was standing directly in front of them. Holding a hat sized red plastic box in his arms. 'For you,' he said flatly.

The smaller reached out grasping the package in a huge hand. Placing his free hand under it he flicked the lid off. His face twitched with an unintentional rasp of recoil. The waiter had left.

'Holly fuck.' He was staring at a two inch tall flesh and blood perfect likeness of himself. It was sitting naked, looking quite comfortable in an oversized armchair of wood and metal moulded from the floor of the box. It was intent on the luxurious spread of food laid across the proportionally scaled table by its feet and held a goblet of what could be claret. It stared back. Its eyes too small to read as fear or disgust. Its head moved slightly and its voice, *his* voice poured through the boxes speaker. 'He requires your immediate indulgence..third door to the right..you will be met at floor 4 at the lift.'

He turned to the twin, 'Ugh' and dropped the box. As it hit the floor he crushed it under foot. A red stain oozed over the carpet.

'Summoned,' said the larger, a semi pained bemused expression across the folds of his face.

They skirted the sculpture and made their way past the exhibition. A table and some German tourists got knocked over in an incidental act which could have been read as either arrogance or laziness.

The lift was empty but too small. They squeezed their way out into partial darkness. Three metres in front of them was a glass wall reaching to form a dome some thirty metres above. There was no one else there. They rolled forward, having flicked their eyes right to left, and pressed their faces close to the glass to look beyond...in amazement.

Below them, at first what seemed a long way below, like the view from a low hovering aircraft, was a perfect panoramic landscape. As they looked longer and harder, they realised it was in miniature. A vast desert plain enclosed by tall mountains to the west; a wide slow flowing river running through it. The scene stretched for the length of a sports field to either side of them. It looked real but was impossible to be sure. To the base of the western mountain range was camped an army. Its left flank protected by the foothills and its right by the river.

'Another fuckin' holo,' groaned the larger.

They recognised the domed glass as one way visibility as they could see in but the view on the other side reflected the sky. They ambled on round to the left.

He was standing with his back to them in discussion with two Company military officers. As they approached his voice became focused and clear, and directed at the twins. 'This is *not* a hologram. Flesh and blood. Clones...like *you*,' he said turning, smiling at the larger. He paused then added 'They do not, of course, possess your *outstanding* intelligence. Cloned from the D.N.A of none the wiser donors. He turned his head inwards to the scene below. 'Their virgin minds were never fully developed, not even sentient exactly, but capable of basic behavioural tasks and of taking orders. Each is downloaded with suitable programme generated memories. Real enough to them.' His introduction had created its own silence. After a while he filled it.

'Dawn 24th November 1221. The battle of the Indus. Shah Jalal ad-Din, son of Shah Muhammed 11 Al ad-Din, ruler absolute from the Caspian sea to the Persian Gulf deployed an army of 50,000 men against a Mongol hoard lead by Genghis Khan 'Khan of Khans'.

'Huh..so what's so great about Genghis Dan?' sneered the larger to a sharp look from his twin.

'He was renowned for his ruthlessness towards those who opposed....or *failed him* in their duty..' Vortex left the sentence hanging, reflected on the glazed look of incomprehension in the larger's eyes.

'Strategist.....a great strategist...I heard', butted in the smaller. He also knew nothing of Genghis Khan but had heard of Vortex's keen eye for military strategy. Of how in the LoTech incident he had reduced potential lengthy resistance warfare to a decisive battle won in a matter of days.

'Exactly! *Rapid mobile warfare* - he would have ruled Europe had he not succumbed to fever,' acknowledged Vortex. He continued talking as he walked some thirty metres or so, the others following. 'He structured his armies in units of ten. Ten men formed an Arban, ten Arbans a Jagun, then Mingans then Tumen of ten thousand men each lead by those selected on merit from the ranks.'

'And you what....watch?' asked the smaller.

'The actions of the leaders are controlled through chip link from here,' Vortex replied.

Below them, the half moon had now fully sunk in the west as the morning sun began to flirt with the shadows, and the second army emerged from the dust. Fifty thousand Mongol horsemen; a mass of blue, red edged tunics and fur clad quilted caps, radiant coloured cloaks reflecting their Tumen; the pace of their advance set by the rhythm of copper kettle drums. At the centre rode a black hoard of ten thousand Imperial Guards on long haired black ponies with bright red leather saddles. At their heart rode Genghis Khan, set apart only by his long red beard and soulless black eyes. Each soldier was protected by a lacquered leather jerkin over shirts of raw silk and carried a thin spear, scimitar and a shield of wicker. Each also carried a short bow and pouch of 60 arrows.

'Neat little hobby,' guffawed the larger.

The Mongol army advanced square on Jalal ad-Din's position. The nine white yak tails standard of Genghis Khan held high in the centre; rows of white and black chequered flags flowing by its side, ready to transmit his orders.

The Shah attacked first. A crushing torrent of cavalry smashed the Mongol left flank turning it towards the centre. Excited by early success, the Shah released troops from his left, pouring them into his triumphant right while leading a full on charge of his main force against the Khan's centre in search of a quick decisive victory. But this day was not written as his.

Genghis Khan foresaw and swiftly countered the move. His Imperial guard encircled their own troops and charged ferociously into the Shah's attacking right flank leaving little for the Shah's main force to engage. By this manoeuvre Genghis Khan had turned and swiftly compacted the Shah's troops to the centre, then the timely arrival of a Tumen, waiting in the foothills, fell on his weakened left from behind. In attempting to turn the Mongol's left flank Jalal ad-Din's army was itself encircled and defeated.

The battle was over in fifty minutes, no prisoners were taken. 'Who is Abigor...why do the defeated troops call his name?' asked the smaller.

'A myth implanted in their set up programmes, along with basic behaviour patterns to ensure loyalty. Those remain uninterrupted when the upper level programmes are later wiped. Abigor, in ancient culture, was a demon conjured to provide military aid and advice. Sometimes I indulge with extra troops, sometimes from another period or specifically pre-designed in anticipation. Such indulgence can tickle the imagination.'

They both stared back blankly.

'Well maybe not,' he added.

'And this time..?' asked the larger, an unprecedented look of disgust across his face. 'Are you going to let them slaughter them all..or send in some.....tanks?'

'Not today.' He turned his head back towards the carnage below. 'Genghis Khan spared none. It is such attention to detail that brings out the true spirit and flavours of the time.' He paused shortly. 'The lower topography and environment are real, identical replicas of the location, the upper tier of mountains and sky is holographic. These ..specimens are for all intent and purpose actual Mongol warriors and Persian princes. Through their short experience of life they have known nothing else. Given life to fulfil this purpose alone.'

'And afterwards you make pies out of them?' put in the larger.

'Their limited intelligence and memories are wiped. Their physical shells form the ranks of whatever venture tomorrow brings.'

'What's the point of it, seems a bit.....' asked the smaller.

'To test history. To establish if the greatest military achievements were in fact that or plain simple luck. And of course to test strategies for use in larger war games against A.I. controlled armies. Or in *real* battlefield scenarios. A little knowledge can go a long way in a close run campaign. I hear that you have had little success to date with our current dilemma. Your friend Claymore seems to have gained the centre of the field.'

'Her army buddies came up genuine cold. They don't like deserters much. There's still one or two others we need to.....'

'Yeah..so what's he want with a dead guy?' interrupted the larger.

'Forget about the others, they work for me and are equally keen to find her,' said Vortex.

'And the dead guy?' said the larger more loudly.

'A family matter..most probably a dead end.'

'So what else do you have for us?' asked the smaller.

'I thought that's what I paid *you* for.....! She has a mother. With a personal predicament of her own. If Claymore is unsuccessful perhaps a more direct approach from you may prove to be more fruitful. Perhaps.. if you were to explain her daughter's position..that as bleak as it may seem, it could get a lot worse..as could her own....or of course that they could both improve considerably and that all we want is what rightfully belongs to us..and so forth.'

'And they are in touch?'

'To my knowledge..not for some time...but she *may* be able to contact her.' Seconds passed then he continued in a slightly stronger tone, 'I could not possibly over stress the importance of finding her and of returning what she stole from me. I guarantee that the reward for success in this...*will* tickle your imagination.'

A waiter appeared, 'Simon will walk you to the hall and instruct you as to the mother's whereabouts. Enjoy the rest of the Sumo exhibition gentlemen.'

Eleven
Rogue A.I.

'Garlic. This bunny tastes of garlic. I hate garlic.'

'That's cause it's small and smelly. The runt of the onion family - just like you,' replied the smaller.

'I'm bigger than you!'

'I was talkin' metaphorically.'

'Yeah..well whatever that is..I'm still bigger.'

'Only cause I got you made that way..bigger and stupider.'

'Yeah well.....I hate *these* places.'

'Hey..have a little heart bro. We're probably the only company the poor slut's had this month,' mouthed the smaller through saliva chewing on laughter.

'Well..*I* ain't ever gonna end up in one of these holes.'

'YEAH..ain't ever gonna take you alive, eh.'

'Yeah....that's right! And *I've* got the biggest dick! So what *are* we doing here? Why'd he not get one of those psi probe types to look at her. Could have fried her brains and told us what she said.'

'Probably has. Like I said..Vortex always plays more than one line in any game. He can afford it. We just get what we can ..and get paid.'

'*Squeeze* the bitch he said..if she don't tell.. didn't he.'

'If she was a tell tale he wouldn't need us,' said the smaller.

'Squeeze her how?' What can we do to her in a Fed Authenticia Prison. Can't hurt something that ain't real.'

'We don't have to. We just make sure she knows that *he* can. *Erase her ass that is.*'

*****

Conscience or guilt no longer existed in Claymore's vocabulary - but *wearing a dead man* was making him feel dirty. Chas Blacker...on the other hand, could be his only ticket to this Sands.

It was two years since she had last met with her son - Chas. He was Company Detroit. Locked out in Company life; as she had always hoped for him. A career, security, in control.

Hadn't aged since she last saw him. His body scan icon looked good. She knew he was immune to vanity, that what she saw before her was the truth. He stood six foot two with a heavy build of army trim. His hair..shorter..but then his visit had been just weeks before signing up to Detroit. She guessed the military got their way. He looked healthy and smiled a lot. More so than she remembered. He looked nothing like his father.

She returned his smile.   'How are you son...you're lookn' real swell.'

'Ah..Company grub,' he replied quietly.

'They don't let you write?' She regretted it as soon as the words came out.   'I mean ...Company rules an' all. I know what..you know I know what it's like.'

'Yeah ..sure.'

'No time..and always tomorrow.' She laughed loud and genuinely.

'Yeah.'

After the silence she said   'So you on leave..or shifting roles or ...'

'Leave..a few weeks in reserve. So how have you been? Still playing racket ball?'

'Sure.. ball, bridge....found a little religion,' she laughed.

'Religion..that's good. Heard you had a neat circle of friends.'

'Pretty much. Of course some of them stay longer than others.'

'Hah..Yeah.'

'And your sister.....you keep in touch?'

'Been a while. Some time. Couldn't say where she is even.. sure she's doing just fine. Sands always could look after herself.'

'I hope you are right. They were *here* last night. Two identical lard cakes with mouths like sewers. Cheap resolution body scan icons. Asked a lot of questions. Interested in something she has.. they say belong to them. Mentioned someone called Claymore. Weren't too *friendly* towards him. Sort of spat his name.'

He breathed in slowly.....

'Who have you been pissin' off this time Sands honey?' she added absently.

'They say what she's got, or who they were working for?'

'Nope. Just that they could erase my virtual ass. Gave me some names of inmates who got switched off..left in the dark until they went insane. I've heard...rumours before. Must be *very* well connected.'

'If they were for real. She still with Company Vortex?' he asked.

'Yeah.....got promoted I heard.'

'She keep in touch?'

'Yeah..like you..when she can. She's living with some girl somewhere. Cathedral Town I'd guess, from what Loki says, but couldn't say for sure.'

'Loki?'

'A friend of the girl.' Visits now and again..passes some time.'

'This girl got a name?' he said forcing a smile.

'Nope. No name. Never met her. Only seen your sister once in the last year. Sends over this friend though, or the girl does, never was sure. I think she hit some troubled water after LoTech. But I heard she's over it now, so she'll turn up soon enough. Loki's an A.I.'

'What was with LoTech?'

'Ah..she did some stuff she regretted. Was seeking some kind of truth.'

'There's not much room for *Company* philosophers.'

'We are *all* philosophers of sorts. At least in so much as we credit ourselves with a set of values. Was having a problem putting hers into perspective. Came to see me shortly after it. Said she was thinking of packing it in..but that she owed them some time. Then again...you know Sands..once she's made up her mind.'

'Yeah. Well truth is I was half looking to chase her up..assuming I can find her.'

'Can't help you there..although Loki seems to think she'll visit soon. So where you been hanging out?'

'All over. Was on the fringe of the LoTech thing for a while. Detroit pulled out before it turned seriously real.'

'Same side as your sister?'

'Not that time. More recently. Was up Detroit Europa for a bit before policing Rajasthan. Could I get in touch with this Loki?'

'Appears and then leaves. No idea from where. Never uses the conventional doors. Never shows up on record as having visited. He did once mention an Authenticia club though....*Solitaire*..where Sands and her girl hang out sometimes. Sounds pretty exclusive. Run by Crescendo Living. Got the feeling that Loki's got a key,' she said smiling. 'I expect she's got some friends there. Maybe they know where she is,' she added.

'Well...suppose I could give it a shot.' Claymore replied.

*****

Her conversation with the twins had been short and ugly.

'*Waste of time!* Does that mean we don't get paid?' the larger had asked of his twin as they approached the last exit corridor.

'Chill it. We're out of here,' replied the smaller.

It zipped past and around the larger's ear; a tiny ball of wondrously coloured light, and flipped onto the tip of his shoulder. Then another; black laced with white slashes. He stopped in his tracks and stared into the one to his left. A tiny frame and impish smiling face.

Lifting his hand he swatted Loki with a heavy slap that sent him spinning head over heals. Somersaulting him face first into a closed door. *Splat!* The massive palm slammed flat squashing him messily against the frame. 'Like popping zits,' he snarled.

As he leered at his sticky palm, the red and black gue spread to form a fine liquid which solidified around his hand creating a perfectly fitted glove...then contracted to golf ball size with a shy crunch followed by his shrill scream of excruciating pain. As he grabbed with his other hand, the gleaming liquid ran between his pulped fingers splashing off the floor.... then it rose... rose to form the full bulk of a heavy framed muscular man. Tall.. brownish dark skin.. short black hair.. and a grin any demon would have been proud of.

Beside him stood another. Long flowing straight blond hair. Scents of yellow and bronze. Looks to die for.

First impression...he had been punched. *Recognition*...the fingers which pushed into the roof of his mouth had torn through his throat and now gripped the back of his tongue....his feet were lifted from the floor.

He focused hard, mentally punching *emergency escape,* desperate that it could somehow be milliseconds faster than the inevitable. Nothing happened. He just hung there..then punched it again, and again and again and.. as the glint from perfect diamond teeth turned his heart cold.

The fist which hit him next crushed the bridge of his nose driving him backwards through the air. He hit the floor hard, his good hand pulling at the hole in his throat, eyes bulging at the dark man who stood four feet away holding his tongue.

He mouthed a gargled plea as the dark one, flicking his wrist, sent the tongue bouncing, pursued by an estranged liquid pool which transformed instantly into a monstrous golden dog bounding after it. Scraping to a halt on large claws, it threw back its head and swallowed, bared diamond teeth in unison with its blue and silver black double, and plodded heavily towards the fat man sliding slowly away on his backside.

A deep throated growl said 'Welcome to fairyland.'

*****

The trees stood absolutely still. Ancient oaks mixed with light strokes of silver birch. Branches heavy laden with folds of soft snow cascading a sea of shadows. A winding level plain of snow telling tales on the frozen river.

The outline of the small humped bridge was barely visible through the puffed layers of recent falls. As they crossed, the dusk's glacier silence was broken only by the teasing warmth of an orange glow reflected against the inner walls of archer's slits set high in the castle tower. Welcome evidence of sanctuary and comfort within.

It had taken two long wintry hours to reach. Through a magnificent white land of glowing villages, lone barking dogs and crisp countryside of snow laden silhouettes. A pleasant journey for those guaranteed a warm welcome at its end; a reward to match the effort. An effort designed to deserve and enrich the reward.

They had come on war horses. Large sturdy beasts veiled in heavy cloaks upon mail. They dismounted, and Claymore stepped several paces into the covered gateway. He stood by a man sized pile of wind swept snow lodged in the corner of a massive wooden and iron studded door to the great castle. Stamped three times returning the blood to his feet and dislodging the thick snow from his boots and shoulders. He was dressed in weighty layers of fine woven fabrics, over which hung a long mail encrusted coat of dark rich cloth. The hilt of a jewel stamped two handed barbarians sword reached above his right shoulder.

Savannah's face was reddened by the frost. Blond curls poked out beneath the short iron and fur clad helmet. She appeared alert and eager to take pleasure from whatever lay ahead.

Their escort, who had lead them down through the pass and across the forest, braced his back against the icy wind holding their horses firm. Oblivious to the cold and snow, intent only on continuing the argument he had been having with himself throughout the journey.

Together they raised the massive circular stone knocker till their muscles began to yield and let it fall heavily against the door. The deep thud seemed lost to the open air.

Through the flame lit aisle they walked, casting shadows over damp moss inlaid walls, each step echoing across the chilled air. The five metre tall barbarian guard, left side cast in bronze armour, two metre club by his foot, did and said - nothing. Two goblets of steaming peppery mead by his side acknowledged their welcome.

Tides of warmth fulfilled the promise. Smells of spiced oils, rich wine and roast meat flooded from the great hall. Flavoured by the gruelling journey. Teased into them every inch of the way. For a moment he almost forgot why he was here.

His eyes cut through the colourful maze of activity that filled the hall in search of Sands. It was created of five tiers. Like a three dimensional chess table where the designer had cut the surface of the board into five uneven pieces and randomly staggered their level. From below, each piece appeared as a pool of sparkling crystal water, back lit in a soft orange glow. The hall had no distinct edges. Each time he focused on the furthest scene another would appear beyond it. Winding stairs pencilled on air and long knotted silken ropes connected each level. The silence startled him, then he realised that volume and focus of conversation was his to control.

'*Cybertramp.....Bagabundo pl..ease!*' exclaimed some pseudo aristocrat, followed immediately by explosive false laughter from her young companions. An immaculate angel refilling their spilt glasses. Either was a lie. He knew no one rode piggy back here.

He shifted his attention from scene to scene. Each was very different. Unique sets customised to the requirements of each group of guests. Each had its own host, someone very much in the know.

Sands wasn't there. His third Jack Daniels and second full visual tour of the party and no trace of baby sis. Felt a strange sense of relief and realised for the first that he had been uncomfortable about meeting her. Well, no point in missing a free party; since he was here, he might as well flow with the glow. A glance at his blond companion told him she had already gone down that end. He slipped in.

Dinner in the presence of the Gods. Aristo slang blended with a taste of jeans and worn oil, docmartins, polished choppers, buckets of noise. Sensation - charged to the heavens. Distraction - surpassing conversation at any level. Two places at once: a chat with friends while screwing the girl serving behind the bar; walking the tightrope across a pit of half starved bears while laughing lightly over the poor choice of wine; smiling at waiters while pleading insanity through tears and taught stomach muscles.

Sliding into your friends parallel thoughts... collecting olives from bulging vines, black clad peasants walking serenely in the shadows of dry stone dykes; burning ragged torches in the pitch dark, alone on a shallow raft, 500 miles from land. Gentle waves lapping over your bare feet and thighs, the periodical bump of something large, fins all around.

Deeper still... Over indulgence - stuffing your face with the things you love, while sunken pitiful eyes stare in silence by your side, hands outstretched..but you can't feed them all.. so you don't feed any and gorge on without a word. 'This is no Crescendo Club. This is an *A.I. interactive.* I could do with some of this on the permanent - given my recent sharp decrease in quality of life!' Savannah sighed, 'Multi-level sensation interface drawn from banked pools of emotion, inhibitions, guilt, secret needs - reshaped and focused to touch that unsuspecting G spot.'

'Sure does,' he replied. 'Set up by A.I's and strictly by invite. This is as close as anyone gets to Shadowlands. And as secure as it gets for a meet.'

'Well.. if our lady is here..Vortex ain't the only one well connected.'

*****

'You *enjoy* that bro? teased the smaller. Tell me. Is virtual death any different from the real thing. *Pain's* the same...the *fear's* the same..and when you pissed yourself on the floor there..it sure looked the same,' he howled in rapturous wheezy laughter.

'Didn't see you hangin' around to help me out - bro!' replied the larger defiantly.

'Hah Hah Hah..hah..ahh..wasn't like they could really kill you.. hah hah ah..just appeared that way! hah hah ahh.'

'I heard they could. If you're in deep enough.'

'Yeah..or if your set up for it. Some assholes like it that way.'

'So who were they?'

'Rogue A.I.? Someone our little girlie friend concocted to stop the likes of us doing our thing?'

'Concocted, what's concocted?'

'Arranged, set up, sorted.'

'FUCKIN' BITCH!'

'Or maybe not. Could have been somebody else.'

'Who..........Claymore?'

'Na ..too expensive..not worth his effort. Those were evolved AI's....cost more than money. You got to pal up with the likes of them...or get involved *long term*. There's always the boss himself though. Wouldn't put it past him. In fact it's right up his street. Probably splittin' his face laughin' right now at you crawlin' around in your own shit and guts squeelin' for the release button. Guess that would explain why you couldn't go anywhere...besides being a moron incapable of focusing hard enough.'

'You think Vortex would do that?'

'Sure..why not.'

*****

Sands saw his silhouette first. It registered *familiar* as her mind threw up a shutter, and questioned - *do I know you?* Then he turned face on, and through the space where her friend had sat, smiled - that childish protective smile that she had grown up with. That had always been there for her. She remembered his strong fingers stroke her hair and wipe away her childhood tears. Soothing her with words that said someday they would all be together and free. Of course he was wrong, but they were both too young to have known.

He was walking towards her. Her reaction flashed unmeasurable pleasure encased in shock, capable of nothing more than staring - *then* the explosion of fact crashed through her head, retracting the room in sharp jolts. *She had watched him fall..* just like she had watched Faro fall. But there had been no freeze, not then, *not for her brother,* no reprieve, no Honey Wagon..only cold empty death....so absolutely *final.*

'Hey sis looking good as always.' His beam was huge.

'*Alive!*' she whispered unintentionally, having accepted that she'd never hear his voice again.

'Feel good about yourself and the world will always end up being kind to you,' he laughed.

His words. A secret oath from a childhood universe, which she had always blindly, loyally believed in and remembered at times when the world turned bad - until *she saw him fall.* Kimmo's head turning away eyeing his next target....his AK100 *Deliverance* still spitting death into her brother.

Jack-knifed adrenalin kick started her chip, enacting enhanced memories into crisp magnified clarity. Dragging out the past silenced since the tears had ended, since she had watched him fall and fall and fall and... fall again and again and again....

She had met his eyes in stark recognition. A milli-second too late. Her blade having already done its work. His external oxygen pads slashed, bleeding air into the sulphuric atmosphere. Hunter seeker viruses instantly etching their life into his bronchial tubes, paralysing his lungs. His weapon dropping from his arm, gripping her shoulder..unblinking eyes staring back in disbelief.

She had slammed her gloved hand over the tares in pointless instinctive reaction, then her training screamed at her - SECURE YOUR SPARE PAD. He had lost consciousness and fell towards her as Kimmo's AK100 introduced itself.

His weight had shifted, thrown backwards, pulling her forward as she slipped in the phosphorous mud ...then the ground swelled like a vision from hell towering towards her as warrior tanks ripped from beneath the frozen lake churning the battlefield into a chaos of broken land bergs and poisonous pools. Kimmo pulling her..Vasos urgently yelling, spiking smart mines to aid their panicked retreat.

Passing months; sweltering dreams, unable to breath. Each night shouting his name into the soundless void of her helmet. 'Alive ...are you alive?' The words tumbled forward.

'Alive *and* breathing,' was his grinning reply. 'New lungs. Your partner's a lousy shot.'

Chip recoil... she saw it again..slowed down..*three shots.* Two to the head, both puncturing the helmet. The plate had change colour instantly, its inner shield engaging the self seal programme, attacking the helmet breach. But the shots had been good, point blank, and with the slashed pads - *certain death.*

'Hey...say your pleased to see me.' He laughed openly.

She smiled back....the most attractive smile Claymore had ever seen. It struck him as a strange thought given the crucial nature of the moment.

She locked her eyes onto his, took her own time, then asked 'How did you find me?'

'We called at the pen,' said the cool Southern accent of the woman now standing by his side. Sands turned towards her. The woman was tall and good looking - even with the word BITCH cut into her face.

'This is my friend Savannah.' He said.

Sands smiled again, but narrower this time. 'Lets find a closed environment. Where our thoughts are not for public consumption.'

He sensed the sadness in her voice, and her attempt to hide it. *'Blown it!* She should be ecstatic,' he thought. Later he found out just how right he was.

As she turned he missed the rest of what she said. It sounded like broken French and was directed at two of her seated friends. That in itself didn't make sense as her chip would have translated perfectly for her. The friends, who had for whatever reason, chosen to appear as black and gold demigods, took little notice. She then led him and Savannah across the hall.

She stopped at the base of a massive central pillar. Abruptly the gaiety of the hall ceased as the curved stone split apart. A reflective silver wall announced itself displacing images receding behind them, theirs excluded. A rush of dread triggered by the need for decisiveness hit him hard, but without hesitation they stepped through the mirrored light after her.

Had he read her right? Then again, without being sure, he had little choice - he couldn't throw his cards in just yet. Then again, he now entered *either* the realms of a fully conscious A.I. mind as play thing to an all powerful, emotionless and unforgiving enemy, or, he hoped, to an agreed real time meet with his target soon followed by game over. Trouble was, if he *had* read her right he was about to find himself with no choice left at all. Shadowlands had no known exits.

The texture had changed slightly but the floor was still there beneath him. He could sense its presence in the blackness within which he now stood. He felt it pulse as if testing the downward thrust of a new weight imposed upon it, firm up as if in acceptance, then melt beneath him to liquid.

It seemed that he was falling forever, his stomach racing to catch up. The impact was fierce as he hit the water, his knee smashing into his nose. Gasping for air, retching Jack Daniels, his stomach and lungs half filled with heavily salted sea water, he realised that his head was finally above the surface. Savannah was already treading water beside him.

'Guess she made us', she said with heavy sarcasm, blinking rapidly, clearing the salt from stinging eyes.

He said nothing, twisting his head side to side trying to work out where they were. *A harbour..* they were in a wide harbour.. enclosed on three sides by rough stones held by a metal net. Two small colourfully painted fishing boats tied together rocked peacefully some hundred metres away, bright sunshine catching the white buildings beyond.

Mediterranean. Calm. Then the panic struck - *Shadowlands!* *..GET OUT..GET OUT NOW...GET TO SOLID GROUND...NOW* - but swimming hard the harbour walls wouldn't get any closer. A small wave lifted him breaking over his head. He turned, saw the boats tilt then rise as the bulge of a three metre wave spanning the harbour gate rolled towards them. He swam harder, tiring. The wall was getting closer but not fast enough. Felt the edge of the wave catch him, then the roaring in his ears as it tumbled and pulled, rushing him forward...slamming him into the wall fighting for breath, clinging to rusted metal..sunlight again. No sign of Savannah.

He pulled his upper body onto the cage, pressing his face in exhaustion to the wire..then lifted his eyes towards the noise like thunder, as a mountain of water rising over the hill town collapsed upon itself exploding in a mass of curling tormented rage blasting everything in its path, its shifting white and sheet black dialogue stabbing fear into his gut - a thousand metre high wall of smooth black ocean swelling over the ridge, drowning the valley below.

He heard her shout as if from a distance then realised her face was pressed against his. 'Great.. just great!' Savannah yelled accusingly.

He found himself half through a '..too much reality for you?' reply when he realised the worthless words were lost to the roar as a wave slapped them apart threatening to put him back in the sea.

'*Why*?' she yelled. 'When *she* knew her brother was *fuck'n"* *dead!* What the hell did we go there for?' They thumped into each other again.

'She only saw him fall,' he shouted. 'She felt real bad about it. Thought maybe she'd grab for a straw..let her emotions override common sense......kinda like when I downloaded your ass.'

'Yeah..guilt's a real motherfucker killer ain't it.'

Again the sea slammed them hard against the wall.

'Can *you* die here?' she continued to holler.

'Yeah....no one ever gets back. Haemorrhage.'

'You think Vortex will dig my chip out of your head?' she screamed maliciously.

The words were blocked by the deafening roar as a wall of crumbled houses, mud and ocean raged towards them.

'*Se non e vero e ben trovato.*' '*What?*' said Claymore, more in exclamation than question.

'In Shadowlands..*If it is not true it is well invented.*' repeated the golden haired friend of Sands as he lifted them both, one hand a piece into the air and dropped them hard onto the stones. 'All the time in the world. And some.' He added as the turbulent mass hurtling at them froze inches from their breath.

They stared back in silence as he spoke again.

'And you are of Vortex we presume. A particularly sick icon of the flesh. *Did you know* that it was *he* who sent her there. To the same scarred land as her brother. Sent her unit to the same coordinates as her brother's unit. Sent her team to the *exact* pinpointed spot as her brother. His doing. W*e checked.* Your boss gave destiny the day off. *And now* he sends you back to haunt her.'

'*The bitch has something he wants!*' Savannah spat the words at the top of her voice. Then realised the world was now silent.

'Well then... you'd best tell him he can't have it. Hadn't you. Not at any price.......not for him.'

After the silence he added 'Yes...she wants you to live. Her brother dying *once* was enough. There is a soft side to humans that *we* will never understand.'

*****

A softness, like the warm bubbling of skin milliseconds before the acid bites, tingled from his ankles up through his spine, bottling in his throat. His eyes blinked open. Metal walls. Back on the road. Back in Vortex's Transport. *Vortex's trans....*

He sat motionless..ten seconds..then moved his hand a fraction and sighed as his mind shifted gear allowing him to accept that it was over. He moved his eyes, his head still..found the bottle of Lock & Load Jack Daniels. Courtesy of Vortex. Pre trip. The transport was cut bland, smooth edges, bucket seats moulded in hard light, censored to move in the flow. No visible tech. Everything built into the frame. Software the market never knew existed. The kind of expense only a Company would choose not to display.

Externally it looked like every other transport. Except for the worn graffiti and some serious looking dents. Beneath lay a second fabric frame spun with attitude; fitted with enough sentient firepower to hold its own at warrior class. When Vortex guaranteed privacy - privacy was what you got.

His foot tapped the table just to prove that he could move. The glass hanging over the J.D. chinked in response as he caught his reflection. He breathed slow and deep through his nose. Re-tracking his mind into frame. Refreshingly chilled air. His body relaxed. *'What was that doing here?'* A bottle of *his* brand of company. *'Gesture* to a thankless job well done? Maybe?' His contempt for Authenticia was well known to Vortex...as was his contempt for.. predictability. 'Had *he* known? Had the cold bastard guessed that she would get to him? Is that what it was...*a small token of his amusement?'*

He paused on the image of Vortex he had grown to expect over the years. 'Who the hell cared anyway,' he thought. A minute ago he was accepting his death..now he was alive *and* back in control. He returned the bottle's stare. 'How could he let her get to him like that,' he thought, unable to leave it. He had never even met her in the flesh..but then..he had *known* her all of his life - Chas Blacker's life that is. He felt himself reach for the glass. He knew her alright; what she looked like, could taste her scent, could relive every tiny minute fuck'n' mannerism that was her. Understood every thought in her head. Yeah...he knew her alright. He felt the J.D. ignite the back of his throat. 'Yeah.. he had downloaded a lot of good vibes on this woman.' He reached with his mind to delete Blacker, but found himself hesitate. It was more than that. It was bigger than Blacker. Layered on top of Blacker. He respected her, *he,* respected her. He realised that - he *liked who she was.*

A full five minutes passed. His mind caressing the glass held absolutely still in his hand. Then with a frustrated sigh he forced himself to snap out of it. 'Where to go now? When things didn't work out...set up and wait. It usually turned round in the end. He checked out her exit trace.' But *her* trace didn't register...and the club didn't seem to exist. No real surprise there. Pointless anyhow. As long as she was nestled in with her A.I. pals no one was gonna find her.'

He focused into his chip to delete Blacker. He had carried and run Savannah from an isolated room. Her *cage* as she preferred to call it. That way, her access to his thoughts or past actions was strictly on a need to know basis, without any threat of contamination to his chip.

Blacker however, was non sentient information. In effect, just a bunch of immaculate graphic memories formatted to interact with whoever happened to wear them. He therefore had to run *him* directly through his chip.

As he focused, the chip flashed *intruder*. A surge of panic froze in his stomach. He concentrated for a trace, path or time. There was none. All evidence of its presence had been erased. The intruder echo was calling *him* the intruder, even although it recognised him. That was its role. Backup in the event of an initial unregistered infiltration. At least he was post warned. As all external links were sealed, he realised that it must have followed him through from the club. He ran the necessary checks. No apparent damage or anything left behind. Reconnaissance, or at the very least, an inquisitive mind. He grinned a half begrudging frown; justice in a way. Whoever it was now knew everything there was to know about *him*.

He mentally punched delete. Chas Blacker was no more. He felt a weird sense of loss. Not of Blacker - of her. Of a woman who he very much wanted to touch. He felt strangely bad about the whole thing. It tasted of betrayal. Coloured by earlier mixed messages, brotherly love and his own impulse of something very different. *'TO HELL WITH IT,'* he said aloud, he was a mercenary, *she was just another fuck'n' job*. It was Vortex, not him, who was her problem. He was just the messenger..if not him, it would be another like him.'

But..it still tasted bitter. The moment had left him dazed, 'last time he'd mess with someone else's head.' But this.. this was something else. He needed to get her face out of his mind.

....Vortex's *Transport*. Then it struck him. *Savannah* was there - sitting motionless in a bucket seat. *Couldn't be!*

Staring at something behind him, her mouth half open, but no words ..for once.

It dug into his neck, picked him up and hurled him across the cabin. Dazed, he slumped to the floor. Lifting his head, his vision was full of green piercing eyes and saliva dripping off diamond teeth. In the corner he saw another golden hound siting on top of Savannah.

'A little personal bon soir from us,' growled Loki.

It was the only time he had ever heard her scream.

Five minutes later the same cabin materialised around him. Alone. Her voice in his head said timidly *'Is it real now?'*

The pieces were back together. 'Guess so.'

'Next time.. leave me at home.'

Twelve
Piranha on acid

Hi. My name is Roland. I am a fish. A trout to be precise. A Mark Four Boston Expo Cyber genic Trout. Class of 33. I live to be pursued - but *never* caught.

I live alone in the mud and ancient machines that bleed amongst the rushes and darkness, deep in the depths of a small lake south east of the river Diepe.

My world is a silent world. With the exception of Monday nights at 7.45, when I treat myself to an interlude of two soft hours of World Service brass bands. Glen Miller is my current favourite. I would indulge more often; it is not as if the passage of time is of any consequence to me. Of time I have plenty. But to spoil myself with longer interludes could, I believe, lead to boredom and ruin the pleasure that I have come so much to relish.

When I say silent - it is through choice of course. The world around me is full of sound and different tones, should I choose to hear them. Sometimes in the course of my duties it is necessary to partake in them. To listen to the echoes from above, distorted and reshaped by the current curving through and around the hollow objects embedded in the sand below me. I isolate each sound, and search out signs of activity that may mean danger and the need for cunning play. The whisper of sinking weighted lines, for example, each with its own brand of brightly coloured heads. Or the thrashing of some unlucky fellow on his way to lie with the sauté potatoes and butter sauce.

For most of the time, life is peaceful, with a slow and pleasant pace. Listening and waiting; forever on my guard. Periodically however - there is the call. The tune reverberates around my head, luring me to the direction of its source. It is often close to the same old spot. By the sunken barge in the newly flooded lands where the stone quarry used to be. It is quieter there, with less lines and nets to avoid. It is here that the pace quickens, for the call not only takes me into the path of danger but installs those momentary flushes of excitement which cause me to zip speedily through the water, much too close to the surface for comfort, and hurl myself into the air. Confoundedly, I have barely hit the surface before the same irresistible urge forces me to repeat the motion.

I must however, somewhat shyly admit, that I do on occasion enjoy those heated moments. As I have said, I am a trout not a salmon, and trout by their nature do not presume to leap. For this reason, I take pride in concluding that this eccentric inconsistency must have been purposely added to my early programming to counter my efficiency.

I must add, smug as it may appear to those with less avid interest in the matter, that all done and dusted, my record of avoiding being caught for 58 years, clearly speaks for itself.

For most of the time though, life has an easy rhythm. Well - except for the odd instance, such as last year when I gave that pike a particularly nasty fright. With retractable blades for cutting free on occasions where I have had the misfortune of becoming entangled in a strangers net, and a built in mark 33 laser for greater emergences, I most certainly do not amount to easy pickings for just any old hungry pike. I may look pretty with my shiny blue scales glinting beneath the surface, but when the chips are down, I can boast a fearsome mean streak.

I have *never* been mean to *him* though. Not once in all of the years that he has tried so hard to catch me. Not even that time when he tried to sneak up on me, fifteen years and two days ago, while I recharged in the sun. I suppose, that there were times when I have deliberately allowed him to get much closer than I would normally permit. Then, as I could almost taste his excitement in anticipation of the catch, just as he was one step away from his prize, I would dive changing colour in harmony with the bubbles and mud particles that he had disturbed, then shoot off to the left or right and settle still as dead on the bottom. I would lie there content in listening to his big rubber boots and net thrashing around in frustration once again. But even those few times could hardly be construed as acts of true wickedness.

Of course, if playing the game were to be considered as mean, then I would, I suppose, be found guilty. It is as if some instinct buried deep beneath my central programme drives me to play so hard. And of course it has been a long time. Over the years I have become wise to all the old tricks, and tickling my belly no longer holds the appeal that it did in my youth. Should I ever be so misfortunate as to actually get caught, it would be by way of tackle and line, I should think. My programme requires that I swallow all things of a certain pattern, which I must say I have always thought to be a trifle unfair. It does however, allow me to be otherwise more choosey than the other fish, who incidentally, are incredibly stupid and stare a lot.

Yes it is in my nature to play to win, but otherwise I do not seek excitement much, and some I suspect may find me rather boring. Yet I am fulfilled by my contentment. Although.... I do regret that he does not come as often as he once did, when we were both young. And rarely does he come now when the water falls from the sky. That used to be our favourite time. It was then that we shared the most fun.

*****

Marie cut the throttle as she pulled out of the bend approaching the two churches. They were identical and yet different. Both were tiny with short stubby spires which she remembered as being huge as a child. The first was painted white with a cross hanging at a slight angle, off centre from the door. The second was also painted white but had no cross. It had always puzzled Marie when adults referred to them as being identical, when they were clearly so different. Beyond lay the first of seven cottages which led down to her uncle's house at the end of the road.

As always she stopped on the brow of the hill.

'It *is* breath taking,' Sands said, her helmet retracting. Marie had always claimed that the view over the valley was the most soothing tonic ever.

From their vantage point the valleys converged directly below; where the river left the lake, then slowly widened again as the hills grew tall and became more distant yet closer at the same time. It reminded her of an artist's play with infinity. It was couched in cheerful greens, indigo and yellows. The longer she looked the more colours she saw and the more perfect it appeared. Now she knew Marie's love of this place was built on more than just nostalgia. 'His house is the one beyond the trees, where the smoke is rising?' Sands asked although she already knew the answer.

'Yes, and he must be home,' Marie replied excitedly.

'Best go visit then,' laughed Sands, as Marie revved up the bike.

He was not in the house when they finally arrived, having wound their way down the weaving unkept road, avoiding the deep holes and riding between the grooved tracks left by his pickup. They could see him working amongst the trees and vines of the aviary, a hundred metres or so away. Despite the roar of the bikes engine he had not heard them arrive, having set his hearing to a frequency more suited to his favourite pastime. Birdsong.

The aviary itself was open to the sky and not really an aviary as such, although for most of the time it was full of birds. He had dedicated much of his later 79 years to the study of birdsong and had published several papers on it; mainly on the subject of comparative resonant tones, drawing parallels between the rhythm of natural and caged water. Marie liked to use his work in her Authenticia sculpture.

As they approached closely he turned and saw them. He was not startled and instead smiled as if they were in the middle of the most beautiful conversation. Sands found herself instantly return his smile with all sincerity. At a glance she saw Marie had also responded in kind, her eyes full of tears.

'Oh.....h! Uncle ...are you well. Are you well.. you look just fine.'

He just continued smiling and slowly lifted his arms welcoming her rough embrace. Then he kissed her on both cheeks, held her at arms length for a second or two then hugged her softly again.   'And this must be Sands,' he said still holding her by the arms.

'Qui, uncle this is Sands..I'd like you to meet my friend Sands.'

'Hello,' responded Sands, meeting his eyes.

'I am delighted. Having heard so much about you.' Taking both their hands he gestured towards a very old and twisted wooden bench. Lifelong cycles of sun and rain had blistered and peeled its youthful flame red charm; turned and shaped it, giving impressions of life to new contours which now were one with the vines and knurls of the tree, which provided shade over the southern part of the aviary.   'I shall get us a cold drink in a moment or so. But first sit and tell me your news.'

'Let me uncle.'

'Very well my child. It must be hot in those suits.' Moving his hand slowly in the direction of the house he added 'There is iced wine and apple juice in the parlour. You know where it is.'

The next few hours passed quickly. Talking face to face; repeating everything Sands knew that everyone already knew, as Marie never let a week go by without getting in touch. But in person it all seemed to carry its excitement fresh again. When evening arrived they moved indoors and sat themselves around a robust and very large oak table. Marie pointed out the scratch marks where her first cat, Jasman, had sharpened its claws on the leg as a kitten. The room was wall to wall old paper books. It smelled dusty and dry. In the corner blazed an open fire burning large rough blocks of some pleasant smelling local fuel. Sands had never sat in front of one before and was intrigued by how it continuously drew her attention.

Roland made his own wine; from just about anything it seemed. They drank his favourite, which he said that he kept especially for Marie's visits. It was made from the same local vines but of an older vintage. Made by Gregio Dublionni before he passed on. Roland's life long friend and almost a second uncle to Marie. He had been renowned locally for his skill at blending and had always said his success was down to a small secret which he would reveal in his will. Which he did. But having tried on several occasions, Roland could never seem to match the taste. In addition to the recipe Gregio had also left Roland the last thirty cases. Roland had laughed as he told Sands, saying that at his ripe old age that was more than enough to see him and his old friend out.

'The summer is almost done.' Roland said. Before he could finish Marie was laughing. 'You always say that uncle as soon as it has begun.'

'You are of course right Marie. When I was younger it was a kind of foolish logic to make the summer somehow last longer, and now that I am older, I still say it, but I am secretly glad now when the heat subsides. Lately I prefer the cooler evenings of late summer and autumn.'

'You never bothered getting air regulation installed?' asked Sands.

'I'm not *that* frail yet. I never liked the cities, as everything is the same. I like it when it rains unexpectedly. It's good to be able to complain about the sun being too hot or the air too chilled. And anyway, when otherwise would I get to wear those wonderfully coloured sweaters Marie brings me.' They all laughed together.

'What kind of music is that? I have heard something similar only once before?' asked Sands.

'Do you like it?'

'It's got some interesting sounds. Sounds like people.. locked into having fun.'

'Well.. I knew that I would like you Sands, Marie never brings me anything but good. It is Glen Miller. A brass band of the 1950's. Bands were large then. Huge. Music charged the world like some new form of energy swaying across continents.'

'Sounds familiar,' said Marie smiling.

'Yes. Synology, the science of cerebral undercurrents, was the medium; Authenticia the crescendo. Music is I suppose the poor distant relative,' responded Roland.

After a few moments pause Sands laughed and said 'Well yes... and the fish, tell me about the fish!'

'Hah! Ah qui mon ami elusif. It was a gift of friendship and endurance, almost a lifetime ago. There have been times..let me tell you ...that I have loathed that fish. Times when I have sworn that I would return with dynamite and end our relationship once and for all. And I have meant it. On each such occasion I have returned home, drunk some wine and talked to myself with such fury. And each time I have always, without intention, talked myself out of it. It is after all, I always remind myself, only a fish. And not even a fish at that. I mean... it is not as if I could even eat it!' He stopped talking, looking embarrassed at having allowed himself to overstep his normally reserved and polite opinion. In the silent moment of smiling faces, he laughed loudly at having been so keen to conceal what everyone around the table of course already knew. '*Yes*... I am pissed at not being able to catch Roland the Trout for over fifty years. But it is a much larger and better picture than that. Roland is not my enemy. Quite the contrary. I consider him as a friend. He has been the source of endless hours and many years of shared pleasure. He *is* my friend.'

The game, was originally set without agreed rules, but has now been played for so long that the rules have formed themselves. And the rules have evolved in favour of the fish. To break them would be like losing fifty years worth of hard earned credit. To break them and win would be to lose. So each of us play to the rules. Yet.. both of us increasingly slip dangerously in and out of the edges. But when we do so, it is always to the supposingly unknowing benefit of the other. Like when Roland the trout comes answering to the call. For years now, I have known that the frequency receiver which demanded his presence has been broken, yet still he comes. Like for the years when I have declined to use multi hooks as clearly prescribed as acceptable in the manual. And, although it may not exactly be ascribed to gentlemanly reserve, the time when I declined Gregio's invitation to use his 12 bore shotgun as our blue and silver friend leaped insistently to and fro from the water some fifty metres in front of me. Each time, I have felt that somehow he understood.'

'Do you think that you will ever catch him?' asked Marie.

'Do you think that he will ever let me?' laughed Roland. 'And the two of you, how did you meet?'

'We met through Authenticia. I was recovering...long term Company rebuild. Marie gate crashed a party. Neither of us were looking for a friend but we both found one. We just went from there.'

Roland smiled and looked around at Marie. It gave him great pleasure seeing her so content. He had been quietly concerned about her passion with alternative realities, but now it seemed that she had found something very real. And he had a good feeling about Sands.

*****

Sands saw his face in the fire. Buried deep amongst the red and black edged embers; sculpted from hollows in the shadows of the crumbled, folding ash. It was a face she knew well. A face that she knew *very* well. Of that she was certain. Yet... she sensed that they had never met. So familiar....definitely familiar, a friend, soulmate, an old acquaintance, but from where? Why couldn't she remember?

A trick of the light, of the fire? Flickering between past images from her subconscious.

She snapped out of it looking away. No way....*she was certain that she knew him.* She returned her gaze into the fire. He was still there. She could hear Roland talking above her thoughts, but she couldn't concentrate on anything except the image. Couldn't resist the overwhelming urge of seriously, absolutely, needing to know. *She even knew his name* - she just had to somehow find it.

She stared intensely, trying to freeze its semi fluid motion - only to watch the flames lick it away. Then it shot back, spread across the coals. Burning softer, though brighter than the spirit of the fire. *Then* it was engraved - branding hot behind her eyelids. Then it was all she could see.

She focused into her chip. Blank..no resolution..this was external. Virus. Customised, DNA reactive..Company installed - a little extra Company security? But *here*...in central Europe, 8000 kilometres from where they would expect her to be? Possible ..a genetic code activated through high stratosphere reflectors could pin point her location for them. But why would they wait until now? No..they would have enacted it earlier; why risk a panicked sale? And why would they let her know?

No, a trace didn't make sense. Maybe just too much time messing in Loki's world, combined with a day's bike ride in the sun and a gut full of wine. That sounded about right. But the flames licking *his* face were burning *her*. Not badly - but enough to sober her up, and get her attention.

She rolled her eyes and mentally shook her mind in an attempt to throw it off. It faded, but then he was there again, brighter still. She felt driven by a sudden urge. His urge. He *wanted* her to know his name. *She just had to know his name.* Like knowing it was singularly the most important detail in the world. It trickled into the rooms of her mind, and grew. It pulsed, fragmented and smudged, threatening to form, bursting to be made known. It...his name was ... Ye....Yenxal ...Jenxa.....Jinx.. that was it...*Jinx*. His name was Jinx.

Her body felt weightless. Stunned in her instant of acceptance. His name, she realised, was only a key. It was his mind, his very essence that he wanted her to know. His mind had touched her, flowed through her. She had sensed *his* confusion, his innocence, the burden he seemed to carry - and a trillion other incomprehensible complexities which were not his.

Those felt layered in the background, each hustling, smothering a throng of others to be heard. She tasted uncertainty, self doubt, and desperation. *Those* were his. And envisaged dry lips and a sweat beaded forehead.

She tilted her neck and quickly shook her forehead realising that the sweat was hers. Droplets of moisture spun from her damp blonde hair to sizzle in the fire. He was still there. No longer burning behind her eyelids, or stretched across her thoughts, but flickering calmly beyond the glow of the fire. She heard herself inhale deeply, and after a long pause exhaled slowly. Her mind slowed from racing pace in shallow terraced jolts, towards her normal calm. She stared at his face. She had been touched, brushed - but not by him alone. By a *shared* conscious. Yet he was no advocate. *The message* was his alone.

She had beheld the unveiling of primal patterns, *rhythmic blueprints for life* - a universe die and another born, but most compelling, most simple, most direct of all, she had been engulfed by his desperate need for trust. Her trust. Whoever he was, however he had managed to contact her, whatever he wanted, he was definitely in way deeper than she was. If she could believe *that* to be possible? This had been a plea for help. *Then he was gone.*

Her attention was returned to the room by the rich smell of roast pheasant. Marie was carving the bird which lay surrounded by an array of locally grown steamed vegetables. The room was lit entirely by the firelight and candles, which flickered slightly against an effortless breeze entering the open window. The idyllic peacefulness of the scene was both novel and remarkable to Sands.

'It is wonderful to have you here, my child. Although I never truly feel that you are ever far away,' Roland was saying in French as he lifted his head and saw Sands looking at him. 'Ah, my apologies. I thought that the sun had taken its toll, and you had nodded off for a small while'.

'Perhaps I did', she replied. We can talk in French as you prefer, the quality of my chip allows almost instant translation,' she smiled back at him.

'Not at all. I am enjoying the change, and the challenge. My chip also has excellent translation capabilities, but I prefer to remember. My English was once very good.... a long time ago.'

'Yes, I remember Marie once saying that you discouraged the chip based rapid track learning, and used to help her with her lessons.'

'There was a time, when everything seemed to become too easy, and the sense of satisfaction was lost. I wanted Marie to *appreciate* the knowledge that she would accrue in her life. A decision with regard to which, I can now look at her, and proudly say was the correct one. He turned towards Marie, and smiling said 'Appreciation, made you look more deeply beyond what you were taught, and helped you become the sparkling genius that you are today.'

'That is ..partially true...the appreciation part,' laughed Marie. Without understanding the mechanics of knowledge, which otherwise was so easily attainable, I would probably never have questioned, and may never have entered Authenticia and got to meet Thor and Loki. Which would be like never having been born.'

As he tested the heat of the plates Roland asked 'And Sands, tell me about your family.. brothers, sisters?'

She took a slow sip of wine then said 'Just a brother. He was killed. Then more slowly 'Quite recently....Company.' Roland stopped for a long moment, then quietly asked 'What was his name?'

'Chas'.

'I am saddened.' There was a short silence, then he lifted his glass and with a most genuine smile 'To Chas...and his lovely sister'.

The remains of the evening passed at a pleasant pace. Roland retired first, and bid them both goodnight with a shortened version of a tale of northern gods, which Marie had compelled him to retell on a nightly basis when she was young. It had been a good, and a long day, and they were both glad to shut their eyes. Sleep hit them fast, partly due to the wine and partly as they both knew that tomorrow they would have to be razor sharp.

*****

The tyres bit into the road like red hot rivets. She tore into bends as if riding for laughs in some game. Hit a tree at 180 kilometres per hour - switch it off and start again. Not here. Marie hung on real tight. She loved when Sands drove like this. Which was pretty much all the time.

The bike was Marie's. Had cost them mega to hostess it on the drive-on carrier. Ridiculously excessive relative to the fourteen minute Atlantic crossing. Most people hired flexi cruisers on the other side. Marie had been insistent about the bike however, given the need for the absolute purity of its genetic transmission system. A privileged clean download was essential. Anyway, she liked riding pillion and wanted to show off her recent toy to Roland. He had always kidded her about the beat up wrecks she had insisted on driving as a youth.

They had disembarked the previous day at the Stagecoach land port north of Perugia and cut directly over the Florence-Pisa Bridge, the city in miniature a quarter of a mile below. Two lanes of solid white magnetic inertia wisping lightly in the air. Invisible lasers blasting energy into the neo turbines which pushed the sections of plates together. Rumour was that four hundred lasers fired simultaneously during the same milli-cycle.

Today they re-ran the ground route from Roland's to the bridge then took to the air grid, shooting above harvest bulging valleys, over red tiled towns and postured villages, reflected as shimmering light over still blue lakes. Trees and spires below appeared and vanished in a shared instant, too fast to recall. The air lanes of old Europe were narrower and fewer but still by far the fastest way to get around, assuming you could afford it.

Sands drove with a vengeance. Colours fading into a smudged spectrum. Shapes left behind. Marie knew that Sands focused control was natural. Slowed down to the subliminal, multiplying her reaction time by three fold. Enabling her to react three times as fast without any degree of stress. Inverted concentration....nicknamed *marine talk* in the Company.

The technique was chip taught. Set up and triggered by a chip command which shut down the more mentally fluid sections of the brain, allowing the mind to look within itself to the purpose of its survival at that particular moment in its life. To the exclusion of all other thoughts.

Its use always induced a chord of pleasure deep inside and lingered there, for three times as long, before settling her conscious waves to dissect each individual instant as it happened, enabling a speed of reaction of almost premeditated hindsight. With the world moving so relatively slowly around her, it seemed like she was dwelling in the moment before the event. Her mind being tugged back, and held, then allowed to think and react at a surreal rapid level. Against any non-marine in the scenario, she had all the time in the world. Marie always got exited in the knowledge that it was real. A technique, so often practised that it no longer required the chip trigger, and could be enacted for relative short periods without spillage into parallel real time. Marie knew that Sand's chip was inactive at present.

Sands knew that Vortex would come. Not in person of course. She would not see him, or breathe his dry orange scented cologne. She involuntarily retracted her lips, recalling the salt taste of cold dead air that shrouded his presence. But he would be there all the same. Present in every movement, every gesture; directing his troops from behind distant walls. They would be hand picked. Selected by experience specific for this particular job. With particular peculiarities known only to him. The directive would be simple and rigid. No room for interpretation, or tolerance for error.

She twisted the throttle hard in reaction to the flashing thought of his thin lipped soulless smile, recalling his sharp edged profile as he stressed the absolute importance of ensuring safe delivery of the disc, that he had entrusted her with.

As the bike soared through the traffic, she slid into memories of her brother, faces of fallen comrades, faces of comrades still with Vortex, of stricken burnt out cities, warrior tanks, landbergs, Lotech.... She slipped between two pot bellied express trams, causing their track lights to blaze in annoyance, and in the same movement dropped three levels and shot straight across eight lanes to the inside slot for exit to the city.

They were forty minutes ride past the town of Carrara forty kilometres north of the bridge, where they had stopped the previous day to set up stall, and now approached the hills of Rome. Marie gripped the bike hard as Sands braked into the automated buffer zone, where the air lanes blurred to merge with the ground traffic. The city map lit up their helmet plates, as Sands tried to relax her thoughts. She focused on the gentle gestures and notions of Roland which had so much impressed her, and on Marie's calming innocent smile, but converse images raged from the world that was her past, and which, until very recently had been everything, to her present which remained confused and very possibly held a short and unpleasant future.

Truth was, it had been *reaction* rather than *decision*. She had jumped ship without any real rational thought. Provoked to the extreme - she had taken the bait. And now... looking to parley. But with what? What could she.. what was she *expected* to take to the table? A package which rightfully belonged to him, and for which she gambled on its value without any idea as to what it actually contained. And in return.. what.. absolution.. *from him!* Or..her life..which she saw as already rightfully hers. And would he be willing to deal, or would he simply assume to take it? Whichever - she knew that he would come, and that he would expect to get what he came for.

'Cities inner ring. No more *bullshit play with words. No more self doubt. Not a hint...time to en..gage the bastard.*' She wiped the bikes upload, erasing its current presence from the Federal Roads Network and enacted the loop with Loki. The plan of Rome was instantly replaced by the boulevards of Free Paris. The bike's chip, clean and of minimal capability, was unconnected to any prying Company eyes. Just another clever engine. When the trace was run they would appear at the very worst as cruising through the streets of Central Paris where Company action was frowned upon and could be met with force. At best, the loop would ensure total non detection.

She enacted the link. The plan of Paris faded instantly, replaced by the cracked unshaven face of an elderly market trader. Once sharp piercing green eyes, now filled the screen with a glazed seen it all before, bored expression. 'Trois kilos de pomme de terre,' shouted a voice outside of the picture. She backtracked the zoom displaying the town of Carrara's weekly market in full flow. At its centre sprang the fountain of Ugual Mente, its clear spring water hanging softly in the air before eventually floating downwards to spill over its shallow marble plinth, creating trickling streams which ran off the pavement's edge.

Within the fountain lay a small glass beaded ball. It rested amongst the wet leaves behind the path of the jets, like a discarded child's toy patiently waiting to be found. Overlooked by inquisitive eyes it introduced itself at 1.25 pm precisely. Thirty five minutes before the market started trading.

It was alive and bright, and it brought something new to the market. It shot a sculpture of three dimensional theatrical ambience, yet with a casual form that gave its presence a sense of having always belonged.

The sculpture was small and designed to appear like a cheap holo of a group of impoverished children. As people passed, some of the children would lock their eyes onto them, and with outstretched palms stare at them until the passer-by turned away. The children would then sit until, out of compulsion, the passer-by turned to look back. Then the smallest boy, dressed in rags, would stand up crying loudly and thrusting both hands open towards the startled shopper. Occasionally one of the older children would step from the water to kneel at the feet of someone who had hesitated or stopped. Those who did, looked confused as the sculpture was unattended with no indication of what it stood for, or what was expected, if anything, of them. Some threw coins into the water.

It had been fashioned by Marie. It was no work of art. A purely professional, functional tool created to deliver the necessary effect. A tableau which could keep them alive. Entwined within the intricacies of its tarnished kiln light, slept the carrier for a score of eyes which she and Sands had released into the town square the previous day.

She flicked through the screens for signs of his presence. The exchange was supposed to be one to one. Between her and one Company officer, who was to be readily identifiable. She was twenty minutes late. A lifetime to Vortex who demanded split second punctuality. She had timed it just so, to get his full, albeit infuriated attention.

Eye five froze displaying commotion. At the far side of the bar, a huge marine with a back shaped like a pool table was breaking someone's leg at the knee. From the group to his left the eye amplified the sound of *traitor*. Sands reclined as she caught sight of the marine who had uttered it – Vasos.

The huge marine then turned and she recognised him – Kimmo. There were two broken looking bodies by his feet. She hit the other eyes. There were troops everywhere. At least thirty. The blue and black of Company Vortex merging unconvincingly with the tangled coloured mass of carts, merchandise and locals, along the edges of the converging streets. She outlined one soldier and instructed the eye to *seek*. It immediately highlighted similar clad shapes on the roofs and set back in the shadow of windows. 'Well I guess..that answers that,' she muttered to herself.

She returned her attention to the bar. By now they would have figured that they had been stood up. Now it would be time to learn what they could, to gain *something*, even the smallest clue may yet turn into an answer. Kimmo had turned his attention to a youngish, rather scruffy looking barman, who given that his employer's bar was getting trashed and his customers abused, seemed relaxed about the whole thing. Which was why he had caught Kimmo's eye.

Kimmo's frame filled the screen, then another voice burst in from behind him. 'You...!'

The young man looked up at the figure behind Kimmo and eye 4 filled the screen. *'Faro,'* she exclaimed, his name gushing from her lungs. She couldn't properly catch his face; the eye showed his upper body and side of his head. His shoulders were as beautiful as she recalled, and instantly recognisable. An absolute 90% from the line of his spine. He was without extra body armour; the only one. He wore an AK100 hand gun diagonally across his pelvis, heavy and overkill at close range, relatively all but useless in the field. She couldn't take her gaze from him and fumbled for the eye control to display his face. He *was* alive - it had been true. 'Faro.' She had been so certain that he was dead, that his second chance was nothing more than rumour. The eye was filled by his face, 'Faro.' She stared for a long time. His posture, his frame, body language, the subtle texture of his movement screamed out at her - as alive as he had ever been. She wanted to burst, shed tears of relief, of thanks. She wanted to shout his name, to grab and hug him.

But there was something slower in his mannerisms. His taught facial expression, his apparent lack of emotion, and there was a dull wet look across his eyes. She unconsciously held her breath, checked her emotion - and held it suspended. She knew him too well. Had shared his self too closely to accept anything short of the total truth. Something wasn't quite..as it had been, *AND ...for fuck sake ...it was her that they were lookin' for!'*

His voice was slow and cold. 'We are looking for a woman...a traitor....a once upon a time marine. Mid twenties, blonde... attractive. Blue eyes. Vasos slapped her wrist strap projecting an image of Sands in front of him.   'Familiar?'

The young barman stopped polishing the glass he held in his hand and stared into the image. He looked at it for a long time and had adopted a broad smile when Faro interrupted him.   'Have you seen her?' he asked again in a cold steady tone. The barman looked back at the glass, then replied in a loud professionally talkative manner for all to hear 'OOO....h yeah... I saw her alright, Yesterday. At the start of the lunch crowd. He paused, then looked up at Faro. 'Reminded me why I wanted to be a barman.'

'And why would that be?' Faro asked with an edge that carried an atmosphere all of its own.

The barman sharpened up, as if suddenly getting wise to a bad situation ripe with potential to get a lot worse fast. He broadened his smile and in an exaggerated professionally joking way delved deep into his repertoire. 'Hey... he flicked the damp cloth in the air.. good looks and charisma may well have fled me at birth...well so bloody what, I spit, metaphorically speaking, on all those who would like to remind me of it. Every Friday night they fill this place. Fill it with their phoney smiles and big mouths.....'

'We have a connection of sorts Sir,' grated Vasos through the fused end of their insignia chip connection. Somebody trying to scratch our link.'

Faro turned intently, looked at her, but said nothing.

'Want to talk about the Hollow I suspect,' said Kimmo through the link.

'I never said that! exclaimed Kimmo. *'I never said that ...that wasn't fuckin' me!'*

'Sounded like you. Motherfucker.'Said Vasos.

'It wasn't me...never opened my mouth.'

'Enough.' Faro interrupted. The link. Room it.. and let them in.'

'Gone Sir...it read like one way. Looks like they said all they wanted to say.'

'Over enthused wanker wanabees,' continued the barman unheeding of the sealed exchange, '..up their own assholes and looking for *me* to make 'em feel good. *Demanding* that *I* feel good, to make them feel good. But the truth is...they don't really even notice that I'm here. Too busy looking at themselves - *well until she walked in that is.*

Caught my eye..right through a crowd of fifty plus. Looked straight at me and smiled like we were old friends or something.' He looked at Faro again, laughed and said 'Felt like..*hey stand up straight*..you know..invisible silky music in my head. Sucked deep on my cigarette. Warmed me in the belly she did. *Made me remember why I had wanted to be a barman.*' He placed the sparkling glass on the counter beside another and filled them both with brandy. Then picked one of them up.

Faro left the drink where it stood. 'You talk to her?'

'Sure. I felt stupid. A woman like that. Might even have got myself a red face. I mean what the bloody hell would *she* be lookin' at me like that for?'

'Somebody's watching,' interrupted Vasos, with a ring to the tone.

Faro turned and followed her gesture, looking straight into the eye. 'Find the source.'

Ten seconds later she replied. 'That was easy,' and pointed in the direction of the children.

'Find the link...then tell me it was easy.'

'It was easy,' she half grinned. 'Company Detroit.' Second later the grin vanished. 'And Company Senate.' Two seconds later she added 'And Company Yamato.. and Company Montreal. They are all projecting it!'

Faro flexed as someone spoke in his head. 'None of them are projecting anything. Check it again. Interface it with your mainline chip, you've just been upgraded to class A. Interface room 14.'

She took two to three minutes then sighed blowing air out of puffed cheeks. 'Now it says it's being projected *from* room 14. And...I'm get direct link feedback from at least two other Companies. If they ain't projecting - they are as sure as fuck listening in.'

'Not possible,' interjected Sergeant Kimmo. '14 is Company V secure. Nobody but nobody can get in...and its *interface only*..doesn't work as a source.'

Faro slipped into the silent distance voice again. 'They couldn't..didn't...till you entered it..then they did. Sucked us in...cannibalised our link...then projected it themselves. They already had a multi level loop giving direct visuals to any Company nosey enough to be a little interested. Then, through your interface via the room we gave them direct link to our chips - *vocals to edit*.'

'What the fuck for..Sir?' asked Vasos.

'A picture of an elite unit of Company Vortex troops staking out some insignificant market place a long way from home... and a confused reference to a Hollow bomb. A clear message that somebody has, at the very least, got something that Company Vortex wants real bad. *They just got an invite to tender*...that's what.'

'So why can't we find the source?'

Faro's attention had turned back to the sculpture. 'Because the loop terminates inside Detroit and the other Company systems that Vortex can't access. It stole in, told them it was there, told them why..then invited them to kill it.. or to watch.'

'We've been set up. We ain't any closer to her..and now we probably got some serious competition,' grated Vasos. 'It ain't really the blueprint for a Hollow.. is it Sarge?'

'Whatever it is..she just upped the ante,' grunted Kimmo.

Vasos refocused on the signal. 'That sculpture.. ain't just reading local.' A couple of seconds later she added 'Yeah.. it's the medium,' gesturing with her head.

Faro moved out of the bar towards it. The children saw him coming and started to cower together, the smaller ones moving behind their older sisters. As he got closer, the smallest boy broke loose from his sisters hand and stepped out in front of him. The child tugged at his leg and with a huge smile held up a silver disc. As Faro looked down the child said 'For you maybe.. but not today... you ugly fuck.' With the smile still in place the child tossed the disc high into the air where it burst like a firework of black words reading 'SALE POSTPONED.'

Faro stood still for a short moment then walked back into the bar. The barman now stood facing the mirrored wine studded gantry. 'You were saying.....you talked to her?'

The barman renewed his broad smile and continued as if his sentence had never been interrupted, in his loud get out clause routine. 'Sure.. she had made me feel a bit.. well.. stupid...so I turned to face the wall, but then when I turned round several minutes later - there she was, standing right in front of me. Startled me I tell Ya. Then I thought..wo, Jesus bloody hell *it is a bar*. I laughed at myself.. then I saw that she already had a drink in her hand, and was smiling at me.......*only me*.

Well.. my mind wa..sss putty. Then.. her friend called her Sands. Wanted to know if she wanted frittas or cheese frabbas? She didn't answer her. She was too busy lookin' at me. 'We have never met..I think,' she said. He let out a huge sigh. She felt like an ice cool drink on a hot summers beach. I never spoke.. just polished the glasses and smiled cooly. As if it could all be said without saying it.. like it was an every day event. Then she asked what my name was..and my allure plain vanished. But.. I recovered well. 'Just call me *Barman*,' I replied. She just smiled the best ever smile.

Yeah... I talked to her.' He placed the last glass to start a second row, and re-arranged the towel, the satisfied smile still on his face.

It was a look that Faro recognised. He knew that somehow, this barman had touched a spot that *he* had once shared. No.. that wasn't it. It was a spot that had once belonged to him. It sparked some deep emotion, lost and long twisted out of comprehension. He snicked the AK100 from its moulded housing, levelled it and replaced the barman's lungs by two gaping three inch smouldering holes.

*****

Roland the Trout recognised the slurp and splash of the long rubber boots fighting their way through the mud some five metres from where he lay. He would often begin his day at this spot. Where the big tree had stood before the reservoir had filled the valley. He often waited here. Silently. This was where he and Roland had first met. Where they had introduced him, to light, to contemplation, and to the river.

He would lie in waiting at this spot until he heard the familiar rhythm. Sometimes, he would wait all morning, then return two hours before dusk. He knew that Roland never came when the orange glow was highest in the sky and the water heated more quickly. He had wondered, if this arrangement was for his benefit, as this was the time that he could re-charge himself most efficiently in the safer central channels. There were the other fishermen of course, in their flat bellied floats, but they were little or no sport and he paid them little heed.

He sensed a relaxed mood in the rhythm. It told him that Roland was happy. His tail rippled in a slow unconscious gesture of companionship, for he too was cheerful. Had it been possible he would have worn a smile. It was a new day; yet another day that they would enjoy together. Perhaps today was the day he would be caught? He thought not.

Thirteen
The guy in room 8

Splicer lived in a cell - he used to joke. Said his girlfriend, ex girlfriend, was a walking pork salami with a craving for vegi food. That when she left him, she had said it was because *he* couldn't understand the little, but important things in life - like why Christmas trees couldn't be deciduous or why they had to be green.....while *she* stuffed her toothless face with chicken tikka flavoured furry cabbages.

He lived uptown next to the abattoir. Ran a small but honestly filthy nine room hotel. It was favourably set amongst the *four hour a day* diner cafes: the less time they were open, the more they were in demand, the more people that couldn't get in, the more money they made. He got the throwbacks. He was swell about having the prime spot - location, location, location. And the race track opposite still had that vacant charm. His real name was Bill.

His wake up call sprayed ice cold oxygen onto the bare soles of his feet causing him to piss the bed. It was the only thing that could get him up. It wasn't the thought of lying in soiled sheets; the cold, wet cloth clinging to his skin. No - it was the pleasure in the comforting warmth as he let go, relaxing his mind, arousing him to think of...food. FOOD. An overflowing plate of eggs, sunny side up mixed with sliced salami with the dregs of last night's tortilla chips on top, fried to perfection in a world consisting totally of odour and expectation. And each time way better than the time before. Busy day. Busy busy day ahead.

The guy in room 8 had looked like trouble. Hardly spoke a word when he arrived the night before. That always raised Splicer's suspicions. *Then* when he paid in raw creds, pulling out *that* wad without a care as to who may have been watching, well that had just confirmed it surely. Yip.. sure smelt of trouble. But not *his* trouble.

Now - as his face squashed his Paris France memorial ashtray into the desk he remembered what it was he had forgotten. Yip..*trouble brought trouble.* The soldier who was squeezing his neck wore the emblem of Company Vortex; of which he had once been proud to belong. He had tried to tell them but they hadn't seemed much interested. Got irritable real quick. All they wanted to know was what room the guy in room 8 was in. Well now that they knew maybe she'd take her thumb out of his wind pipe?

Claymore was back in Cathedral Town, though not by desire. His only lead having almost end gamed, he needed *some* kind of fix on this mark or she would be gone. He had slept late, having lain awake till the early hours her face burning behind his eyelids, trying to work it out. He knew she was here - somewhere. Her A.I. protection and the girl organising it, whoever she was, said so.

He had cruised the night markets in a poor attempt at a long shot based on the knowledge that it was the one place all the inhabitants used regularly. But more to let his mind work overtime. Out of ideas - how to find someone who doesn't want to be found in a city of eight million lost people? Or the girlfriend - with no name and no face? *But he knew what she did - or could do.* Somebody must have trained her - someone capable of training her *very well*. So he gave the name *Loki* to Vortex who gave him the name Splicer and an address in Cathedral Town by return.

Splicer wasn't what he had expected. He had been once - a high ranking Company Authenticia technician. As named by Vortex he should have been able to run a personnel history of everyone *ever* officially instructed in the field cross referenced tangentially to the name Loki, in addition to twenty years personal memories of every student who passed through him during his pre Company Vortex days. But Company security had terminated his chip on retirement along with other *dangerous* pieces of his mind.

Claymore had recognised it almost immediately. He gave his name as Loki and nothing else. Got no reply and left it at that. He'd probe in the morning when Splicers mind was fresh, just in case. There was usually something, if not much, in Vortex spoon fed games.

His sentry boomed silently in his head!

His room had the makings of basic tourist security. Reinforced bands had slid into bolted plates as the outer door shut and a security eye whined into action, displaying an optional corridor view onto the room wall, accompanied by a recorded reassuring statement in some eastern language which Claymore hadn't bothered to translate.

Instead, he had placed his sentry on the corridor floor the previous night and watched it scuttle into the cover of the shadows. It looked like a large wet cockroach and blended just fine with the kind of place he usually stayed in. Now it boomed *ALARM* through his chip, projecting images of Splicer's unfortunate predicament.

As the house key released the bands and the door sprung open he followed them back in, speaking to their backs and the otherwise empty room. He held the AK100 in his right hand. 'Nobody speaks. Nobody moves.' It was Savannah's voice, projected through the gun. Crisp and southerly sexy. He alone picked up on her unusual pleasurable tone. Had he allowed her access to the trigger instead of just the voice they would most likely be dead already.

After a pause so that everyone had grasped the idea, she drawled 'Everybody turns round real easy.' As one of them was wearing 360 combat wrap-arounds, and they would all be chip linked, facing their backs wasn't any real advantage. And face on, they would see for themselves that they were talking to a semi-sentient AK100. Reason enough in itself to at least try for a conversation.

The four soldiers slowly slid around to face him. Three male and one female. The nearest ranked Lieutenant and carried a holstered AK100. All had empty hands, except for a large framed Sergeant with the name Kimmo engraved across his gun butt, who had instinctively drawn his weapon on entering the room. The Lieutenants eyes looked dangerously dead.

'They named me *Ah Dare Ya* for a fuck'n" good reason,' she added, directed at the Sergeant.

The gun was really a negotiating tool. If it came to it, the sonic dealer implanted in Claymore's palm was ripe for this kind of point blank deal. Assuming they weren't tooled up with some kind of counter. Safer to let them have both.

It fell into place - the insignia..same unit. *Her* unit. He had thought of talking to them some weeks back, but figured they would clam up - protect their own. His mind laughed at his own stupidity. Of course *the man* was already on that! Vortex didn't ask - he got them to *go find her*. Like it was their fault; like they were personally responsible for her choice to screw up. He scanned their body language. Veterans.. cool..four metres from the wrong end of a pissed of AK100 and none of them looked uncomfortable. He figured that if the move came it would be from the big

Sergeant. The Sergeant's huge frame filled his memory - and he recalled the shells burst into his chest – *Blacker's chest.*

'Your friend there,' said the Lieutenant, 'sounds a little on edge.' After the silence, he moved his index finger in a half arc indicating Kimmo to sheath his weapon. 'She's just feeling frisky, nothing a little exercise wouldn't cure,' replied Claymore.

The Lieutenant's stare remained unfocused. 'Sexy sound for an AK.'

'Vortex said you were a little off the regular,' added the Sergeant.

Claymore lit up with his free hand, sucked in and spoke while exhaling. 'Did he also mention that it was *you* who wasted her brother.' After a shocked silence he added. 'Guess he forgot that part.'

'Who's brother?' uttered the Sergeant, having understood in disbelief, and in need of confirmation.

'Sands - the *mark's*. Cause that's what she is. Now - perhaps you'd like to share with me just exactly how you feel about all that? And what you're doing kicking my door in, so early in the morning.'

'And get it right first time,' drawled Savannah.

'She has the blueprint for the Hollow.....and she's holding an auction,' replied the Lieutenant casually.

'Least so *she* says, added the Sergeant. 'And where'd you get that brother stuff?'

'From Vortex...with a little help from her dead brother.' Said Claymore.

'That fits,' interrupted Vasos. 'Would explain why she got weird after... '

'She's attracted quite an interest,' continued the Lieutenant. 'Needless to say, that our mutual benefactor is far from pleased at having to compete in the market for his own merchandise. He seems to have been under the mistaken impression that *you* would repair the situation without the need to involve us.'

'Well... now that you're here.... how exactly do you intend to get *involved*?'

'One... to inform you that she intends to sell. Which we have done.'

'He could have done that much himself.'

'We just obey orders. *To inform - to progress- and to deliver....the merchandise ..and the traitor.* She raised the stakes and brought the timetable forward.'

'And how exactly do you intend to *progress*?' asked Claymore.

'The sale will take place real soon. *We* will be there.. to make sure that there is nothing to sell.'

'You know where?'

'That's your part. We expect it to be a Company sale. We don't know who or where. But when it happens - our orders are to prevent it at any cost.'

'Detroit already has a Hollow. What about the others?' asked Claymore. When no-one replied he continued 'How did she put it out?'

'She had us do that for her,' the Lieutenant replied frankly. 'She's got A.I. help.'

'So why the drama?' said Claymore gesturing towards the broken door.

'Vortex was kind of complimentary about you - in a way which suggested caution.'

Savannah's voice drilled through his head. 'So don't disappoint the man. Let's down these fuckers now....we don't need *them* to take the bitch!' Her excitement pulsed in his chip, her self image projecting across his mind... *a beach... standing barefoot on white sand... the edge of an ocean...*

moonlight... the glint of thin slashing blades through the rain.

'Well it seems he wanted us to get acquainted....' said Claymore, '..and now...?'

'Now *we* wait while *you* find out where the sale is. Vortex said you had a lead. You *do* have a lead?'

'Yeah....*lots.*'

When they had left, Claymore looked for Splicer. He found him sitting all quiet in a rear ground floor room.

'Not really been your morning,' remarked Claymore as cheerful as the moment allowed, as he crossed the large and pretty much empty room. Standing by the oversized dusty and torn settee on which Splicer sat, he said 'I'm lookin for a piece of your past.'

'I don't have a past. They removed it,' replied Splicer in a matter of fact tone.

'Earlier than that. From your teaching days. You remember your teaching days?'

With a frown he replied 'Some.'

Claymore asked the question slowly. 'A girl.... a girl with potential..real potential.....possibly a *French* girl. Would have been young then, mid to late teens. Someone who could eventually be capable of crossing into Shadowlands.'

'Then she'd be no good to you. Anyone good enough to get in - never gets back out.'

'Unless they want you to..it seems,' said Claymore, suppressing an involuntary memory flash of salivating jaws.

Splicer poured himself the gritty dregs of the mornings coffee. The start to his day had definitely been all wrong - and, as for the vibes from this guy... *that* scared him a lot more than Vortex's troops. Best foot forward, he concluded. Get this over with as fast as possible. Co-operate and what happened next would happen next.

'There were two principal schools back then. I'm going back ten years. I worked mostly out of Milan. Spent some time at Florence. I was on Vortex's payroll even in those days. They equalled my salary to hand pick and develop *special* students, the ones with *exceptional* talent. The Company would assess them, and if there psych's matched the bill they got their dream break. There were a number of good French students over the years, but none of them got picked up by Vortex. There *was* one in particular however, a girl, who shone particularly bright. They looked her over, she never knew of course...but rejected her. She was too interested in the art side. Yeah music as I recall..didn't fit the Vortex profile. She got picked up later by another Company. Marie....I can't recall her last name. The school will give it to you. That was Florence Accademia Conservatorio. Would have been nine, ten years back.'

The thing that always struck Claymore was that Vortex was always available. He *must* be an incredibly busy man - yet he was always there. Never once had Claymore been put on hold or talked to a p.a. What's more - he always had an answer - like he had been given a week to think about it. This time was no different.

Claymore supplied the name Marie and requested that Vortex ran it. The answer was seconds in coming back. There was no current or past address. Company Senate had erased all her records at the time of her employment.

'Get Splicer to contact the University direct.' Vortex instructed. Claymore was then given the name of a current Professor of Authenticia whom Splicer had once had a close friendship with. 'As it seems that this sale may actually take place ahead of our endeavours to prevent it...as a matter of urgency you will find the *builder* of my merchandise and ensure that at least I can have another made. I will at worst therefore have a competitor.' After a short pause he added 'Ah..I see that you are confused. Indeed it is *not* a Hollow.'

'And the girl?' asked Claymore.

'See that Splicer plays his part. I will have someone contact you for any lead as to her whereabouts. Let them break the shoe leather, but if it comes to it - be there for the sale. The sale is yours and Lieutenant Faro's.'

*****

The day had developed its own random pace. First - the uninvited visit from Faro..new players, then..someone else to locate - the *builder, the builder of what?* Followed by a dead four hour wait while Splicer got hold of his long lost Professor buddy. Least Vortex had supplied him with a straight address for this *builder*.

Harbord's address was in a neighbourhood similar in every way to Splicers, but on the other side of town. It crossed his mind that he was probably the only person who had ever happened to visit both. The urban form, like most of the city read like superimposed layers of a confused dream; original blocks and buildings replaced or enlarged at random, and entire new structures overlaid and interspersed to staggering heights, and postures which betrayed thousands of years of architectural thinking. The end result was a splendid chaos of urban mayhem punctuated with architectural gems, relics of the past, for which any leading architect would proudly have taken the applause as their lifetime achievement.

The flat took some finding. There was no door as such. Rubbish; bamboo boxes, bottles, boxes of bottles, bamboo bottles, were piled and strewn across and along the alley leading to the wide grey stairs that lead past a number of smiling faces to what eventually turned out to be a very popular grocery store, that had turned its back on the public square. The square was open to the sky, and enclosed on three sides by the Cinema Coustou.

The stone stairs to the Cinema crawled up and along the fourth wall, enclosed at first floor level by a much too low wall, then disappeared into a black arched abyss. For the past decade the building had never fully justified its designers vision, although the occasional film show was run for free. Instead it had found purpose as a semi legal squat, housing non paying tenants who kept it wind and waterproof, and had a handshake agreement with the proprietor to make themselves scarce, or blend with the characters and ambience, during the shows. The owner, Raji, was known to everyone in the locality - or everyone in the world, if you considered the world as defined by Raji. Her world was the world of classic cinema. Classic, of course, according to Raji.

...OY ROGERS..July 24th/25th.. ROY ROGERS..July 24th/25th.. ROY ROGERS..July 24th/25th.. ROY ROGERS..July 24th/25th.. ROY R.. read the sign rotating above the head of the plump elderly woman sitting inside the door, surrounded by piles of Raji stencilled shirts and boxes of Chinese beer for sale. She looked genuinely amused when Claymore asked for a word with Raji, and said nothing with her eyes stretched wide, until he realised that she was Raji.

He picked up one of the blue stained cans, brushed the powdered ice away and dropped a wad of cred's, thick enough to buy all the beer on display, into the topless tin box by her side. 'Do you have the forwarding address of your recent tenant Jason Harbord?' He held a second wad clearly in view, and caressed a T shirt admiringly.

She continued staring, as he opened, drank and finished the beer. He shook his head ever so slightly, then nodded and smiled. 'You collect these, as well as show them?' he said gesturing towards the screen. She returned the nod, gently.

'Must be difficult to get hold of ....good ones.. that is,' he added. She nodded again.

'The really valuable things in life always cost more than just money.' He crushed the can in his hand. 'Got a favourite. One that *you* can't get hold of?' After a few moments she shook her head.

'No!' He placed the can lightly back into the box. 'You like this place? Lived here almost as long as its been here I heard. Were married to its founder.'

'I am his *daughter*,' she corrected proudly.

'Ah! Past its best. Always a pity when good times come to an end.' Looking around, focusing beyond her for the first time, he said 'The structure has definitely seen better days....crumbling.. looks like it could simply turn to dust overnight. You must have a favourite...everyone has a favourite. Maybe yours is locked up somewhere...in some bod's private little hoard.. for their eyes only.'

'Maybe.'

'Mr Harbord and I are colleagues in a sense. We both work for Company Vortex. Mr Harbord recently vanished from sight, and while the Company fully respects Mr Harbord's privacy, they would very much like to contact him regarding the matter of his back pay..... and to fulfil the Company policy of ensuring the safety and good health of all its employees.'

She continued to stare blankly back at him.

'As I'm sure you are aware...the Company has extensive connections and access to unlimited resources. I'm sure it would be delighted to furnish you with the beginnings of a collection of your own, as a token for your help in re-uniting them with Mr Harbord.'

The short silence was interrupted by a sharp reply. 'He left suddenly. Three months ago. There is no forwarding address.'

The world seems to be filling up with people who don't want to be found, thought Claymore. 'Mail?'

'I leave it in his room. It's still empty.'

'I'd like to see the room, if I may?'

Her stare never faltered. 'Now Voyageur....Betty Davies and Paul Henreid. There are two originals. The same collector has both'.

'One of which is now yours,' he replied with a thin smile.

The stare remained, but he caught the distant light in her eyes.

As she took him through the auditorium to Harbord's room he laughed inwardly. The insane part, was the fact that Vortex, who would gladly rip the heart out of an entire nation for only the marginal chance of achieving his purpose, would actually deliver to this woman as promised.

The room still looked lived in. Clothes dropped casually on the floor by the unmade bed; spent beer bottles, many only half drunk, littered the Indian rugs and table. His foot hit with a solid thud against a half full case. He picked up an open bottle and slowly turned it on its head. A layer of green fungus held the beer in place for a while, until gravity finally won releasing it in a single glug. He turned his attention to the centre of the room where a set of weights and bells were set up. Some of the weights had been rigged from engine parts. The room smelt of cat.

In the corner, propping up a heap of delicately balanced relic papers, stamped with obscure University heads, rested some apparently clean, and *very* expensive looking electronic equipment. Clearly the lady of the house ran an honest and trusting household. There were no locks on the door. All the equipment was disconnected but appeared fully functional.

The noise from the crowd gathered in the level below drew his attention to the far end of the long narrow room. He walked its length through what had once been a number of separate rooms, their connecting walls now removed, and looked down from the open gallery which gave the room its special light.

The bride and groom looked stunning from the air. Their individual outfits, linked diagonally by strands of fabric recycled from their past, gelled like one huge black top hat. Her legs moved perfectly through the circular folds of dark linen which set them apart from the guests, and bonded them together forever in the snap; the current fad expression of selfless union. Their reflected image gleamed back at them from the perfectly polished glass floor.

She more than equalled the height of her man though they looked perfectly matched. The folds of cloth draped round them made it difficult to be sure where one started and the other finished. The intended illusion of singularity rang true; only her 3mm wide glades gave her the edge.

The movie screen facing them and the other diners displayed black and white scenes from some old film; sounds of the ocean and warm winds encompassed them. Both beamed easy smiles larger and more genuine than they had ever done in their lives.

The voice came from behind him. He turned instantly - but there was no-one there. He stared back into the depths of the room for a long time. He was certain that someone had spoken, but hadn't quite caught what had been said. After a full minute of standing absolutely motionless, he qualified that it had felt more like an idea thought aloud, than a statement or a question. He ran a circuit with his eyes around the room one more time, then dismissed it as a quirk from the film below.

Then he heard it again. This time it was unmistakeable, with absolute clarity of sound, but from nowhere in particular. *'Do not give him the address!'* It was expressed as *his* idea - it was *his own* voice.

As the impact faded, as unsure and awkward as he felt, he replied 'What address?'

'What address..are you talkin' to me...what are you talkin' about?' he heard Savannah ask.

'Not to you. Did you hear anyth...'

'The address with which the Professor furnished Splicer. *Do not give him the address of Marie's uncle Roland.* They will use it badly. Nor will they learn anything to help you find what it is that you seek.'

'Who are you?'

'What are you doing...who are you talkin' to?' interrupted Savannah.

'I am the one who Vortex refers to as the builder.'

'Don't you have a voice of your own - Jason. Lets see you. Where are you?' He turned and scanned the crowd below for a hint of who was talking through what must be a speaker.

'Are you linked up?' asked Savannah.

'If it was a speaker she would also hear it,' Claymore realised. 'Is this conversation chip based ...why does it sound like its in the room?' he asked.

'Because it *is* in the room. I am not linked to your chip at this present time,' replied Jason.'

'Then.. if it's on speaker..why am I the only one who can hear it?' Claymore said, continually focusing on the crowd below. Wherever Jason was, chances are he would be watching. 'I am not in the crowd...or in the building. The *speaker* that you alone can hear is the sound of your own voice ..as my thoughts are located within *your* mind. It is quite separate from your chip or any link to or from it.'

'That's not possible.' Claymore replied flatly.

'Well... it seems that you can hear me..can you not. What Vortex has you seek is *very* precious. It has several facets. It also, could be used badly, or not. You have one address already - now I will give you another. *Iglesia y Conventa de San Francisco de Asis; Plaza De San Francisco; Habana Vieja.'*

Claymore's focus snapped to attention. His chip's four second auto cleansing run de-railed at three. The suspected external virus, housed in some bored defence unit amidst all the techno crap in the corner and triggered by any trespasser without a security code, got a second's grace to extended life, should it exist. The last exchange said that it did not. As the image of the club projected across his mind - he knew instinctively that he had just been given the location of the pending sale.

'Yes,' said Jason. 'It is the address that everyone is so keen to know.'

'And the time?' asked Claymore without hesitation. He could question the who's and why's later.

'Two days from now..at 12 noon.'

'The buyer?'

'You should take much care - there will be more than one,' Jason replied slowly.

Claymore lit up. Smoke danced with the reflected light. After a while he asked. 'Curious......why now? You ran from Vortex just like she did. You gave up a lot, an elevated Company position like yours doesn't come easy.'

'*Her* location is not known,' replied Jason, guessing the direction of the chit chat. I didn't run. I fulfilled my employee commitments to Vortex to the full, and as far as I am aware, much to his satisfaction. Having completed my work, I chose to pursue an alternative path in life. That was all.'

'Then how are you aware of the sale?'

'Because I am *the builder*.'

The answer made no sense, but its tone implied that it was the only one he was going to get.

'Well Mr Builder...you are required to resume your post, for the time being at least. He needs a duplicate of your work.'

'Had it been possible to simply duplicate my work, it would have been done at the time. The work would have to be done again from the beginning. It is possible, but would take a considerable length of time, a full year perhaps. I cannot offer such a commitment. Perhaps you will reclaim the original, now that you have re-found your direction.'

'Perhaps. Unless Vortex finds you first. I think you will find that the decision to end your contract is no longer yours to make.'

'Yes. Assuming of course that you decide to deploy your energy in *that* direction. Would it not be simpler for all concerned if you were to retrieve the original, before your rivals. Then there would be no need to go looking for me, or for a duplicate to be made.

'And why should I trust your information?'

'Look into your soul. You will find *me* there.'

Claymore sensed that the conversation was over.

As he passed close to the bride he saw that the slithered glass was much more than a fashion aid; her eyes were stone cold blind. Her vision was total chip dependent.

The breeze was hot. *Nothing* else tasted like the air of Cathedral Town. It was distinct beyond mistake. Not quite foul but definitely nauseating. Unless you were a veteran Cath - then it tasted *good*. Claymore recalled the smaller twin say '...it hung like the sweat from a leper's skin.' Like everyone else in the city, Claymore was uncomfortably wet.

Savannah's mood however offered up some distraction. It was a first. Must have been the familiarity of it all, he concluded. To date she had been a passenger. This morning, without access to the trigger mechanism she had been little more - but she had played a *real* part. And they both knew that had it been absolutely necessary, he would have given her the trigger too. She had got high on it - and now she was coming down.

He sensed an extended blink, as she cleared wet impotent tears. She blinked again.....she was remembering..finding herself..who she was. Cascading colours flashed through her eyes..his eyes..then settled on a yellow which matched her hair. The image froze... a cute blonde child standing very alone amidst a faceless city of graphite. Nothing else worth remembering.

The child disintegrated, replaced by adult thoughts, she remembered *what it had been like* ....to awake from last night's early mornin' blitz, head pounding, mouth stuck in dry regret, alone. Or at best, lying next to some ugly yob who'd be bragging to his mates as soon as his head cleared. ..She mouthed her regular first sober thought ' Sav.. you stupid f... ', as other little bits floated across her mind ...again bare foot on an evening beach, but this time just walking, crossing each foot over the other in small steps as the tide rolled over her toes...smiling...happy...and stretched out under the mid day sun wearing nothing but her favourite glades, relaxed, feeling good about herself. Then a frown....had taken too much for granted, had been top of the world, no-one could touch her..had never really properly noticed the warmth of the sun - *but* she had still always felt good about herself..about it all, about who she was - *is! About who she fuck'n' is!*

Now she recognised the pleasure she had once got from the little things ..the taste of cumin sauce on pasta waffles ..the sting of cheap British tobacco ..sleeping naked on cool satin sheets, well at least on that one occasion...and her memory *cooed* over the bigger things ..the hit of adrenalin, as she felt her eyes go smoky, her mind contract, focusing absolutely at moments of truth during her chosen profession - her ears hurting, threatening to burst as her AK80 thumped out its tune to an audience frozen in her eye. Death standing there, invited, but always held at bay. *Until that stupid fuck Claymore misjudged the kick!*

Appreciative as ever. Claymore thought. Damned lucky I bothered agreeing to her download in the first place. Not to mention the one in a billion chance that Vortex wanted to finance it. Well.. she'll get her shiny new clone when this is over. Soon enough for everyone I reckon.

He was mid way to discarding the thought when they interrupted.

'Send a boy to do a man's job.' Said a sickly wheezy voice. 'You have something for us...time to give it up.'

Claymore sighed inwardly. 'Marie Dupont - left Florence Accademia Conservatorio nine years ago - was picked up by Senate - was a founder of Authenticia - past address unknown - current address unknown - no credit address - current occupation unknown - no known family alive - she's a cyber tramp - has strong A.I. links. All yours.' Claymore said flatly, and cut the link.

The link was down just long enough for them to stop laughing before a new link opened. 'Don't worry *we'll* finish what you started for you. It's not your fault. The man just wants the job done *professionally*'.

Claymore made no reply.

'Talkin' *professional*....you learned to shoot straight yet? How is Sav baby?'

A second almost identical voice added 'Heard you guys were.. kinda intimate. Does she hold it for you when you piss?' His head filled with the sound of gravel laughter in duplicate. He could hear it ringing even after the link was gone.

'When I'm sorted..and walkin'.....I'm gonna' enjoy meeting those boys for the last time.' Savannah said quietly in their wake.

Fourteen
Jude

The siren from the fire engine was deafening. So intense was its shriek, he was convinced its origin lay within his skull, piercing his brain to a degree that hurt his eyes. He had definitely brought his hangover with him. The kids hanging perilously onto its rear end grinned widely at him, oblivious to the cold, intoxicated by the thrill of their ride.

As he walked, the wet drizzle and snow drove against him in swirling sheets. Occasional icy blasts forced his eyes into slits, his chin tucked tight into his neck, his arms across his chest holding his coat firm. He now realised what it was that he had missed in his choice of dress - buttons. His wide brimmed trilby hat at least protected his head. It was bloody freezing; Phil hadn't said anything about *the weather*. He was probably licking his lips in laughter over a pint of Guinness right now back at the Smuggler's Inn.

The idea of coming back didn't seem so exiting now - that he was sober. But he was here, and as here he was - here he'd stay - for a bit at least. Give it a shot. If it sucked he would leave and join them in the pub. Maybe - just maybe it would work out like he had figured it in his head when he had found it so irresistible.

He remembered - he loved fire engines. Yeah, even that fitted. He smiled as much as the cold would allow him. When he was a kid, he used to chase them with his uncle John in his little black car.

Yip - fun wise, that was about it for school, but College had been better. Much better. With College came his inheritance, and with the inheritance came the girls. The fact that he, Andy Branston - affectionately known as randy Andy, was an ugly bastard didn't seem to figure in it at all. But that was then and this was now, and lately it hadn't been that great. Until last Friday.

Tonight - he had arranged to meet her in the glass enclosed roof garden of the Imperial Hotel. The food was recommended as the best in the city. They would eat while watching the swimmers breath ice the air in the heated open air pool. 'Rather them than me,' he mused, feeling warmer for the thought.

The place was surprisingly busy for so early in the evening; mainly middle aged monied couples. There was no one here that he recognised - of course not. He studied their faces anyway. It was easy to spot those on their first date. This was their second; the first had proven much harder work than he had expected; not that he had really known *what* to expect.

The waiter returned to the table with a small silver bowl of chilli ice cream without having been asked. 'This will warm you Sir, until the lady arrives.'

Once the waiter had departed, he discreetly stuck his finger into the bowl and found that it was not the frozen ice cream, with specs of chilli, sauce, or whatever on it, as its name had conjured. It was indeed hot with largish flakes of iced chilli peppers mixed through it.

He glanced at his Rolex again; she was late. The ice cream had warmed him, but his thoughts were still on wishing that he had worn a heavier jumper below the woollen coat - when he saw her cross the floor. She looked fantastic.

He kissed her hand, and eased a chair out for her, while wondering what they could possibly talk about this time. As she plucked her fingers from her Italian leather gloves he felt a surprised rush from the conversation of their last date.

They had sat by the window, in a Hungarian patisserie in the busier part of town; the evening had been black and the rain even heavier than tonight's sleet. The patisserie's windows were streaked with ragged vertical rivers of raindrops, racing in joined up jig-saw trickles down the black panes lit from within. It was warm and comforting inside. They had flirted with a discussion of poetry; she had said that as a child she had believed that it was all already there, like science - the words, the rhythm, the beauty; that all that need happen was for it to be found and shown to us.

She had drunk double espressos like she was late for an important business appointment, contrasting appealingly with her happy carefree charisma. He had found himself intrigued by the way the heavy folds of her hair would fall across her eyes, and how she would gently tuck it back behind her ear only for it to fall again a minute later. He had admired the way she sat, her posture relaxed but her mind alert, missing nothing taking place around her; and enchanted, by how she laughed for no apparent reason each time she asked for Drambuie *with cream.*

Since the patisserie, he had found a shop in the back streets of the Georgian part of town where they made flour and raisin biscuits the old fashioned way. She had made a light hearted passing remark that as a child she was partial to them. He had bought her a bag of mixed animal shapes. He hoped to see her eyes light up.

He was certain that he would love the smell of her hair.

Fifteen
Ambassador

The rubber soles to his boots made an unpleasant sucking sound as Jake moved across the glass floor. Inlaid sand blocks, set one metre apart in two neat rows, marked the path through the public gallery to the exhibits. The message had been non specific. *Museum De Quincy - exhibit 21 - tomorrow 11.15 a.m. - something of interest to you!* The lack of a signature alone had been enough for curiosity to demand his presence.

The museum's frame was entirely made of glass; constructed in the later part of the Nouveau Renaissance period of the forties. Its walls, ceilings and roof were moulded on site, from glass selected across the history of the globe. Set pieces of Louis Comfort Tiffany, Charles Rennie Mackintosh, and many others filled the best spots; Marc Chagall's memorial window from the original United Nations Building New York took central stage above the entrance. The floors were constructed abroad, in what had then still been Europe, and shipped in at phenomenal cost to be slotted into place and complete the largest and most magnificent work of glass ever created. Only the yellow sand stones which lead the visitor through the blushed coloured shadows were not of glass.

Journals had debated whether it was Art or Architecture. Cynics condemned it as " *symbolic of the transparent and brittle facade of current social thinking* ", and on that sunny day when it shone most brightly, of " *reflecting - the soul of social integrity* ". The insurance companies had attempted to invade *all* illusions by insisting that the buildings structural integrity was ensured by more than the subtleties of its buttressed design.

The headaches were more frequent now. And the blackouts longer. It wasn't his head that ached - it was his mind. He couldn't really rationally distinguish the difference, but knew it to be true. Like he knew everything else important to be true. Everything he trusted. When the blackouts passed, he could almost, but never *quite* remember. He did however awake, if he could call it that, with some fuck'n' good ideas.

The Order Of The Jake had been one of those. His background had made it easy to set up once the idea was in place. Then all that was needed was to start spreading the word. The power of word of mouth backed by a contrived lengthy track record would do the rest. All that Jake had to do was to play himself. He was a God after all so he wasn't deluding anyone. Not that, that mattered a shit anyway. And what's more - it was Federally legal.

Before he had time to realise that he was on a role - he and the boys were - well - on a role. And things could only get better. The money was flowing in. Disciples and converts growing in true pyramid fashion. Lately however the blackouts were irritating him more and more. Huek and the other monks had began to question his long periods of absence, and to top it, there had been that business with Loki.

Clearly, The Order Of The Jake was crucial to his life style; his only source of income.. and.. well it was who he, Jake, was. And....of course when it peaked....he would be at the *very* top of the tree. Loki's message however - had been crystal clear and forcefully made.

The fact to focus on was - *facts* were - don't fuck with Loki or anything Loki had any thing to do with, including - no especially - the thing with Sands. Yet, while The Order Of The Jake was capable of making him personal millions should he leave the other well alone - he was driven by this impossible frantic itch to pursue the thing with Sands to its very end. For he knew - beyond any doubt - that somehow there lay his true confirmation as a God.

'What you thinking about hon?' asked Sop.

'Paying the rent. Or not,' he replied stroking behind the panther's ear.

'Hope he doesn't piss on the floor an' embarrass us all.. or anything,' she added from behind her gum, subconsciously folding another loop of the cat's chain around her slender wrist. 'If you don't pay the rent hon we will have to find somewhere new to stay. You got somewhere in mind?' she suddenly perked up excitedly.

'Was thinking more of ...the grander scale of things. Existence. Macro or micro..assuming that they can actually be distinguished from each other.' He removed his sun glasses. 'So that's why it was so dark in here!' He began polishing them looking around at new colours in the glass. 'I met with a God very recently - a real God. His name is Loki. He felt it pertinent to advise me on a number of matters - which by no coincidence were also of interest to me. In particular, he advised me as to the benefits of giving the lady Sands a wider than wide berth; expressed mainly in the form of the serious disbenefits of doing otherwise.'

'Like what,' she blurted annoyed.

'Like... demonic visits to major clients, or more subtle, replicated visits from non other than my good self, but with less than virtuous intentions in mind. He was inclined to foresee the very rapid fall of the Order.'

'But he only exists in Shadowlands. How can he hurt the Order?'

'He clearly has access across Authenticia from Shadowlands. Most probably has a long standing pact with some cybertramp.' He hooked his glasses over the top of his white T shirt. 'He also made time to relay the *illusion of reality*....as perceived by a God. He illustrated it by way of a short story. A true story. Would you like to hear it?'

'I'll scream if you *don't* tell me.'

'Well........the scene is a closed, and very private, virtual city designed exclusively for visitations by the rich. Those who choose to visit this decadent world can, for their pleasure, flirt with it..manipulate it..as they please. Prior to their arrival, they may assume any fantasy role of their choice, and the city and its inhabitants will re-design itself to fulfil their every desire.

Of the inhabitants of the city, only one in ten million are visitors. As for the others, it is *their* reality, their normal world where they live and where they will die unaware of the nature of the visitors or the virtual state of their own existence.

The story's character ...let's call him Andy... was such a visitor. Andy was a pretty ordinary guy in every sense, save one - he was excruciatingly rich. After some encouragement from a friend, he decided to instruct the City Masters to ensure that he could *not only* indulge, absolutely uninhibited, in pleasures of the flesh with a deliciously beautiful woman - the demure and intelligent kind of woman who would never normally give him a second glance - *but* that she would also slowly and without any effort on his part, fall hopelessly in love with him.

He was ..somewhat embarrassed to make his request at first, as he knew it exposed him as the sad and selfish bastard that he was. Then he thought ..well..what the hell..indulgence was their business, and he was paying through the nose for it. And of course.. behind his slightly reddened face and his openly sceptical attitude, lay a thirsty curiosity.

Anyways......Andy took to it like a duck to water. His scepticism soon overcome, he found the world he was visiting to be as real if not more real than the real thing. He full heartily played at life without the down side; parties where everyone laughed at his jokes, and where he always said the right thing at just the right time, and where gorgeous girls never ever tasted like ashtrays. Andy couldn't get enough.

And of course there was Jude - the reason for his visit in the first place. Jude was everything and more than Andy had ever wanted - was ever capable of dreaming up for himself. A gorgeous, intelligently witty brunette with light olive coloured skin and a laugh that lingered in her smile; small white even teeth and lips that.....well..

They had made her perfect in every way; a mirror image of his desires, or as he concluded, the mirror image of every man's desires. He certainly had got his monies worth.

Then - disaster struck. What Andy could never possibly have expected to happen - happened. Andy fell in love.

What to do? Well........one day, when he has worn himself thin agonising over his impossible dilemma - he tells her everything. He had to. He had to tell someone.. and who else could he tell? Any friends he had made in the city would simply think him mad or put it down to too many drugs. Tell his mates on the outside? That he had fallen in love with an AI generated image.. they wouldn't stop laughing for a week. No he had to tell *her* - even if only to break the spell.'

'What happened?' gulped Sop.

'Well.. Jude got very visually upset when she found out that the man who had become her best friend, with whom she had shared her most private feelings, and who she had grown to love - was only having a laugh - a holiday from his tiresome old reality. That their relationship had been a lie from the start.

She also, not surprisingly, got very distressed by his claim that she didn't really exist. Whether it was true or just some sick cowardly way of dumping her somehow didn't appear to matter. What was clear was that it was over and he was leaving.'

'How does it end - did he tell you? Did he stay? Tell me that he stayed!'

'Perhaps?' Jake teased.

'Tell me.' ..she punched his shoulder, accidentally pulling on the cats chain.

'Yes......I mean.. Loki told me how it ended.

'The end......well.. he swore to her that he *would* stay. That he would never leave her. One day, shortly afterwards, when he was due to meet her at their favourite cafe, she was late. He thought perhaps that he had got the time wrong as she was always so punctual. He waited for two hours but she never arrived. He went to look for her at her flat, but it was empty, and the landlady said that Jude had moved to another city and had not left a forwarding address. The landlady asked him what she should do with any post, and he replied that she could forward it to him. Months passed without a word. She never turned up at any of her friends' parties, and no-one knew where she was. There was no post. She had simply disappeared, as if she had never really existed.

Andy slipped deeper and deeper into depression. After a few more months he decided that he should leave, return to his own world, resume his life. But when he tried - he found that he couldn't. He realised that he couldn't because *he was already in his own world*. He had never left - it was Jude who was the visitor. It was Jude who had played the game that he had so much wanted to play.'

'What did he do?'

'What could he do? Nothing. Andy's world, his programmed world - his reality, was realer than real - but that wasn't enough; because *he* didn't have the power to change it. In Shadowlands - Loki does. That's what makes him a God.....and what makes The Order Of The Jake a crock of shit.'

'This Loki and Shadowlands - could that have something to do with your dreams?' she asked without her usual teasing tone.

'Visions.....*visions,*' he corrected. 'No - they come during the periods when my chip is de-activated. They originate from my mind not from the chip - there can be no link to Shadowlands.'

'Then why does this Loki want you to stay away from Sands?'

'He is Guardian to her friend. Talking of *dreams* though.........I did have a very serious dream... evening before last.'

'Tell me.'

'Well...... I was stranded in an strange universe.. with 50 million women..... and 50 million other men.'

'So what was so wild about that? '

'I was the only one who had a dick.'

She coughed her drink onto the floor spraying the panthers back. For the next five minutes she cuddled, hugged and apologised to it lovingly while rubbing the sugar thick pop from his coat.

'You poor thing...sorry...sor-ree...sor-eee she almost squealed, arms wrapped around its powerful neck, while it sniffed and occasionally licked the wet floor. Eventually, she poured a little puddle for it, having looked around to make sure no-one other than the twelve security eyes were watching. 'Well..dammit it's glass.. so it won't *stain,*' she said as she felt she had to.

He was gazing at the cars. They made his heart smile. Polished hard, to shine far greater than they ever had during their working lives. They looked so heavy, so solid and fine, set there on the glass surface. There was about thirty in all, arranged in apparently random fashion. He knew however, from the poster at the door, that when viewed from the upper gallery the pattern read as a cartoon car.

He recognised a number of them; two mid-20th Century blue and silver Corvettes; a yellow 19th century Rolls Royce; a British Triumph Spitfire; a Cadillac from Graceland - all metal and spotless chrome, not a speck of rust on any one of them. Attached to each was a small oval shaped magnetic backed brass plaque carefully placed to avoid any possible blemish; detailing a history of car and owner. He moved through their ranks, paused at each to marvel over every detail, soaking up the vintage of the era in which it had been king.

To the rear of the cars, announcing the entrance to the adjoining *Scents of Yesteryears* exhibition, stood a gleaming square steel box in bright red. He had passed a disinterested eye over it when a familiarity struck him. *'Something of interest for you',* the note that enticed him here had read. He *remembered it now*, printed neatly on a sheet of Mulberry bark paper and folded around his key card in the pocket of his jeans. As he had unwrapped it, the briefest vision had struck him instantly. He had not recognised it at the time;

the view had been too close, inches from his face... a dashboard... at an angle just off central plane, and a lop sided basin of reflected light resting in a gleaming chrome ashtray... the corner of a music player - *his* music player, in the dash of an *Ambassador*. There was no mistake; he had customised the player and fitted it himself. Yet here it was...fitted...no, slotted into the larger hole...in the dash of what had once, according to the brass plaque, been the Ambassador of Ambassadors owned by a Maharajah of Rajasthan. 'Well...you won't be driving anywhere again,' he said softly to the hideously sparkling square piece of art, black rubber eyes protruding high from its frame with a pleading expression of *kill me*.

The immaculately turned out museum guard, Julianno, had glided his impressive physique alongside them, and was displaying perfect teeth in his perfected friendly smile, more inquisitive of the panther than anything else. After all, what could possibly spoil *his* perfect day; thoughts of *Conquistador* and *Luna,* his latest Mexican catch of the night before, licking his mind.

'Time to *get real!'* Jake whispered in the guard's face, appended by an almost inaudible half hiss to the panther - and a click, as its chain freed itself from its collar. Three inch, pearl white incisors bit deep into the guard's calf; razor sharp claws dug into his thigh pulling him to he ground. His screaming froze as Guido placed a huge padded paw on his chest, and rubbed a wet nose into his face. Luna's silhouette flashed momentarily across the back of Julianno's burning lids ...replaced as he opened his eyes by the insane thought.... that if it wasn't for the mind numbing pain from a semi-severed leg..and his look of frozen terror that threatened to break his jaw - he might have been minded to kiss Guido and tell him how gorgeous he really was.'

'I feel like breaking the furniture,' said Jake at no-one in particular.

'There isn't any,' Sop heard herself say fumbling to fix the chain to Guido, as Jake stepped over the unconscious guard into the first sculpture. He tore free a 130 year old fireman's axe from its paper Mache mounting, stepped in front of the Ambassador, and drove the axe hard into its shell. An embedded headlight exploded; rivets bounced on the floor; the sacred sound of glass shattering resounded throughout the temple.

They left the hall to the sound of Guido's claws gouging parallel lines across the glass floor as Sop tried to drag him both hands by the collar. 'Wait!' she shouted after Jake. 'Guido needs to go.' They waited ...then left.

As they followed the sand stones out of the building and across the piazza, he flicked on the player and re-ran the message twice over...*Iglesia y Conventa de San Francisco de Asis; Plaza De San Francisco; Habana Vieja*. The same address that had come to him in the vision - confirmed in the flesh. He knew that he would have gone there anyway; having decided that what she possessed - somehow belonged to him, regardless of what Loki had to say on the matter. 'Guess someone just wanted to be sure,' he thought aloud. He unhooked and slid on his glades. 'Well..... looks like we are going to Havana,' Jake said smiling into the panther's eyes.

Sixteen
Salt beef

'**Y**ou wearin' a breaker.... sunshine?'

'*What....... !*'

'A breaker. Your DNA insurance up to date.........?'

'*Waaiiit........!*'

'Bounce.........can you bounce?'

'Can clever prof bounce?' added the larger, in a raw husky laugh exhaled from lungs in need of a purification job.

'Or you just gonna splat out like a slug on salt beef .. ha. ..ha....ah....' said the smaller twin.   *'Hey*...remember *Angel*, bro?'

'Angel........nah.'

'Course you do. Real cute. Tightest little ass *you* ever licked,' wheezed the smaller, his huge fist clenched around the third mans ankle. The swollen balloon like fingers of his free hand playfully slapped the larger on the shoulder hard enough to rock a transit. 'They called her *free fall Angel'* he continued, to the third man. 'From some heavy gravity hole on the dead side of the galaxy...mining bitch...all muscle...tits like tennis balls..looked like a fuck'n'' cartoon - but smelled all woman. Till she pulled her little game on bro here, that is. Got to free fall alright........370 floors in 10g......*without* her grav suit. Bro here punched it's tank out.'

'Dented the concrete when she hit. Left her imprint there forever,' said bro.

The smaller peered over the edge. 'You've... only got 40 floors though. Tell me ...is it true that you reach a certain speed after a while..then it don't get any faster? Clever man like you would know that kind of thing.'

'Yeesss!'

'Well.......40 ought to do it.'

'No....waaiit..!'

'Less your wearin' a breaker. But I don't feel one.' Said the smaller.

'Drop him. I'm bored with this. Lets go,' said bro.

'Ok.....*beer,*' laughed the smaller.

'I owe you eight case,' scowled bro.

'Quits...twelve seconds till he hits.'

Bro tilted his huge head into the wind looking down. 'Ten seconds.'

There was no sound for a while, each twin holding one of the man's ankles.

'Let's hear him go,' said bro. The smaller's huge arm moved to the right, opening the mans legs, and bro's left hand dropped like a sledgehammer from some nightmare machine into his groin.

The man mouthed a long silent scream....which broke into a yell of '... *NO BREAKER* ... ...NO BREAKER....NO BREAKER....NO BRE.........!' He twisted violently in their grasp, urine running down his chest and over his face to splash as floodlit droplets onto the ground 40 floors below.

'What did we want again?' asked the smaller.

'Senate,' replied his twin.

'Oh Yeah. Where did she go after Senate? Everybody knows that students keep in touch with their masters...least for a while. So where did Senate take her... Professor?'

'I don't know...I swear to God ..I don't know! She was just a student. One in thousands...'

They held him, said nothing, listening to the wind, for twenty seconds or so. Then the smaller asked 'Your car.....expensive?'

'Yours ...take it ..please take it ...it's yours...for God's sake ..just ....just do not drop me!'

'Ha ha ha.....Your lady in the car ..she like salt beef? Must be wondering where you are.'

'*Don't drop me......*'

'Gravity dispenser.....expensive car like that. Must have one fitted. You'll be just fine. Will slow you down and roll you off like you just fell out of bed.'

'She doesn't use it. She leaves it off! It switches *itself* off ... ...it switches off!'

'Well fuck me. An expensive piece of ass like that .....and it switches off just when it's about to get some, now don't that just sound familiar. I'm sure she's got it on tonight though....just for you.. eh. What do you think? I think we should find out.' He turned to the larger. 'Quits if its *on*..double if he *slugs*?'

Bro nodded in agreement. 'Quits it is.'

The scream lasted all 40 floors.. Then the hollow thud of meat hitting concrete replaced it.

'Oops.......missed,' laughed the smaller. 'What you reckon?'.

'Eh..'

'Was it on or off?'

The larger peered down at the mess on the sidewalk. 'If it come for free, should at least switch the fuck'n' thing on. *Slug!*'

Then you owe me another eight case,' laughed the smaller.

'Like fuck. You pulled him to the left. You think am a moron or something?'

'Ha ha ah ...spotted that did you. Lets get a beer.'

'An some salt beef...all this fresh air's made me starvin'.'

*****

The bourbon tasted class. Jacob had lifted it from a small locked cupboard under the bar.

'For special visits,' he had nodded as he poured them both a large opener. That was three hours ago. The good bottle was gone as was the best part of the second, non-plussed tourist J.D, and Jacob had long since shuffled back to his clientele.

Claymore was feeling good. The world suddenly made a strange kind of sense. This target ...was crisp... ..Marine...with shadows he couldn't see. Loads of metal - attitude.. *and* a brittle background. Solid but..yeah, messed up at the same time. Running scared towards a frenzied fight.

Reminded him of Cooper, Lieutenant Cooper of Company Senate - for all of 3 days - before going hand to hand with a smart bug deployed by Detroit. Got all four limbs ripped off or pulled out, depending if you viewed it in fast or slow motion. Deval, his Sergeant, had engraved an over lengthy lament into Cooper's AK butt. Claymore had inherited the rifle along with post of first Lieutenant, and had relied on it for two years.

'Cooper's Triumph'.
Leaking tears of shard glass;
confused bloodied pity.
Why care you who falls laughing terror.
...went the chorus.

He couldn't remember having paid too much attention to it at the time, but the words engraved like braille against his cheek had played their part in shaping his character - and had kept him alive.

*****

He had smelt the pig before seeing the bikes. Three bikes; each fitted with two side cars. One of the cars had a large live grey pig in it. The pig was tattooed in the same colours as the short flag on each bike.

'Two chics.' He laughed to himself. One of the larger multi continent gangs. Originally called *Too chic*, and had dressed the part. Then, somewhere, it got translated. Now the pride was in two girl one guy teams. Each member required two women or they were out.

He had put faces to the machines as he came in. Not difficult. Eight in a row along the left side of the bar. All looking inwards, at anyone in particular who might feel uncomfortable about their presence. Jacob looked happy enough about it.

Not the usual clientele for Jacob's bar... but it had been some time since his last visit. Numerous licks of paint; smartened up, and only four pianos left. The base layer for an oil painting lent against the wall where the fifth had played. Four was noisy enough, he thought. Jacob hadn't changed though. Still wearing that sleeveless string vest; showing off his Federal tattoo. Claymore hadn't known him as army. Their association was instigated by Vortex, intended as an irritating reminder that some people actually took pride in, even respected, the concept of authority. Claymore had laughed at that thinking 'Respected it to the extent of boring everyone to death some ten years on.' But Jacob sorted things for Vortex - like silent passports into places like Cuba.

The biggest biker was a woman. Well maybe? Least she might have been once. With her, was a smallish man who wore a silver studded dog collar that matched her bracelets and the pigs collar.

The leader of the group was the only one facing the bar. His reflection made him look sick; a sort of distorted greyish green with a brownish stripe that belonged to the bottle between him and the mirror. With him, it had to be said, were two stunning looking women, each with an arm in his. They both looked out of their skulls.

The third trio was two men and a woman. One of the men was sitting on the floor, while the others made a big deal about getting over friendly at the bar. Looked like they had been there a while. Most of the other drinkers had given up noticing.

*****

Claymore's life had never felt suppressed by rules. Oaths sworn, and allegiance to the code of honour they instilled had always been enough. As for the question of values, ethics, or moral judgements; such concerns were already entrusted to the Federal State. That is how it had always been, and how he expected it always to remain - *until* - that day in the sun bleached fields of Kerala, where he and Cherco, against every sinew of their marine grain, challenged and shattered that trust. Stepping forward in a sweat trenched moment of instinct; ripping the guts out of an inbred lifelong belief in respect for the chain of command. For several years after, he had convinced himself that it was a one off - never to be repeated. The rules - the hard lines of responsibility were there for good reason.

Then....... at 3.15 am on a perfectly ordinary Tuesday morning, sky watchers glimpsed what the world first took as a rogue satellite burn its way through the earth's atmosphere.

At 3.19 a.m. Captain Yositshne stared past the brow of his beloved fishing boat Karoshi (*Death through over work*) at a ball of fire which sketched a crimson shimmering path through an otherwise demon less sky - at what must surely be an unearthly rate. As he hurriedly cleaned the mulled wine steam from his father's glasses it quietened to a broken red streak, stretching for as long as he could see, far past the stern. 'The sea of Okhotska already overflows with monsters.......yet tonight another is soon to be born,' proclaimed the elder.

At 3.19 a.m. plus twenty seconds the Federal research satellite *Settler* displayed the anomaly clear the coastal cities of Abashiri and Hokkaido by two thousand feet ....eight seconds later it recorded its crash deep into the black waves of the Pacific Ocean ninety kilometres north east of the city of Tokyo.

Four minutes later the tremor awakened seismographs across the planet. The blast responsible was confined to a hazed impenetrable ring of energy. Its outer wall holding its shape as the centre *slowly* imploded as a burning mass. Unseen before - an impossible freak of science. The term *containment* became public speak - then the label HOLLOW emerged.

Silence - was the unanimous reply as to who had placed it in orbit. Then one by one all nations denied ownership of it; then everyone began to blame everyone else.

The circular wall of energy glowed yellower than the rising sun. Slowly, it gorged itself to smooth dark orange; then copper lined shimmering crimson sheets incinerated everything in its path to the centre.

The blast had erupted as compact fluorescent beams shooting in every direction. Like overstretched elastic, they stopped at some invisible critical moment - recoiled, twisting at incomprehensible speed into a raw mesh of blinding energy, lasting decades of seconds, then pulled itself together to form a perfect inescapable circle. The circle remained intact, relentless, drawing its strength from its tortured centre as its apocalyptic heat quenched its thirst. Then simply faded as a gentle breeze. Its final death throw likened to a barbecued ice cube.

Where it had raged - an area of ocean bed six miles in diameter lay naked and scorched for the world to gape at in awe. 127 minutes after conception, the Hollow's outer field collapsed. The inky smooth three mile high vertical sheet of jet black hostage sea exploded in anger - to fill the greatest abyss ever witnessed by man.

The wave that rose from its depths peaked at over a mile high as it hit the eastern shore of Japan. Western papers for once were struck into dumb silence. Front pages carried huge black question marks as to how, why and - tomorrow? Company Yamato filled the pause - launching a strategic nuclear strike against those it claimed to be responsible.

The war which followed was global. It became known as *The War Of Nations*. Why - because there were no nations left when it was, some seven years later, eventually over. Only Companies remained.

The nations had already been weakened by the preceding decade of cultural and nationalist erosion. It was during this time that Cathedral Town's sovereignty was Federally endorsed, and from which the Companies first revealed their presence. It soon became evident that it was they who were effectively the real power behind the multi facades of Federalism. There were even untested rumours that it was the Companies who started the war.

Claymore had trained in Japan. The wave struck close to his heart, yet despite this, and the confused accusations as to who was responsible, he had made the decision with ease. He had no second thoughts as to where his loyalty lay. It lay with the Federation. The Linear Assembly which crossed Eastern Europe, Russia, China and onto America was Federal funded. He had served in it for eight years, since its initial foundation to provide financial and military aid to struggling economic sectors. When they renamed it Company Senate at the outbreak of war, it was only of minor concern to him.

What was soon to follow changed everything. Instead of the advocate come negotiator role that the Assembly had undertaken in the past, a new and more direct doctrine emerged. Senate, like the other new Companies, was clearly a power unto itself; self financing, contagious and hungry. It spread with a rabid intensity that appeared to be independent of victories or defeats. As did the other Companies.

The war itself seemed to be never ending. When it looked like it had burnt itself out, or had reached a critical impasse, it would take on a new twist, and resume with reinvigorated fury. For the best part of its later years it was running on empty; while Nations collapsed one by one, and the Companies grew stronger.

For his part, he spent two solid years in mindless head on assaults against an enemy which changed on a whim. " Enemy of the day ....! " became standard prefix to role call. The Company's part in it all was never clear nor had anyone felt the need to explain it. Company loyalty was demanded and given.

Sleep arrived in scrambled lapses. Thin and ghostly. *Dream intruder*s studded the walls of the clay trenches; protection for those who slept where senso wire crawled through the debris till it found something warm enough to die for. Dug low within the ruins they were safe from pattern fire, but, the retro shots released randomly with enough energy to seek a live target on a six hour tour, would still find them in their sleep.

In the night he would wake to gladiator trolls playing havoc, singing their sweet tune of death amongst the crowd. They would slip in quietly, armed with unscrambled codes and abundant politeness for the alarms, and waddle in martyrdom through the trenches to stop wherever bad luck or fate determined the end for those who slept. There, they would commence to noisily rip the life out of everything within their death wish parameter. Small childlike metal frames, top heavy with hydraulic overkill armament with toy faces, intensified the taste of insanity.

Semi-fluent dreams rolled night past day. In the beginning, he would spend starless nights alone, motionless in some distant vantage spot, tangled randomly as camouflage amongst the piled dead. The eerie quiet split only by short smothered bursts from his AK as he released mercy targets. He would track them as the trolls cut them loose; as they crawled away from their playful catlike cross slit stares, through acid pools of the chemical laced soil. The trolls would make it easy, flaring the location for any one soft, wired up, or stupid enough to think about going out to do something about it. The wounded would crawl all night only to wish they were dead in the morning.

He would track them across an inverted landscape of filtered shadow, into trenches, out of blackened ruins, until the gun sight told him that for flickering seconds they were *framed*, isolated; the trigonometry linking him to the trolls broken by something, anything. His muted AK and scattered deflector beacons would fragmentise the dull sound, and chill his body heat enough to prevent them locating his exact position. Though their retort was still always much too close for comfort. There were many times when the wounded crawled...and crawled...until he couldn't see them any more.

The passing days turned to endless months. The slow light of each new dawn soothed pain into need; blurred the edges of reality and branded routine into the sogging layers of fading humanity. Replacing it by a cold edge of veteran steel.

Harsh reality dominated his days and his dreams. The fighting and bloodshed became routine, and he got better and better at it. Comradeship - a forgotten cause. Trust - in nothing, in no one - other than himself. Switching off became a sickening way of life.

Thoughts froze at conception, deep within his mind. Sheets of memories, often only hours old, folded quickly, forming neatly woven blankets of conscious nonplus forget. Solid barriers between what should have been and what was; an impenetrable wall exiling the man he knew, enslaving the man whom he had become.

Surrounded by chaos, with no evident sense to any of it, where troops had undistinguished short projected lifespans, his world became one of introverted self preservation. He built his own personal fortress; a mind state, insular, immune to the screams and havoc of the outside world. Accountable to no one, to nothing. Driven only by his mood at any particular moment; safe from conscience or guilt. Behind cold blue eyes he survived. A reputation built on dangerous unpredictability, from passive non intervention to total ruthlessness soon pursed him.

The war ended, and the years whispered past. He never did recognise the exact moment when he finally lost it. Survived he had, but the toll buried his past in ghostlike shadows. The present - he did what he did best - and he was good at it. Small hard hitting jobs that no one else would touch. Jobs that getting your fingers burnt meant that you were dead. Jobs for men like Vortex.

Vortex had picked him up during a temporary lapse in Company Senate's economic credibility. Sort of part exchange involving a Company trade in an item that Claymore was couriering for Senate. He had worked strictly to Senate until that point. At the exchange of the said item, Vortex had explained to him that he was now officially freelance. Which in plain speak meant that he now worked for Vortex.

That in itself was good. He could work alone; his retainer was premium; the jobs plentiful; which kept him busy; which stopped him thinking too much. And Vortex never asked questions. But the dull ache in his guts - the ache that seemed to respond solely to his best and only friend, J.D, remained.

So it was; as he waited for the third night running in some pay by the hour hotel room, for a crippled stratabike pilot with a Company grudge and something or nothing to trade - when Vortex, in person, showed up saying the other had been taken care of and gave him a new target - some AWOL marine with something Vortex wanted back *real bad*.

Maybe *that* was it. he thought. Maybe that was why he got interested in her in the first place - someone else who had broken *their* rules. Maybe he had sensed some kind of an empathy with this Sands, even then. Or maybe it was just something fresh to occupy his tired mind. Whatever - it was a wake up call, and unknown then, would ignite the road of a long forgotten crusade.

Now - sitting in Jacob's bar, drunk, reflecting on the pleasure of having denied the twins the morsel of information that they needed, and more than likely having kept her cybertramp's one and only living relative alive by doing so, not to mention having blocked any chance that Vortex may of had of finding Sands before she made her sale - it was plain that *her* self inflicted problem, and where she thought that she could possibly go with it..... had sparked something to life *in him.*

Empathy - yes, *and* he had come to know her *through her brother's eyes.* He had shared in her life. She too had changed, had lost something precious by the LoTech event, and by her brother's death. She was army, through and through - just like him. She had crossed the line, broken their rules - just like him. Had lost faith in her code, and like him - had invented her own. *To live for the moment* ...to him it meant to live without conscience or guilt. What did she want?

The thought was interrupted. The image that hit him was slightly out of sequence. Like a dream state waiting quietly on the sidelines until it felt that he might feel curious enough to sharpen the focus and give it his attention. When he did, it was Savannah's voice which filled his mind   'Well, well..... finally decided to grace me with your presence?' He saw her standing there before him, her hair sleek and wet from Cathedral Town. She retained her detached air but her body language was slower, full of hunger. 'I wasn't *always* a bitch you know.' She smiled her slow even smile. 'There was a time... she let the moment linger ...*when I was just plain truly bad.'* She laughed afterwards with a sexy husk that made him shiver. It was the same line she had used the night that he had ended up in bed with her. Now it seemed a fitting opener for what recently had become a string of verbal abuse, fit only to be ignored.

'Get lost.' He replied, then switched back into his thoughts. Normally he would have indulged her some, at least until she began to grate, but the timing was wrong. He had been thinking about Blacker. About a juiced up link to allow him to carry Blacker again. Stupid he knew..but he had this need.....to see her smile.....to see *Sands* smile like he had seen her smile for Blacker.

'Nursing scars.' Savannah laughed. 'What an ass.' She had picked up his vibes, and snippets of drunken mumbles slipped unintentionally from his mouth, for her and all those in the bar to hear. *'This marine was something else'* she had heard him mutter.

'Of all the heads to get chipped into,' she cursed. He had swallowed enough J.D. in the last hour to put them both down. She could almost taste it. She remembered the pleasant sting in her throat. How she had made it flow..and would again. But for now - she would have to make do with watching. Watching this fuck'n' retard lick his mind. It wasn't as if she could even access what he was thinking, or even look where she wanted to look. The chip enhancement helped but she could still only see or hear whatever *he* chose to look at. She smiled, 'If he had not already erased it, he would probably have re-opened Blacker's mind..in search of what.... a smile - from some sad bitch who he would probably have to waste when he met her in a more sober moment. Stupid fuck.

Now *her* smile... she laughed. When she ..*Savannah*.. smiled ..it was sharper than any icicle; this she knew to be true. Some men it turned on. Scared the shit out of others. Left nice guys with a stupid bemused look on their face. The ones she really enjoyed, were those who took it as some kind of macho challenge. She kept her *favourite routine* for them. For those lucky few, she would transform her cool exterior into an aura of unblemished sensual warmth, radiating from a smile so distant from the mask she had *presumably* worn; portrayed in a look of infatuated innocent delight, eyes wide open, almost tearful, sending messages of gratitude and admiration for her saviour who had unlocked the femininity in her. Freed her from herself. Then as self righteous satisfaction registered across his face - she'd crush the spell with coarse ice cold laughter, or if the timing allowed, complete the scene with some cold hearted extremely violent act. Now that - really made her smile.

Whatever pathetic thoughts were going on in his twisted mind...he could at least have the balls to share them. That much he owed. He had agreed to carry her after all. She was his god-damn partner after all. Wasn't that what partnership was about. Well - if he wouldn't talk to her - she could still sure as hell remind him why she was there!

She bit deep into her memory. *'Hey.... sunburnt Cadillac's; chilli flavoured bonnets; tail fins to die for....remember..? Red hot steel crashin' through the surf.'* Her voice echoed throughout his head. Her tone was soft, almost soothing. The image was of an Indian sunset beach. He could almost smell the burnt evening air. Sri Lanka .....two nights stay after a messed up hit; nothing intimate. Probably the closest he had come to relaxation in a long stretch, and the closest he ever came to seeing the alter professional side to her. The little girl in the big boys game - as she always claimed to be. She had traded a Vortex eight wheeler, triple skinned fire-cat for some revamped ninety year old Cadi, only to leave it parked in the ocean for anyone who wanted it to save in the morning.

He stretched his eyes in a vain attempt to increase his drunken focus, his attention momentarily captured. As always, her silhouette looked good; blonde locks filtering hints of her silver laced Celtic tattoo. The silhouette remained, but the image behind it mutated into a more recent scene. *His head was filled with flamenco music ...he was staring back at himself - through Savannahs eyes ...he was one of a few left standing in a body strewn bar, his handgun pointing straight into her face ...he saw himself pull the trigger ...felt the shell impact ...her head recoil as the room spun and she hit the floor.*

'Hey.... remember... ladies bite,' she cooed. It was her idea of smart play. To touch his guilt. She laughed and said 'Do you think this marine would respect you if *she* knew you as I know you?'

He laughed aloud. She thought she saw his eyes sparkle against the reflection on the table. 'How pissed off you would be if you knew *half* the truth of that!' he replied into the blank faces of the nearest drinkers. And pissed off she would have been. For there was no guilt. How could there be - the shot that killed her was intentional.

She was the target - and the instant had presented itself. The kick of the gun had played no part. He had always worked alone. At the time, partnership to him was no more than something that had its moments, and that wasn't one of them. He had shot her without hesitation, or remorse. If she *had* known him she would have known better.

Slowly, and with a more sober edge, he smiled for the second time of the evening. *"An obligation written as a gentleman's oath. A last right of partnership cast in penitence,"* he recalled. Her words, not his. He had chosen to carry her not from guilt, as she had presumed, but because *Vortex had asked him to.* No guilt, only surprise - as it was Vortex who had ordered her shot.

Surprise, and a hint of curiosity as to Vortex's motive; later intensified when Vortex said that she must remain unaware that the order had come from him. There was no guilt on Claymore's part, only regret that he had partnered her and more, in the first place.

He hadn't just slept with her. He had asked himself afterwards what it was he had really been looking for.

Yeah..the sex was good..real physical.... which was the way he had wanted it. With Savannah, he would have been surprised had it been anything else. The emotional psychotic edge didn't exactly arrive unexpectedly either. Yeah.. but there was more.....he later wondered, that if without realising, he had wanted to look deep within her; as though he might find something remotely close to his self. An *explanation*, more than anything, of who he was, through understanding someone as cold and lost as himself. If that was it - he hadn't found it. *Her* ice was all natural. Anyways... the thought was short lived, and was lost after the first caffeine hit of the day.

This marine - now she was something else entirely - though they still had some qualities in common; both physical - both dangerous. Both with wicked smiles. Except Sav's had a razor-like edge to it; whereas any teeth marks from Sands, he thought, would kind of fade with the morning light. He had been with a lot of women. Most, he couldn't remember in the morning. This one - he had never even been close to, but..... he knew exactly what not to expect. She had edged him towards the *was meant to be syndrome*, fit for drunks or kids. But crazy or not, it was starting to feel good.

In his mind's eye he shook his head sharply. He gathered the floating layer of soft crushed ice from the table water jug and rolled it across the back of his neck. 'Snap out of it,' he heard himself say aloud. 'Don't need this..... don't need any of this. To hell with them both.' He reached for the bottle, and pulled the cork out with his teeth. As the J.D. stung the glass he was sure he heard a silent sigh.

'Well this party sure ain't going anywhere,' Savannah said flatly. 'Hell.. enough of this one way bullshit.....let's see who else wants to chat?'

The voice was not his own. It belonged to........ some heartless bitter female? He could feel her presence itch through his frame. His family name was Kuznetzov. When in Moscow, his street name was Misha. Both names were interchangeable with that of his masters - Mikhail.

For a rucksack, Misha was extremely polite. He always took great care not to bump into any of the other bags as he slid his way silently along the airport check in floor, even the slow, or worse still, the dead ones. The dead ones always saddened him; their power cells having popped their clogs, sometimes years earlier, and no-one having taken the little bother involved to revive them. Sometimes in the odd moment of low esteem it made even he question his loyalty. But despite it all, even on extreme occasions of all time low, like the time when his master risked him in a game of sorts, for the chance of sex with some Brazilian dog - he never faltered. That had turned out to be a bad night. He did however, eventually take strength from the truth, which was, that his master was after all human. And if the absolute truth be known she wasn't really a dog. In fact she was a rather choice cut - well at least in the opinion of the other rucksacks in his friendship circle.

Politeness, loyalty and obedience was his game. *No point in pissing me off.... all you'll get in return is a smile* - was his plan. And it worked, always had. Twelve short beloved years of globe trotting, with only four months total spent brooding in dark dampish cupboards, in idyll places. Until today - when he experienced what could only best be described as an itch. It had trickled up and down the length of his secondary rear straps, as if trying to get a handle on him, shot his vertical bar support rigid, then paralysed him on the spot. Then *her* voice caressed its way all through him.

'Tell me now...the *truth* now...you ever get horny? Ever get jealous...ever want to swop places with whoever it is he is *favouring* at that moment? No....o! I don't believe you. *Course you do.* You little devil.'

'What *is* she talking about?' was his initial thought, followed closely by 'who is this?' He tried to reply but the infiltrator was either unable to hear or refused to communicate. Whichever, it clearly wasn't worth pursuing; obviously someone was jealous, bored or seriously messed up. Either way it was of no consequence to him.

'Wrong.' Replied the silky voice, as if having fully anticipated his conclusion. 'Want to play?' she continued. 'Let's play shall we. A little game called.....*let's strangle the boss.*'

He suddenly did not like the sound of this - not one bit. The paralysis - he then realised was not a flash circuit reaction to the interruption as he had initially supposed, but was very real, and very strong. No matter how hard he strained he just could not budge. He switched his thoughts to Mikhail. Best make him aware of whatever this is. But Mikhail was fast asleep. Curled up neatly in a foetal ball, out to the world on some 'Aqua de la Cathedral Town' cocktail of urban mythical reputation.

'Shall we wake him? Perhaps best to let him sleep a little. He looks so..o tired... like he could sleep forever...just never wake up at all,' stroked her voice.

He could feel Mikhail nestled comfortably into his retractable straps, relaxed and in absolute trust of Misha's watchful protective eye. A placement of trust that had proven true over the years, and one which Misha was very proud of. To Misha, his purpose was one of companionship. His retractable straps would inflate to pillow like head rests when he sensed tension in his masters neck; his back plate would cool in temperature to chill the heat out of long hours in the sun, and he would provide soothing words in moments of tired travel stress. His easy temperament was of crucial benefit; never had he raised his voice. Even in moments of threat by not so bright would-be thieves, had he easily resisted the urge to shout either in aggression or warning; but simply made their presence known to his master, and then his to them in some subtle way that ousted their attention. Never once had he used the slicer wire or pacifying spray. But this was different - he could sense the urgency - and her confidence, as if she had anticipated his every move. He yelled into his chamber...then yelled aloud.. but his voice was silent on both counts, as if the mechanism had never been inserted.

'So what are we good for then my little musketeer? Ah ... Tokyo mace - a little squirt of that would sure to spoil his beauty sleep... eh.'

'Yes indeed it would,' thought Misha, instantly seeking to release a micro amount, which would certainly catch Mikhail's attention without being too offensive. But it was not to be, her hold was too strong.

'No.. something.... a little more subtle.. I would say. Let's try.....'

Mikhail grunted and shifted his position slightly as the straps began to deflate and tighten around his throat..........*then*... her grip suddenly ceased as something much much more interesting caught her attention.

Her voice ricocheted through Claymore's head, jolting aside his blurred double visioned view of the bar. He caught familiar echoes of *beware* from her tone..unintentional..but too sweetly laced with welcoming anticipation to go unnoticed..a neon sign which read ...*Come on then!*

'*I smell smooth delirious chocolate,*' he heard her breathe. He turned a fraction late..the blade cut deep into his face, its serrated edge zizzlin'... catchin' on bone. The woman who wielded it was already dead; eyes glazed over before she reached the floor. Thoughts crashed across his rapidly focusing mind... 'Reacted..should never need to..should have seen it coming,' as he felt his cheek flap against his jaw, and drove his chair up into the second biker's throat, right hand slashing hard tight across her lower rib cage, body and chair hitting the floor simultaneously..his small samurai knife already wrist sheathed.

'Oh babe.....icy..... you could at least have given it time to glint,' whispered Savannah. No one else in the bar moved. Drinks froze mid air. The leader lunged forward... stalled, growling instead at the sitter still muttering to the ground. The sitter threw back his head; petrol loose eyes illuminated the void between him and Claymore...then on some pathologically mutated personal death wish, tore vertically from the floor throwing himself arms spread straight at him - only to recoil body elevated parallel with the floor, as the shells hit him clean centre of the chest battering him backwards to land with a thud in the same spot as he had spent the evening. One and a half seconds later the third shell exploded in the leader's head.

Through adrenalin boosted vision he heard the smoky echo of Savannah's voice 'I wanna walk bare foot. I wanna feel the cold floor through his warm blood.'

From his rear left, a thick masculine voice rasped through a heavily braced tooth line 'oVer..oVer...', as Claymore turned Ah Dare Ya in that direction. The gun had sighted on the largest biker, who stood with a short lived palms up gesture, uttering the words again and again. Then the massive bulk of the smaller twin rose behind him, and in one short gentle movement embraced the bikers neck and snapped it.

The body slid from his grip to thud heavily onto its knees. The twins huge hand pulled the bikers head back and stuffed a wad of cred's into the open dribbling mouth. 'Not such a waste of cred's as it may seem. Least we got the entertainment value,' smirked the twin looking directly at Claymore. The remaining two bikers were already on their machines, having decided to leave their payment where it was.

Ignoring Ah Dare Ya's sight spot illuminating his chest, he continued 'We've been to Florence......Florence Europe and back in all of the short time it took you to get here and get sloshed. Not bad for such large though elegant statutes. Met with a not overly helpful professor.'

'We're sick of getting your scraps. We deserve better. And we don't like to be left out,' hissed the larger.

'Vortex says *you* know where the deal is,' continued the smaller. 'Also told us you were here.......which seemed a little strange to us...having just told us that our services may not be called on for the next play.'

'We got the feelin' that he thought you might like a little company tonight. Why do you think he would do that then?' added the larger.

The smaller chuckled. 'Maybe he thought you were in need of sharpening up a little...eh!'

'*I wouldn't!*' interjected Savannah swiftly and silently. '*Not a good time to think like that,*' she added, reading Claymore's alcohol laced mind. 'Fatboy's got a lot of body shields round him.. and this was *their* call. Ugly as they are - the're not that s*tupid*. And *remember* - if this ends wrong, no-one else is going to bother remembering about *me* - *this is both our ass's.*'

The frank crispness of her tone snapped him out of it. It wasn't the kind of call she liked to make. Which meant that she was probably right. It *was* their game - whatever went down, they would have an angle.

'Now is not the time,' she added calmly, sensing that the heat had passed. 'When I'm walkin for good again... we'll look them up together.'

He ran his index finger back over the grip as he holstered the AK100 smiling broadly at the larger twin. He knew that they had taken this as far as they would for today - unless he forced it. No. He would focus on the current. He had got what he needed from Jacob. He knew what he needed from Sands *and* where and when to get it. The twins could wait.

Seventeen
Baby blue eyes

'Know your enemy.' Loki had said as he filtered Claymore's psych profile into her chip. '*Never* pre-guess his next move; but - know what he is capable of....know what his preferences are....what, if anything, he would normally seek to avoid.....cut down the odds on particular plays..but be prepared for anything. Especially this one - for his trade is unpredictability.'

She stared across the water. The muscular horn of a mammoth tanker filled the midnight black of the bay. As its massive non ship like frame of pinball red lights slowly slipped past her towards the ocean, it unveiled the silhouette of the island behind, the tall white catolica statue standing guard high on the hill gently illuminated in a foggy green shroud. Would the fortune teller, this Jinx, be true to his vision. Is this where it would end - where she was to die? She felt her AK purr beneath her jacket - she thought not.

This time *Vortex* would be more prepared. This time she would get in and out fast. No elaborate set up; no need for Marie's toys. She turned her eyes to the flare as another industrial chimney erupted into a godlike scaled torch, its reflection floating pink in the still water. Would Faro be there? And the others? 'Cool frictionless minds free of dogma,' she had once heard Vortex proudly describe them. 'We'll see what we see,' she whispered sadly.

She used the wrap rounds to see 360 degrees from her spot; past the ferry terminal building, past the eloquently crumbling apartment block where Marie waited, zooming in across the public square to the punched out shell of the Catedral de la Habana. They were linked directly to her AK, which purred loudly as it tracked multiple targets, eyeing everybody, everything that happened to move. The glasses extra thick heat shields countered the Cuban sun, the colder they were the more efficiently they behaved.

All quiet on the western front, she thought. No trace of any early risers. The sale was set for tomorrow, mid day. Company Senate had bid the highest. Their representatives would most certainly check out the meeting place before the exchange, but would not arrive until the agreed time. They had no reason to feel threatened from her, and had been given assurances that the sale was both private and beyond the eyes of Company Vortex. Nor did she have reason to doubt or fear them. Exchanges of this manner rarely involved treachery on the part of the purchasing Company, for reasons of precedent. The warning from Jinx - this voice-over fortune teller, did however cause flashes of concern. He had suggested without being specific, that he and others knew the location and details of the sale - that she and Senate would not be alone. He had entered her mind two nights ago in a much more direct manner than his previous contacts. She grimaced, recalling the polythene take hold; stretching itself over her face, distorting the shape of her mouth, pressing dry against her teeth, tightening the skin against her cheek bones, and rolling up over her eyebrows forcing her eyelids back. Stuck to her pupils; frosted vision of Marie's fright. She had stopped breathing, clawed at her face. Nothing there. He had later apologised, rather timidly, for the unpleasantness of it all, followed immediately by a desperate outburst and rants about inevitable doom if she ignored him this time.

She put it down to a panicked final attempt to make her stall, after his previous failure to entice her to trust in him, to bring the goods to him - whoever *he* was. The hand of Vortex seemed the only explanation. This in itself was good, for if he was of Vortex and could not be specific as to the details of the sale then there should be no Claymore and no Vortex troops.

It was his passing reference to someone he called Jake which was the real source of her concern. His insistence that this Jake, although extremely dangerous, should not be harmed had definitely been laced with genuine non professional concern. More like.. the need to mention Jake at all was born of reluctant necessity, and had installed panic. His uncorroborated suggestion that giving the disc to Jake would, although not match her financial plans, satisfy her deeper needs and true reason for taking it in the first place...and was the only possible option that any good could come from in the long term - didn't cut any ice. It did however cast doubt on her conclusion that his claim to infiltrating the sale was bull.

Saturday 11.00 a.m. Barro Café, Havana. Omara: owner, manager, and waitress of the best cafe in town by day, best jazz club on the island by night, looked down in disbelief at the black panther lapping up the hot spilt milk at her feet.

Latteccino; somewhere between a cafe latte and a cappuccino, 'the stupid name for stupid tourists had been her stupid mans idea because he couldn't be bothered fixing the frother,' she'd laugh with her friends. She knew that the real reason the coffee was popular was down to her cinnamon and mint marshmallow topping. The cute looking cat sure seemed to like it, and it sure didn't know it had no fancy name. It was *her* coffee bar, and those were *her* shoes. She smiled at the thought that everyone knew that they just had to be expensive as there was so little to them. She had just never imagined the day she'd have a pure black panther lick her toes through them.

Saturday 11.20 a.m. Barro Cafe, Havana. Sands was forty minutes early and had intended a fast recon pass only. Then temptation got the better of her, as Cappuccino had never tasted *that* good before - and well.. wooden floors don't bleed. Least not till now. The red pool on this one was getting darker and bigger by the second. Something beneath the feet of the three brown clad monks was making tearing noises, like someone fitting a carpet. Their sandaled feet were getting wet but they didn't seem bothered by it in the least. She decided to sit somewhere else. Somewhere with a larger sense of normality. She quietly spread eagled a short wooden bench between a huge western looking Sumo, whose very sweaty look-alike had just glided towards the bar. She flicked her eyebrows at the passing waitress indicating her desire for more coffee a la house brand. The waitress smiled back continuing their wordless conversation of four cups from the day before.

The Sumo returned shortly after, a dozen or so burgers from a vender of the square crammed into both fists, his mouth already chewing rhythmically. The seated larger caught the disconcerting glance from two smartly dressed young business men sipping coffee at the next table. His jaw was moving from side to side as a cow does while chewing the cud, salivating in anticipation. Screwing his face into a scowl he lent forward noisily drawing a large lump of dark green mucus from overripe neck glands, and spat it onto the front of the nearest business man's freshly pressed white cotton shirt. Turning to bro who crashed heavily onto the bench, he said with a tremendous full face grin, 'a little chemical treat for the deserving.'

Omara stood frozen on the spot next to the table, a tray with Sand's coffee and someone's food temporarily forgotten in her hands, and said the first thing that came into her head. 'You can't eat food not bought on the premises in here. You don't like my menu you should have stayed outside.'

Bro turned his head towards the tray and sniffed twice at the food from a distance. 'What's that smell...reminds me of pig's foreskin?'

'When did we eat that?' asked the larger.

'You know,' bro said to Omara as he turned away, 'You're very very sweet. You should know...that if you were to be a little bit more polite...I might consider letting you get to know me better.'

Sands too had frozen on the spot. How could she have missed it. Whoever they were they sure as hell didn't belong here. She followed the line of bro's fine silk ankle length coat to the calf of his boot; the imprint of a heavy handgun was clear. Surely they couldn't be Senate? This sale had just got very claustrophobic.

They hadn't seen her yet! Her mind raced. The larger one had his back to her and the other had been too engrossed in his food and exchange with the waitress. Time to leave and re-assess. She stood - and found herself staring directly into the eyes of Kimmo, across the room. She blinked quickly casting her eyes around. Too late - she too had been engrossed. They were all around her: Kimmo, Vasos, lips drawn thinly in a look of *'this is where you get yours'*. Troops with Vortex burnt into their lapels everywhere. How could they have known? Her eyes searched the room for Claymore. Instead she saw the two uniformed Senate officers enter the bar. They were pulling an anything but playful king sized special breed dog alongside them.

She watched the officers scan the bar. What they saw was a very large marine with a mean glint in his good eye ferociously staring across the floor. In his shadow, absolutely still, save for a slow rotation of her head and fast flicking eyes, stood a compact female with Vasos VR1295 burnt into her lapel. She held a top of the range AK110 rested across her forearms, professionally relaxed and posed for instant engagement. She saw them inhale adrenalin as they picked out the rest of the Vortex unit, then briefly exchange words as they saw her standing across the room.

They reined the dog in closer and made their way to a half way point between them and Sands. Kimmo echoed their movement around the other side of the room, never once taking his eyes from her. Two half drunk off duty Company Kladio privates hesitated in their minds, in a mixed objection of Company pride and rank, as their bodies moved to let him pass.

On top of the bar to their left, his outline backlit by the midday sun, framed like a picture by the glass window behind him, sat a de-robed shaven headed monk. Unlike his brothers, he wore tight fitting brown jeans held by elastic braces over a bright white T shirt. He sat poised like a King. *Jake!*

Stalemate seemed set. *What to do* was flashing across her mind faster and faster when she saw them standing on either side of Kimmo - Faro and Claymore! A simple closed sale, she had told Senate. *'Christ - is there any one who isn't here?'* Her heart went cold as Faro walked towards her. Her moment of truth; dreaded in her sleep those past months. She had witnessed his wrath on the barman; seen the deadness behind his eyes. She had woken in the night, hair drenched with sweat as she played through this moment. She could almost hear each stride as he crossed the floor at his usual unhurried even pace. The calm unfaltering pace that had set him apart for her. Now.. as they stood just beyond touching distance.. had the fortune teller's call come true after all? He smiled his certain half smile tapping a cigarette from its packet. 'I believe that you have something that never belonged to you.'

She searched his eyes, pale against the intense fathom blue of the lighter, in the hope of finding something that would give her a clue. Something that would open his mind to her.

'Lieutenant Faro. We have unwanted company,' she heard Kimmo state through his link. The frequency was roomed to Company Vortex, but Loki had his ways.

'She is reading *main* line frequency,' Faro replied on a *parallel* wave. 'When she releases the disc - execute her.' He watched her lack of reaction - but Loki had fitted her out well. 'Room the secondary wave and communicate by secondary only,' Faro concluded.

He then turned, looking initially at Kimmo who blankly stared back, then at the Senate officer as he saw the Sumo rise behind him. 'The Sumo are of Vortex,' he stated flatly, turning his head back towards Sands as something flat and shiny in the twins hand cleanly removed the Senate officers head. The second Sumo slid beside him ten feet from Sands. Her wrap rounds showed Claymore standing firm to the rear, an AK pointing diagonally at the ground across his lap.

When he had sobered up, Claymore had realised that as it was Companies doing the buying he could need Vortex troop backing. Maybe he could have backed out right there, let Vortex military take it from now? His role had been to find the girl and the disc. That he had done. Looking around the room, he had certainly called it right, even if for the wrong reason. Two Senate negotiators would have been simple enough - but a bar full of fanatic monks and the twins was something else.

His decision, prompted by the overcrowded nature of the bar, to rely on his customised left handed pistol and to give Savannah temporary control over AH Dare Ya would also soon be tested. Then again - two eyes were better than one, and this definitely was her kind of play.

Inside, another part of Sands had died on hearing Faro's curt order. As he turned away she had played her hidden hand. As pretty lights as Omara had ever seen had arrived at her bar a week before; a gift from a secret admirer. Sea shells shaped from blazon glass encrusted in a frame of Jade coloured titanium. Within each case sat the guts of a thirty year old riot police pacifier light. The cheerful blush radiated through the pink silken slats cast the warm soft shadows of the setting sun, and nothing more, unless specifically commanded to.

As he turned away, Sands had initiated the pacifier which *should* have reduced everyone within forty metres to a state of stupefied non-action. The average citizen would be capable of nothing other than sitting quietly until the light was switched off, but then this room was full of everything other than the average citizen. Even as the room moved frame by frame in marine speak for her, she could see that it also did so for Faro and his troops. For Claymore, she wasn't sure, his body language was too professionally relaxed for her to be able to detect any difference, and it definitely hadn't hit the Sumos who had decapitated the Senate officer after she had turned the lights on. Not the room full of dazed tourists she had hoped for.

Surrounded by professionals - and none of them in her corner. Then her eye caught Jake, sitting high on the bar like a sleeping king. Her thoughts shot to the fortune teller whose warning had held true so far - *so this Jake who was not with her - was not with them either*. And *he* wanted what *she* had ..and *they* sure as fuck were not just going to give it to him. She switched off the pacifier. Jake never moved a muscle, but released a semi audible hiss which was repeated by the monks throughout the room. Seconds later fourteen beautifully groomed black panthers attacked. A monk called Huek jumped with both feet, as if on fire, onto a table emptying twin magazines of a sub machine pistol at the furthest marines. The panthers targeted the marines as instructed, tourists and regular customers trying desperately to look small in their seats or hugging the floor. Two marines fell from Huek and the dozen other monks' fanatical onslaught, though most of their small arm fire simply ripped up the furniture or lodged harmlessly in Company body armour. She heard the thud of Claymore's AK as Savannah cut the second Senate officer in half as he reached for his pistol, then its continuous thump as three of the monks erupted in bits. She instinctively side stepped raising her own AK level with Claymore's head as her body armour started to inform her that its sight had locked on the centre of her back. Both sights held their marks from 15 feet. Without the slow motion control of marine speak they would have been dead. Instead the moment froze as Claymore told Savannah to step down as she was at risk of damaging the disc, and Sands held firm her aim - then the hum of something much more sinister kicked in.

She recognised the sensation instantly. Used during training camp exercises to harden resistance. Little more than a wicked toy designed to link two minds and implant a subconscious idea, or an equal but opposite action required of both participants; then intensify the rhythm until one of them gave in. This model was military in that it only worked one way, applying increased pressure until you either did what was required or something burst in your head - and it was focused at her.

She could see the small control plate in the smaller Sumo's hand, its calm docile tones asking her to deliver the disc. Around her the carnage continued unabated. A half grown panther which Huek had called Guido had gone one on one with the heavily armoured Senate Doberman who didn't seem to be enjoying it much.

As bro held the control steady, and Sands hand slowly lowered her gun, Claymore heard the Sumo slip the catch of a way too big handgun as he upholstered it from his boot. 'I think this will speed up the transaction a little,' he laughed - but stopped mid sentence as Claymore's handgun caressed the back of his bald head. As he rotated his neck the gun pressed point blank against his face. Claymore's other hand held Ah Dare Ya which was now directed at the other twins stomach - whose gun was levelled at Claymores head.

'I wouldn't be doing that!' said Ah Dare Ya. The voice was Savannah's.

'Hey it's baby blue eyes! I remember you ...... HA! HA! HA! This sad fuck's only carrying you around for company cause he can't get a real woman - guess it kinda warms both ways...EH.!' replied the larger.

'*The disc* - is what we came for,' said Claymore quietly.

'Touchy aren't we. What's the difference to you if I do her or not?'

'The difference is whether *you* live or die.'

'Ha Ha Ha..she goes....we all go..it seems....Ha..Ha...'

'I've never had a problem with that. Have you?' replied Claymore.

Ah Dare Ya made a low pitched whine. 'Grotesquely vulgar explosive tips for grotesquely vulgar fat fucks,' complimented Savannah.

Sands could feel her mind struggle with its grip, like the sensation of cold pearls against hot skin, her hand unzipping the pouch of her jacket, her fingers millimetres from the disc. She remembered the technique Vortex had taught her - the trick was not to focus on resisting but on something else altogether, something vivid in your mind which would act as a release mechanism. *Vortex..* she filled her mind with Vortex, what could be easier or more appropriate. He of course would be watching somewhere. 'Lets give him something to watch, ' she said aloud.

The second's lapse was all she needed - she had levelled her AK and shot the Sumo in the face. The second burst ricocheted off the other twin's gun tearing through his wrist and hand.

Faro had stood almost motionless throughout the entire 45 seconds that Jake had been awake; the length of time it had taken to wreck Omara's bar, kill two Senate officers a Sumo and a large number of monks and civilians. He had smoked half his cigarette. The twins little fiasco had shown that she clearly had the disc with her. He slid his pistol from its metallic wrist sheath intent on the single shot that would resolve the matter.

Their eyes met over the barrel length of her still smoking AK. His gun was only half way home. Her mouth opened as if to say something then he heard her voice echo through his chip. 'You were killed. I saw you fall. You were shot in the head. *You were killed!*' she cried. He realised that in her emotion she was mouthing the words as well as transmitting them. 'If you had lived you would not have chosen to be here. You were the only one who knew that *he* killed my brother. You and I were best friends - much more.' Her words were senseless to him; *why hadn't she discharged her weapon?* gnawed loudly in his head.

'In rebuilding your mind he rebuilt your memories, they are chip enhanced - to suit *his* need. He has sent you just like he sent my brother - to get back at me. Switch off your chip - switch it off - search what you have left ...maybe there is enough to see the truth!'

She had jolted his memory ..one frame flashes...her torn body the second of his *death*..the overwhelming sense of loss he had felt seeing her hit, presuming her dead...together, alone, chinking brandy glasses...her brother..did she have a brother? And the chip ..true it had never been off since his recuperation, he had been advised against it given the seriousness of his wound. Curiosity - he switched if off. There was a nothingness silence slowly filled by a dull growing pain... no new memories. Everything was as it had been. She was the one who was deluded. *Then* he smiled as if having understood the riddle, and somewhat more slowly raised the gun.....

Bro's very dead weight was sitting upright, what was left of his head resting on his chest. The larger twin stood over him staring down at the hole in the back of his skull. He seemed oblivious to the mayhem around him, absently rubbing the stump of his right hand. Then his small pig like eyes sparked alive as he stood straighter than he had ever stood before, twisting the retractable samurai sword through the air in a poetic four beat motion roared aloud 'I am the man.' Pieces of a monk fell to the ground. Again he roared louder 'You have stung my soul.' The scream resounded like the bass echo in the dust storm of a collapsing building dynamited from its base, sucking the ground into its belly. Bro would lie there - not playin' dead - never get up again.

For Kimmo it had been the longest four seconds of his professional life, eternity in marine speak; for Vasos even longer as she had always had her own private passion for Faro. Either of them could have taken Sands down at will - but they didn't have to look behind his chip, they knew the Faro of before and after..and the brother thing..she hadn't mentioned that it had been her brother, it would have been bad form. That explained at least part of it, comrades they had definitely been, and for an instant once again she was one of them. In the long run their private hesitation would be attributed to him rather than her ..as they had loathed what he had become.

As Faro fell his head bounced off the wooden slatted floor.

'Bro..gone. Will be alone. Make all the decisions now! Will be the man. Will get me this bitch - will get *me* a reputation! Double fee!' the sole twin squealed aloud at no-one in particular. He dropped to one knee beside Bro having parried a blow from a monk; reversing the sword, drove it backwards through the monks chest, then slipped a slim magazine into its handle. In a single arced motion he released the blade from the monk and sprayed a Gatling round of twenty four explosive tipped needles into a struggling Vortex officer and three other monks.

Roaring 'I am the man' above the din he crushed a handful of smoke screen pellets in his hand and slid away. From the heart of the putrid smelling smoke the sound of the retractable 0.5 mm thin samurai blade collapsing into itself, each of its 275 perfectly crafted razor edged sections slotting neatly into its handle, went undetected. As did the barely audible whine as they tore on mass through the air as he fired them back on a random pattern into the room.

Sands backed off slowly, the smoke thickening fast around her, her AK levelled at Claymore and the remaining troops.

As the smoke was about to engulf her completely she quickly side stepped into it, ducked to her knees and rolled behind the pillar she had picked from her wrap rounds for the purpose. The room had instantly erupted in a ball of gunfire, AK's thumping out discords of mayhem at everything their heat or motion sensors detected. She had intentionally dropped hers as she rolled and now commanded it to open fire. Within seconds the tables and furniture around it were in a broken heap and the gun itself then ceased having been hit. Both Claymore's handgun and Savannah's AK were red hot and reading empty. Sands was gone.

'Don't look back. Don't look back. Don't look back,' she screamed inside, jogging steady towards the dock. Her vision fogged with tears, she reached instinctively to wipe the glass on her wrap rounds, just like she had the time before. But this time there was no warrior tanks, no poisoned air or landbergs, no drones to freeze and save him - just someone whom she had loved left kneeling, head hanging forward, his blood mingling with the spilt coffee on the wooden floor.

This time, there had been no mistake. She had stood three metres from Faro, whom she had once already painfully lost, looked into his face - and pulled the trigger.

She reached the spot where she and Marie had joked over the *too hot to handle* routine two nights earlier, ran a thorough 360 scan, then stepped off the wall into the darkness landing on the oil stained sand three metres below. Three strides later she slipped quietly down the slope of the concrete breaker into the cool waters of the bay.

She activated the gravity dispenser, which acting as a dead weight sank her three metres, and kicked for her predetermined landmark two hundred metres along the coast. A seven minute swim as the crow flies or a fifteen minute run around the secure chemical plant which lay in the way. The beacon linked to her glasses ensured she stayed on track; the oxygenated liquid smear recently injected into her lung delivered enough air to do the job fifty times over. It had been the most expensive accessory that she had purchased, the straw which nearly broke her bank, but as water had never featured in her military record, she had gambled that they would not expect her to opt for it.

*****

Claymore had stood a full twenty minutes staring out across the bay. Tonight, for him, its dark waters played their own soft calming melody of surreal anonymity. The occasional gentle waves, lapping against the soft orange lights of the silent moored ships; sky lit patches of purple and lilacs flickering amongst his thoughts; dark red explosions of the gas giants on the other shore glowing pink in the water, reflecting as rainbows across his night lenses. 'Blew it....too many hands......'

*****

Sands slumped heavily backwards against the plain wooden door of the room she and Marie had rented, hauling the fresh humid air into her lungs, exhausted. Her head full of rapid confused thoughts, racing in time to the pumping in her chest. Faro - dead! Dead......by her hand..like her brother. Claymore's AK too close for comf.. Faro – dead. Dead..by her hand.. What is this fortune teller Jinx.. Faro – dead. *Those* panthers.. Jake.. Dead like her brother. Like her brother. Her hands slapped hard against the door as she stood straight and rested her head against it. The disc...she still had the disc.

Marie was standing in front of her, relief registered across her entire body.

'I heard the gunfire..the whole town could hear it..the lights..they didn't work. You are ok?' she added, realising her assumption as Sands appeared unhurt.

'Yes,' Sands smiled in reply. 'Fine. And the lights worked well enough. Vortex troops were there - and others.' She never mentioned Faro. 'The fortune teller was being straight. Claymore was there too - the whole god dam world was there. Oh...she lent forward pushing herself off the door.. that's not to mention a whole pride of shiny black panthers.'

'Panthers!'

'Panthers. They were with the monks.'

'Monks!'

'*They* were with this Jake..who the fortune teller, Jinx, told us was our pal..or could be if we wanted.' They both sipped their wine in silence. Marie never asked. 'I still have it. Sands finally laughed aloud. 'Bruised - but we're still in business.'

Marie opened a bottle of local wine and they drank in silence. The bottle was gone in ten minutes, then Marie brightly said 'Lets lose ourselves in the city, lets do a club. Tomorrow is another....tomorrow.'

Sands face registered that she liked that. 'Absolutely.' She took in the view over the harbour through the slit in the curtain, presenting no additional light for any Vortex surveillance drone he may have had the after sight to put in place. Sure, had she returned to a lair in the vicinity who could resist a peak in the dark - but then again, she was not only military, but Vortex trained military, and would therefore be long gone by now.

Eighteen
The brighter side of the bay

Marie was curled up asleep on top of the massive dark wooden bed. She was still fully clothed except for her colourfully striped cloth shoes, one of which lay beside her having almost made it to the floor. Her breathing had found a deep saturated rhythm, worn out by hours of dancing. Sand's mind was still too alert for sleep, still actively burning off the earlier excesses of adrenalin. It was almost dawn. She watched as the silhouette of the island rose out of the sea to reform around the Statue, which stared back at her from across the bay.

The break of morning shifted to *a bright sunlit June day eighteen years earlier*. The foreground had changed some but the picture was still pretty much the same. She must have looked tiny, standing there in the Plaza in front of the vast metal doors of the International Ferry Terminal, she thought. She smiled at the strangeness of the thought; of course she looked tiny - she was eight years old.

She had always remembered how small the boat that had brought her appeared next to the international cruise liners as it made its way back to the island. *Cruise liners*...there was a thought. Little did they know that five years on they would be stripped of their lavish furnishings and refitted to battle standard, only to get blown apart or sunk in unromantic waters. There had been a café then too, but it had been part of a church. The warden who had bought her the ice cream had seemed sad. She couldn't remember his name, but the ice cream was strawberry flavoured. She remembered wondering why he was sad, as he had told her everything was going to be just fine, that she would make many new friends at the Federal Academy and that she would get to visit her mother often.

The visiting part was true, but when she did visit it was very different. She never had to physically leave her dorm for visits, she would simply link up with her mothers recuperation realm through her newly installed Federal chip. At first she thought that this was part of some temporary grown up thing, but after a long while realised that this was the way it would always be. For many years the statue high on the hill behind the prison was what she saw when she thought of her mother. In later years her mother told her that it was this same view that had inspired her to seek religion.

Her eyes moved down from the statue to the prison itself. A monotonous brown streak with row upon row of neatly spaced small windows arranged in straight lines stretching for five hundred metres. She would have lived and played in many of those rooms, she realised, but had no way of telling which were which. Her childhood memories of Fortaleza de San Carlos de la Cabana were always good. The harsh corridors and limited space had been home to her, all she had ever known. Her mothers quarters, which the three of them had to themselves, were much bigger than most, and always full of flowers. When the flowers were out of season she and her mother would make large colourful paper ones.

Her eyes moved to the green embankment by the dock; it was worn now with practically no grass at all. She remembered it was here that she first ever saw daffodils outside of the prison. Bright yellow daffodils, much smaller than the ones she would watch happen in her mothers pots each Spring, but growing by the water in random clumps...as if by mistake.

Her mother's new home had been *Federal Time*, a by-product of Authenticia, financed and run by the Federal Government and known to inmates as Camp Holiday. True enough, prisoners from around the globe diagnosed as clinical downers were given short internments here to straighten themselves out, and many if given the choice would have opted to stay. When the war arrived the prisons were emptied, save for the lifers and repeat offenders. All physical prisons were closed and a policy of mental containment endorsed. For Sands' mother this simply meant the injection of half a million new inhabitants into her world. She had already been interned for several years starting from the date of her youngest child coming of Academy age.

There were more flowers when Sands arrived at the Academy. Those were like the ones in the prison, arranged in neat patterns, shiny and cared for. She recalled later that the registrar officer had called her kitten. She had liked that. He had smiled at her and said to his colleague 'factory kitten', and had raised his eyebrows when he added that she had been raised on death row for seven years. The other one had said that they hoped that she would be as dedicated a student as her brother, who had been there for three years. And she had - she frowned, top cadet of her year when she graduated. Got snapped up on a fast track contract by Company Vortex five minutes later.

Her mother felt close, minutes across the still water. Of course she was no longer there; now asleep motionless in a suspension tank someplace, somewhere; her mind linked directly into everything that she now was. Physically in one world, mentally cruising in another. 'Closer still,' Sands whispered, her smile broadening. The dawn light had begun to pick its way through the delicate chandelier which floated down from the high ceiling, casting soft droplets of colour against the tall plain white walls of the room, printing patterns across Marie's face and the white cotton sheets. Sands turned again, smiled back at the statue, and jacked into the maze.

The bubble Marie had created for her was still in place. With Loki as guarantor, it ensured absolute security for her stay. Her mother was reading a large and rather over embellished original volume of Don Quixote as she approached. There was a thin layer of fresh snow on her mothers sun umbrella. Her skis and others were stuck vertically in the snow beside her. The air was crisp and thin, and the late afternoon Alpine view a sharp awakening from the Cuban dawn.

Beside her mother, lounging back casually in the deck chair, drinking Chinese beer through two straws beneath cool black glades was ....Jake.

Her mother beamed radiantly when she saw her, jumping out of the chair to hug her tightly. 'Are you all right? Jake told me what happened. He said you were ok. Are you ok?'

'Never been better,' Sands replied in automatic pilot. She and Jake just stared at each other silently.

'Thank God,' intervened her mother, in overwhelmed relief, totally oblivious of everything else around her. Then she laughed and said 'Or thank Jake - he told me it all, how his monks intervened and you escaped.'

'Oh. Is that what happened?' replied Sands still staring at him.

'Well...its not exactly untrue, is it?' Jake said. 'They did save y..'

'What exactly is it that I have?' Sands cut in.

Her mother stopped talking realising that no one was listening, and turned to look at Jake in expectation of an answer to Sand's question.

After an uncomfortable pause he said 'I assumed that you knew.'

'No.' Sands said flatly.

'Well if *you* don't know - how the hell am *I* expected to?' replied Jake.

Her mother shifted her gaze back and forth between them, then burst out laughing. 'You mean that all this trouble that you have both gone to - you don't know what it is that you are fighting over!'

'We........didn't actually fight,' said Jake.

'Bullshit. What is this disc to you - and who is the fortune teller?' Sands cut in again.

'Who?' replied Jake.

'The one who calls himself Jinx.'

'I know nothing of fortune tellers. The disc is of the utmost importance to me. An obsessive itch delivered me to its doorstep. It is mine - it is my destiny.'

'Its content? asked Sands flatly again.

He hesitated then said 'I crossed a bridge of sorts, many times, it glistened silver, touched by a hand gifted with creative surreal song. On its shores brisk dancers slipped through its metal tinged shadows vanishing into foliage to dark to see. Canvas for some; was how it felt, unfinished, striking with its razor edged depth of field. Burnt at corners where history had began to fade. They moved speedily, the dancers, through sheet after sheet. Till they hit the blank page; the wall - end of the world, our world. Vortex seeks its power for himself. The dancers fear him. Should he get the disc, and not I..... *'Indulge me,'* he shall whisper, as he steals their futures.'

'And why does this itch consume....*you*?'

He smiled slowly. 'They say that dying dragons never shed light. But children scream to awake the universe of their passing. Such a scream will happen so rarely in the life time of a boy, that it may well go unnoticed, mistaken as a bad dream. Deep within the young man's developing mind however, the seed will grow and form a many forked scar. The shadow of a crack, which if remembered with renewed adult interest can become a canyon from which will spring a fall of thunder enough to wake the sleeping giants.'

'He always talks in riddles, isn't it romantic,' said Sands' mother.

'It's a load of bull..that's what it is,' Sands said still staring at Jake. 'Whoever you are - stay away from my mother. You come near her again and I will find you - and put a huge hole in your head.'

'Jake is my personal religious guru..you could say. Others would call him..the God of my choice,' Sands' mother said quietly.

'I am Jake, of The Order Of The Jake, and what you possess, and which does not belong to you as it happens, *most definitely belongs to me* - is all that is important. That - and that I *will* eventually have it.'

Sands stared back.

'No point I suppose in asking if you would care to give it over to me. Your other playmates will be less than forgiving next time. I could relieve you of that burden. I am sure that I could arrange to have whatever financial aspirations you have satisfied, given time?' asked Jake smiling coolly.

'This is not about credits. This is about Vortex *not* getting what Vortex wants. Until I know better - you and Vortex are one and the same.'

'Well - I wouldn't want to outstay my welcome,' he said as he rose to leave. 'It was an unexpected pleasure having met you today. I only came here, as your mother's comforter, to tell her that you were well. Clearly it would be wonderful if she talked some sense into you, but after my *previous introduction* to her friend Loki, I decided that pressing your mother on the matter could have undesirable consequences which out weighed the likelihood of gain.'

'Thank you for coming,' Sands' mother said as he left towards the ski lifts.' When he had gone, Sands sat and they embraced.

'Are you really all right?' her mother asked.

'Yes.. absolutely fine.'

'It sounded terrible, and I got the feeling that he spared me most of it. Is Marie all right, he never mentioned her?'

'She's fine. She wasn't there. How did he find you?'

'I don't really know. It felt as if I had found him. Accidently one day, after your last visit, and before the visit from *those* two - the fat men, Jake was giving some sales spiel about The Order Of The Jake to a friend of mine, when I got interested. He was talking about the statue above San Carlos guarding the souls of those asleep in the city below. I started to listen to him and found that I liked what he had to say. I found his mood comforting. We got talking, he's a good talker, and over a few visits we became friends. I suppose today's visit shows that we *still* are. I can't imagine that he is *behind* your problems, though he does want whatever it is that you have. When he asked me about you, it was direct. He stated quite openly and unprompted that he had sought me out to find you. He was looking for an address, and knew about Marie. I was very angry and told him that I trusted in my daughter more than I trusted in any God. I had Loki have a word - we told him not to come back.'

'Did he tell you where it took place?'

'No. Where?'

'Havana, by the docks. I can see the statue now, from where I am.'

'This problem with Vortex, can you get out of it? Do you have a plan?'

Sands looked at her mother for a long time, then slowly she said 'Chas won't be coming to see you any more. Chas is dead.'

'I know,' her mother replied quietly. 'Loki told me. He said that he was killed in a Company Vortex event. And that now he wants you.....unless you give him what he wants.'

'You knew? I couldn't find it in me to tell you.'

'Yes..I knew. And the hurt is no less today than the day they told me. But it is *you* we have to take care of now. It would seem that Vortex wants this thing you have badly. Between threats, they offered me a deal.. a pardon for that same address. I never asked him to, but I think Loki had a word with *them* also. Why did you do it? Was it because of Chas?'

'Partly, yes. There were other reasons. Chas was the final straw.'

'What other reasons?'

'LoTech....it raised too many questions, and Vortex kept pushing me, couldn't take no for an answer, too used to getting what he wants.'

'Vortex - *in person*!'

'Yes. He used Chas to get at me.'

Her mother was silent for some time then said 'Well..you have caused him to lose face. That is something, but I don't want to lose you also.'

'I have never really thought about how it would end. Only how to hurt him back - I jumped in head first.'

'Well...I lost your father all those years ago, then they put me in here without a word or reason why. Over time though, I have got to enjoy life here. Then Chas. Now you and this. Well..I guess that you have to finish what *he* started. I don't want to lose you but I trust in the knowledge that you know what you are doing.'

Sands knew that her mother was right. Vortex would never call it quits. Companies didn't do those kind of deals. They would honour most deals for credibility, but not this way round. This was betrayal; un-negotiable, unforgivable. Otherwise she would have done a pardon deal for her mother in an instant, with or without her mother's agreement.

'I'm not finished with him yet. After Chas, he knew how much I hated him yet he still entrusted me with the disc. He had me collect it from an A class Security Unit, where he left instructions stressing the absolute importance of what he was placing into my responsibility. Inviting me to cross him. To show me that in spite of everything he still owned my ass. Well now he knows different. I'm gonna make sure that whoever can hurt him the most with this, are the ones who get it.'

Marie was still asleep; the sun was well into its day. Its rays had finished playing with the chandelier and now displayed gentle red and yellow triangles as it shone through the decorative stained glass of the windows higher panes. Vortex would haunt her forever; she knew him little but well enough to know that he would never let her go. But..she still had the disc...nothing had changed. It was good to have talked with her mother. She would test this Jinx on his offer - find out what it was that everyone wanted so badly. The early morning Cuban sun was bright and cheery.

Nineteen
The hour of the Jinx

It was dusky morning when they came to him. Jinx heard both of them, long before they could see him. What remained of his darker side liked that. The feeling of power it gave to know that they were there, stumbling in the dark, through the towering hollows and debris of rusted crusted sheets of painted metal that once had cruised the cities highways radiating proud aloofness. While he sat still and silent in his nest a mere 100 metres of physical space from them, enveloped and protected by millions of years of humble solitude. They would never find him. They would stumble around forever through his multi-level hive, his domain. Until failure set in. Then he would shyly announce his presence.

He could feel them clearly now. He felt that he knew them intimately. That they belonged to him, somehow. One would smile with patience instilled by military training; the other was uncomfortable and afraid, less relaxed and reluctant to find whatever they came for. Each time he touched them it was different; the clarity of their aura was never the same, not exactly - but his own sense of guilt, like the wash in a watercolour was ever present.

It constantly slipped his thoughts towards hapless tangents: *'If teardrops had minds..... what would they think as they fell? Would they dream of being human? ......Would they dream.....or like us.....simply fall?'* Others he had met along his new travels had tried to soothe his deep pain; sympathetic souls, kind and encouraging but with empty answers.

Water trickled down cold metal walls bringing rhythm of life to the broken strength of folded pylons, transforming cracks and craters in the ancient hull into pools of intent, encouraged by the solemn shadows cast from the three hatches of light, far above. The trickle would soon become a flow and the flow a tide with its own set of rules, until the hull was full to the lower deck where small waves would leave and complete the daily ritual of high tide. This was his favourite time. It was now that he felt at his strongest. When only those of absolute conviction could hope to earn his indulgence. It was also the saddest time, for Jinx knew that again soon, he would have to leave - and another would take his place.

It was black dark. At first. In his head he heard the motors of the lead truck and the muffled tones of Norton bikes, then the unmistakeable grumble of a half-track.. no two half-tracks and ....yes more trucks. He rolled his vision to a higher perspective and flicked it far to the west, inverting the image. *There*..the grey wisps were trees behind which rolled the convoy, lights dimmed and muzzled by rough cloth casting short distorted shadows on the banks of the loch. Yes..his time with the two welcome visitors was limited - but enough.

He flicked back to the hull... yes...she was extremely attractive..in a distinctively primate way. Of no concern to him. Her friend also. She was the one who was AI literate - dangerous. Outstanding; both of them.

Sands' mind became filled with thoughts of blue planets as she sensed his presence behind her. As she started to turn towards him he stepped from shadow directly in front of her, a torch of sunlight back lighting his brown robe, fire red.

'Welcome. Most welcome,' she thought she heard him say above the quiet swish of the shifting tide. His head was hooded; his robe tied in simple fashion at the waist. He wore sandals familiar to her recent encounters. She tensed.. her chip searching for panthers in every silent shadow. Her thoughts fla....

'You have no need for concern *here*,' he interrupted. 'There is nothing to fear from me.'

She moved slowly but steadily towards him creating a diagonal path, placing more light into their conversation zone. Marie stood quite still, where she was. 'Well..you invited me..what do you want?' said Sands.

'Invited you...ha, ha...' he laughed warmly. Somewhat of an understatement wouldn't you say. Now that you *are* here - we have a little less than an hour. Then we will all have to make ourselves.. scarce again.'

'Who are you?' Marie shouted abruptly.

'Yes..of course....introductions. I am already fully acquainted with *you* - both of you. As for myself, I am known as Jinx.' He raised his hands and slowly lowered his hood.

Sands straightened on the spot, the word shot from her mouth '.....*Jake!*'

'No – Jinx,' he replied smiling in a serious manner. 'Some things of insignificant importance we still share....our love of vintage cars for example.' She felt a sudden pulse, like mechanical energy, transform her sight of the rusted shells, which, stacked high, filled the huge ship's hull around her. An instant blaze of colour, like a polished rainbow lit up the bay. The moment passed faster than it had arrived, and the steel floor, having briefly captured the reflection, was once again cold and wet. 'And our attire, of course. Jake's choice actually; but an affected choice reflecting my basic preference. Of no consequence really. Oh..and we share ...a friendship.....loyal to us both.' She turned her head to follow his stare as Huek stepped from a hollow shell; although her chip had already told her that someone was there. 'We are alone. There are no *panthers* here. They are entirely a symptom of Jake and have no place here.'

'You offered me your help?' inquired Sands.

'Yes..and whatever help I can give - you shall have.'

'I need to know what it is that I have been carrying.'

'*That* I can help with. And in doing so..' he turned to Marie... 'will answer your question, *who am I, and for that matter, who is Jake?* The answers I'm afraid are not straight forward, nor can they be best given in words alone. They, and I, beg your indulgence, and your *trust*. I hope that your presence here reflects a degree of trust?' he gestured back towards Sands.

'Coming here seemed the best remaining option open to me. Your previous *interference,* buys a great deal of curiosity - but *zero* trust. In coming here, I weighed up the risks.'

'And you will not be disappointed,' he added quickly. 'Soon - you will understand much more than you have ever dreamed of ..about everything.' He laughed gently, gesturing with his arm for them to follow him. 'You will *certainly* be much more informed than when you awoke this morning - or expected to be, when you go to sleep tonight. Please come this way', he said, neither of them having taken up the offer of his arm. 'It is my hope, that you will soon share the view that our paths are destined to the same end', he concluded, leading the way into the tangle of wrecks.

They climbed for a full twenty minutes. The route was illegible, without pattern or logic, weaving in every direction but mostly going up. They slid, crawled, jumped through the graveyard of twisted chassis and part crushed shells; some perched precariously against others jammed into spaces half their size and always going to get smaller, as the weight of new arrivals crushed them from above. Jinx moved quickly finding inaccessible footholds with practised ease.

Finally he quietly announced 'We are here.' Slipping a key from around his neck he unlocked, lifted, then slid open the heavy rear door of what once may have been an ambulance. Beyond which lay a large open room, enclosed on all six sides by solidly crushed and cubed vehicles. Those which formed the roof seemingly held only by their own mass, relying entirely on the push and be pushed principle of the Roman arch.

In the centre of the room, with no apparent clue as to how it could have got there, was a small, immaculate, highly polished gun metal coloured car. Across its black tinted windscreen ran the words *Praise the Lord.*

'Home.' Jinx exclaimed with the lightest of smiles. Acknowledging Sands' bewilderment, he gave her *the tour* from where he stood. 'This section of floor has nothing beneath it for fifty metres. Then there is water three metres deep, except for a narrow channel where it is mere centimetres. The floor beneath the water is painted black; to the eye it is all an equal three metres depth. The floor on which you stand, once served this ship as a hoist; now within this mountain of unwanted metal, it drops by retractable cables onto the channel. Privacy to think. The car belongs to Jake.'

Marie noted mentally that the room was tidy and comfortably laid out in an organised manner. The light was artificial blue tinging to green where the bulbs radii overlapped; a range of sophisticated scientific hardware stamped with Company Vortex emblems had clearly been in recent use, and covered a make shift table with legs of tightly piled thick scientific books and journals. Jinx beckoned them to sit, then with an outstretched palm asked for the disc. From behind a soft casual laugh, Sands said 'What makes you think that I would bring it here?'

'It is not in your character to do otherwise. You are...impetuous.'

She looked at him long and hard; through eyes trained and experienced in finding the slightest edge, or where none exists, being *very* sure of it. 'And if I give it to you?'

'I will return it with the same goodwill..unless *you* decide otherwise. But first - you will witness its power.. its touch.. and share its truth.'

'First..you will tell me *your* role in this. And your tie with Vortex,' she replied instantly.

'Yes.....your little escapades have rattled certain cages, sparked inquisitive minds into play. *All* of the Companies now know the nature of what it is that you have for sale. Strange that you are now alone in your ignorance, though clearly you have grasped its importance, if not the extent of it. *I* am known as the builder - *the builder of bridges.* I am still technically in the employment of Vortex, in that he continues to feed credits, increasingly large amounts of credits of late, into my accounts. Though, like you I have chosen to part company with him. I now travel my own path. In a sense I created your current dilemma, as it was I who built the bridge which you carry - and are so anxious to use as a weapon of revenge.'

'Bridge to where?'

Marie sparked to life. 'I recognise you now..you looked different.. older, you had.. hair. I saw you speak once at a conference - something abou... Breath of the Gods - you were one of the leading lights of Authenticia.'

'Yes...indeed. And now....the answers you seek.... He extended his open palm.

Sands tossed him the disc. Jinx caught it ungracefully between his arms and chest. Finally, holding it in his hand, staring down at it, his face exploded in involuntary physical release. As the moment of surprise stretched into a comfortable silence, all three laughed together. Then he quickly moved to the table, pushed aside some likely candidate hardware, and injected it into a one meter square glass water filled cube; resembling a fish tank without the fish. The cube was wired along its edges and connected to a simple terminal. Both were connected to the same socket as a blackened copper kettle. Turning to Sands he said 'All yours,' and stood gesturing her to take the seat.

'What now?' she asked.

'Now you share with me the knowledge that only I can give you...that is what you came here for.'

'Share it with you ...or with Jake? Tell me about Jake.'

'Opposite sides of the same coin. He has all of my, our.. anger, selfishness, deceit, ...ambition. We both still share a strong enthusiastically *driven* personality. *I* have always achieved whatever I have set out to achieve in life, having never once doubted myself along the way. That.. fool's arrogance I have shed onto him.

Please excuse me for referring to *us* as *I,* as in truth neither is stronger than the other; save of course for the fact that it was *I* who inherited the sense to retain control of our split existence. Other than what I have, through necessity, informed him of, he is entirely unaware of my existence, or of his past for that matter.'

'How can that be?'

'Because when we entered the flow...as you are about to.. it tore us apart. We ceased to exist as a singularity, our conscious and subconscious violently dismembered by its sheer inquisitive power..then tossed back together in a shambolic confused order, creating two very different shades of the same persona. For each, the subconscious now uniquely matches the conscious creating two very separate and very single minded people.

As with grass, which reflects green light, absorbing all other colours and converting them to life; I inherited the passive, gentler side..while Jake......well let's call him 'a man of action.' Though most would call him a totalitarian thug. Someone at best to be avoided.

Two minds..sharing the one physical body. We each have our own spells of control; our body chemistry dictates when, but not why. I have however learned to recognise the change as it is about to occur; and with each change I have approximately three days to complete my business. During Jake's waken hours I slip into the flow, which you are about to experience, where I can both watch and influence to a degree, what I see. His actions..I cannot directly influence, although I can incur dreams, visions ..hints, to progress our singular goal.'

'Which is?'

'To retrieve the disc. Jake seeks divine power. He believes it to be his right. The disc; he knows through flashes of insight relayed by me, will enable the realisation of his goal.

I have therefore been fully alert for the duration of both our existences. Jake, on the other hand ...wakes up with a giant killer headache, usually in his car, with no recollection of the last three days. Huek has helped the illusion.'

She was staring apprehensively into the glass cube, as he continued. 'I am already part of what you are about to experience. For your protection, I have now created a roomed link between the disc and your chip. To join me, activate the link then switch off your chip; when you relax your mind the roomed link will still be there. Once there, I will meet you. You have nothing to fear.'

'Nothing!'

'Yes...nothing.'

'And in the room...?'

'In the room...well.........you may share a grand vision..or you *could* enter a mind of insanity...or as those of a religious disposition claim, socialise with fragmented souls. Whatever.....I will be there to guide you through.'

Sands sat as requested and paused for several long moments, then she smiled reassuringly at Marie and did as he asked.

She felt her mind expand then rest as if floating upon the water. Then the edges grew light and began to take shape as she entered the darkest folds of a stranger's subconscious, gifting herself, she wondered, to a world of satanic mirth.

Roomed. The walls and floors shimmered in rhythm with the water; *but* they were solid. No way in - *no way out*. Panic hit her hard; harder than she could remember since a cadet. Panic raced through her thoughts... S*tupid ...Stupid.. This asshole could kill her and there wasn't a thing she could do about it. S*he slammed her mind into the wall's silver-blue flawless sheets.

'Relax..deep breaths...you have nothing to fear.. as I said.' His voice was calm and re-assuring. 'I should have warned you..the room I have created is within *my* mind - you have to travel within me; otherwise what happened to Jake and I will happen to you also. The human mind is strong, but we will be moving within its less tolerant, vulnerable zones. Relax ......place both palms on the wall facing you and you may leave at an instant's notice. Her heart was still pounding...his voice was way too loud, reverberating in her head. The

Ambassador snapped back into focus; her hands, face and hair were saturated in sweat.

'Let's just sit a while...there is time enough,' he said softly.

She let her breathing settle. 'Let's do it!' She was back in the room. The walls bronzed ...then punched themselves outside in..then disappeared; patterns in song; language that felt familiar, deep within her bones. She could sense Jinx's presence close at hand, but could not see him. She could spin and turn full circle like in space, frictionless, without warmth or cold and...could perceive infinity. It was pitch black with specs of bright light at unknown distances, too far to even speculate; or were they simply tiny? 'What are they?' she heard herself whisper.

'Yes......beautiful are they not. Like stars pencilled thinly across the heavens forever watching. Touch one.'

She chose a shining emerald child's mooned-shaped crest. As she reached out, the space contracted at a rush, till it brushed her finger tips, spinning her, pulling her gently after it. She reached again to pull it in but this time it moved away taking her with it..faster and faster.

'Stay with it. It is your guide,' she heard Jinx say.

'Your mind, temporarily displaced within the realm of my subconscious travels the threads of the Akasha.....within which lies the soul of mankind. The subconscious is the advocate for the soul.

There you travel sheltered from the others which you see and feel. You may share and learn with them, but they cannot physically touch you. You of course already have a presence here; albeit not at a conscious level. Look for yourself Sands - find who you are.'

'How?'

'Pick a star; focus slowly, you will know which one.'

She did as he suggested, and sensed one with a bashful air..seeking to remain quiet behind the light of another. She reached forward, felt it warm to her and plunged her fingers in....*She was standing at the grand entrance to the Palace of Art, Chicago, on the same spot where she had stood once before, some weeks after her Honey Wagon rebuild. She felt the same reluctance now, as she had felt then, to touch the small statue resting on a plinth immediately in front of her. For she, more than most, understood the gravity of its sentiment.*

The structure was set in blasted sand; yellows, blues, crimson coloured layers, inlaid in gleaming molten rivers of silver. A perfect replica, exact to the minutest detail, right down to the expressions in the eyes of the faces of the people stolen from a millisecond in time, frozen forever, of 500 square miles of LoTech Mars pre Event. It was in all, less than a metre in diameter. Had she viewed it through her chip's filtered magnification it would have presented a memorial, which if one took the time would take a lifetime to read. Standing over it, as she had, refusing to engage her chip, it appeared as no more than the eroded wind blasted remnants of an Earthly Doric pillar. A symbol of a civilisation at its outset. A donation from Company Detroit to the people of Lotech expressing their support, and sorrow of not having been able to lend a hand, for reasons out with their control; post Event. Standing in front of it now, without the chip, she could see its full glory - whether she wanted to or not. She knew that she was staring into the heart of her own conscience.

She felt the overwhelming scent of Faro, and of her brother. She searched for them but their aura had less spark - no longer working sentient minds; more like ideas being passed around, slowly perishing into the whispering wind.

Present also - the strong scent of Claymore. Surprisingly; why here - close to her? *Claymore*..her hunter..her enemy..yet.... something about him had always intrigued her. Hence, she had ensured that Loki provide her with a constant insight into his actions. It was to do with the way he stood alone, unaffected by the demands of others - like a sole surviving tree in a gale force wind, bending only ever so slightly to stay put. She opened her palm and thrust it in.

The cold face of the veteran soldier stared back at her; impenetrable, unpredictable. Once, a self defence mechanism - now it was engraved in the hard lines across his temple. But buried deep within, she could still detect the flicker of a struggle for inner peace; his need to accept what he had become.

This man had once been someone else entirely. Mindless war had moulded him into Vortex's right hand; but what fired her curiosity even more was his perception of *her*. He respected her - he was attracted to her. He had disliked wearing her brother to get to her; it had made him feel dirty - yet still he hunted her relentlessly. And he carried no guilt, as such, for his actions - any of them. Not even the execution of his partner Savannah.

Savannah; now *there* was an enigma. Close to Claymore, she displayed a healthy spark; she had been downloaded using the technology that Sands now experienced..she was still very much alive - *this disc had power well beyond a simple bridge.*

Glancing Savannah's aura she hit an intense wall of resentment - directed at both herself and at Claymore; the confused, overlapping sensation of a razor white double edged blade slashing through salty ocean rain, forming hot spirals in the sand laced wind, enriched by the *pleasant* smell of burnt Sri Lankan evening air.

This Claymore - soldier of mis-fortune, this warrior without humanity, had somehow captured a part of each of them, though a very different part. It was easy to see the attraction he held for one such as Savannah; but for Sands......well.. they shared a common energy.   'The irony of being hunted by one's own soul mate,' she laughed.

There was something else, close by – watching. A source that she could not reach, colder than the rest. Was Jinx holding something back from her?

It presented itself as if some forgotten or misplaced gift. It shone sharply, intensely bright yet portraying an unpolished, unfocused magnetic empathy of mystic. As if a great light burned within waiting to be released, and once released would illuminate all. Brass coloured opaque; the semblance of long buried gold. Black pearl eyes stared outward inviting those of naive brevity to stare back.

'If you focus hard enough you will be able to touch them, but do *not* cross into the light.' She felt his conviction...and his extreme sadness.....then an overwhelming wave of tortured guilt.

'Well..I wanted answers, she heard herself echo aloud. She focused hard, to the point of straining ...then the eyes began to melt before her, fading to reform as pencilled shadows of greys and black at first, then rich colours illuminating shadows of a city landscape; hollow eyes, thin lipless expressions, flat strong brows over a stern sharp ridge of a nose. The lips parted, thickening to form a smile around the infinite dark pit of a mouth...beckoning her to enter; offering the promise of unimagined revelation and wisdom, the answers to every curiosity. Her mind was being pulled towards it, intensified by her own new found curiosity urging her to cross. She could taste the magnitude of the wonder beyond, as it continued slowly to evolve, expressing itself as the changing patterns of civilisation past and future. But his warning had been clear..and there was an edge of *panic*.. of *fear* to his words.

She had relaxed her concentration, and was pulling away when an ice cold hand rested gently over the small of her back; long cold fingers stroked either side of her spine until they caressed the nape of her neck, slipping into her hair, and extended until her head rested gently in its palm. She felt her mind soften to air, and her mouth involuntarily open.
'*Now* - as you threaten to leave, they let you touch them.' This time Jinx's voice was without fear and full of reassurance.

Her mind was floating... gliding over a rolling patchwork of green fields, enclosed by regular hedgerows interrupted by thick clumps of lushly leafed trees..two winding criss cross rivers..horses running..brown pantile roofs punctuated by spires....tiny people on the streets below. It was familiar - the spires of Oxford England. Thin layers of cloud shot past..too fast..the rivers vanished and the buildings now much more tightly packed..fields again on a hill..no, a park....the Heath, Hampstead...Hampstead London. She had visited it the previous year - with Vortex.

The home of the rich, and recluse of the pseudo powerful. Only a few played any worthwhile role in Society; fewer still lived there permanently. An entire urban village of pied-a-terres frozen in time as a quaint pocket of old England.

'These were not *her* thoughts' she was certain. '*What the*.....' the roar of engines was deafening and the freezing air in the bay stung her face... the view flipped; *external perspective lo*oking back towards her..staring at an ancient B52 bomber..gigantic wingspan..blue clear sky everywhere around..the sound on mute...*back inside the bay*..the din again and..babies.....babies everywhere; two year olds, black, white, mediterranean, oriental..squirming..like maggots on a dead something - not her thoughts - definitely *someone else's thoughts*..twenty babies deep..pulling playfully at each other..the massive hold, full of them..happier than happy could be..big smiles..laughing in mute... The hatches opened; *external perspectiv*e..she was falling with them..empty skies filled with tiny Nappied cuddly lumps in freefall..dispersing fast..*projected perspective*..5000 globules of joy splatting their presence across cobbled forecourts; pulverising pretty coloured window boxes; decorating public squares and Victorian slate roofs with iridescent, barely recognisable salty buttery stains, and ruining the quiet Sunday afternoon ambience of the Hampstead Village market.

Her mind was racing - lurching to withdraw..*the scene shot rapidly backwards*..the babies were back in the air..they were falling again..ground approaching at a rapid blur..then - the padded nappy holding a particularly cute, gorgeous in red, little Caribbean gem with Icelandic eyes called Tiana, sprang a mini parachute shooting her upwards and slowing her to safety. Each and every one followed suit to land with a soft plop, still merrily gurgling, on the grass verges next to the road. Each baby had Jinx's smiling face.

'Yes - from the other side they are powerless, locked within their own realm. Ideas alone, without the means to implement them are of no consequence.'

Their touch withered slowly, receding to its host. She raised her concentration again and as a glancing blow to their passage, engaged them. In doing so, she, as Jinx had before her, beheld their ethics of indifference. A vastly superior intelligence, embodied with a single minded, cold hearted callous pursuit of power. Each pair of black polished eyes not only in ruthless competition with its own kind, but *predator* to all, beyond anything ever perceived.

'Yes.' He sensed her question.

'Those eyes....they have the eyes of......*his* eyes!'

'Yes - *the eyes of SHADOWLANDS.'* he replied as she held her breath and they poured into her - cascading vast chunks of knowledge - seeking an exchange.

'I know...*who he is*.....what they want.'

'Yes. More, I am sorry to say, than I had wanted you to see. I am most sorry indeed. And yes - what they want is *to cross*. As we have both now witnessed, our universe was born directly from the energy of another; the same energy then used, by us, to create alternative realities through the science of Authenticia; no less real to those who exist within them than our universe is to us. Shadowlands incarnates those - and watches over us through black oceans of envy.'

'You have created a bridge *to* Shadowlands.'

'*The one and only bridge*....but..ah..if only that were all,' the sadness returning to his voice.

'But I have been there already..many times, with Marie, through Loki,' she said puzzled.

'No - you have visited the fringe of both our worlds, where the energy that holds each together overlaps; a no-mans land, a limbo shaped by those of immense power in Shadowlands as a tool to make contact with those of power in ours. You and your friend are most privileged to have been allowed to venture there safely. It is time for me to tell you what it is *that I* have done.....'

As he unravelled the layers of truth for her - the *interruption* was sudden and felt very full on. A face that was much too close; head and shoulders merged in a colourless smudged blot, lips tightly drawn. Her vision shot into focus.

'Claymore - here!' In his hand he held the wires to the water tank which he had torn from the wall. Her eyes flashed in search of Marie.

Marie's jacket shrank fractionally, re-aligning itself physically to its new command; individual micro resin drops of cloth re-forming into an ankle length dull leather like coat hugging the contours of her body to exactly 9mm tolerance, seamless and flowing as if to its own personal breeze. As she lifted its hood her face fell into shadow as her presence faded, the colour of her garment now reflecting her surroundings to the exact detail. She slipped silently backwards, blending with the ragged rusty wrecks.

Sands hit recall in her chip...she *needed* to know.. how he got here..was he alone..what were her options? *There was no recall.* She remembered - she had switched it off to interface through the disc. She turned her attention back to Claymore. He was standing three metres from her - Ah Dare Ya pointing at a fixed spot in the wall of cars.

'Tell your little friend that military software is designed to overcome such gimmick antics. Tell her to re-appear and to sit in the chair...now. Otherwise... Ah Dare Ya here is liable to bring its own solution to the problem.'

Sands spoke slowly and clearly. 'Marie..do as he says.' She then realised that Marie would not have been party to the exchange. 'Marie, that is an AK100 he is holding. I just had a conversation with it, and it strongly advises that you show yourself and sit quietly in that chair. It is advice that I very much think you should take.' After a moment she said 'You are as visible to it, as it is to you.' Then turning to face Claymore with the same professional tone... 'I *saw* that you have experience in killing innocent women.'

'Innocent?' he replied with a thin smile.

'I trust that you will agree that there is no need to harm *her*. Leave her be..and we can talk.'

Claymore remained silent. Marie coughed and reappeared, seated on the chair. Sands turned to Jinx, a look of surprised betrayal in her eyes.

'I never saw him arrive.' He fired the words at her. 'I was engrossed in protecting you. I am afraid that the others are here too. I saw their approach earlier but.....'

'Others?' interrupted Claymore, slipping the still wet disc into his coat.

'It is not *I* who is..... traitor here!' frowned Jinx.

Claymore's eyes narrowed, as he instinctively flashed the mental command that relinquished Savannah's control over the gun. As he did, he felt her pulse cross his - a milli second too late for her to open fire. For three long seconds he stood absolutely still, staring at Sands and Jinx sitting none the wiser immediately in front of him, when they should have been three seconds already dead. 'I think you just got as close as you would ever want to get to being properly introduced to my partner. *Innocent* ex-partner.' He grinned openly. 'Now....what others?'

Jinx looked skywards. The roof vanished; a large section above them was no more than a hologram displayed across what now appeared true as rather old, but clearly functional, multi dimensional cinema plates, which had probably once entertained thousands in the last of the big screen days pre Authenticia. The actual roof of the building was another ten metres upwards enclosed by stepped walls of metal and crumbling salt decayed ladders.

'Normally I have it portray clear blue skies,' announced Jinx. Then with a genuine hint of sadness he said. 'I am sorry to have deceived you, but I share Sands' just cause to deliver her part of her bargain. *There need be no further conflict,* he said, looking up at the thirty or so Company Detroit and Company Senate troops, weapons poised threateningly into the enclosed space. 'You would have zero chance of success.' He spoke the words firmly at Claymore, looking for some sign of assurance. 'Had it not been for the treachery of your partner they could not have followed you to find us - you would have succeeded. Time to let it go.' Turning to Sands, Jinx said 'The lady here was reluctant to re-market the goods until she could be aware as to their nature. *Now* that she is.....I suspect the disc is *back* on the market.' He smiled at Sands placing his open hand towards Claymore requesting the disc.

Claymore's eyes had locked onto hers. His face was impassive, but registered there in the hard lines, was the shadow of a hint. Sands read the slight movement; his gesture towards the heavy mechanism for the lift cage; heard the distinct click of Ah Dare Ya switching to blaster mode; caught the marginal change in light coloration as his Perspex inner lids slipped protectively over his eyes. '*Know your enemy.*' She remembered Loki's words. '*This one's trait was unpredictability...his position was lost yet he was about to change that - if not, he'd kill as many as he could trying.*'

She also caught the glint of his localised hand blaster as he began to squeeze the disc....grinning at the nearest Senate officer on the stairs. 'Wait! Let this go. She spoke crisply without trace of alarm but a level urgency to her voice. I *now* know what it is....I have seen *you* through its eyes..I *know* who you are....*why* you are....*who* you once were. Trust me.....if you too, knew what it is that you are about to destroy - you would willingly die to protect it! If only to re-find what you instinctively once believed in ..what you lost so long ago.'

The tone more than the words, startled him. *Interesting. Unexpected. But,* not *that interesting,* he thought. She believed in them, but whatever mark she was aiming at - she had missed. He had decided to call it.

The disc began to bend in his hand as he squeezed. *It was history ..and so was every* fuck *who had a problem with that.* The officer on the stairs stomach exploded as his AK re-introduced itself...and Jinx threw up. The lead Detroit officer's scream of 'HOLD YOUR FIRE!!' echoed throughout the hull. 'What you are holding is *priceless* to Company Detroit. Destroy it and you are dead. If not now..later - *wherever you go!* I have this instant been ordered to advise you of this. Destroy the disc and your life is forfeit...even Vortex will not be able to secure it. The *contract has been set* - as from this point it is irreversible. We ask only for the chance to negotiate.'

'Priceless. Such an old fashioned term,' Claymore said mockingly, the disc at breaking point in his hand.

'*Do not damage it.*' The voice ripped across his mind with the impact of a high speed locomotive, causing him to physically sway on his feet. It was the voice of Vortex. It addressed Claymore alone, and for the first time - it has an almost manic edge to it.

In the silence that followed the reverb, the room seemed to stand still. When Vortex spoke again it was in his usual cold calm tone. 'As always.. your life is yours to take or leave. Should the twisted logic that drives you, dictate the former....your *mission* demands that you relinquish the disc now... *or* are such assured of your position that you will emerge victorious with *it* unscathed. For what its worth, he continued in a sardonic tone, given my thorough knowledge of military exchanges throughout the entire course of history...and given a *quick* assessment of your current position..I would seriously recommend *surrender.*'

Reading Claymore's hesitation, Vortex said, should you choose to comply, I will ensure that your..*our*..X partner .. gets *hers* in the most painfully unpleasant way imaginable.

As for your part...and as for the part of our victorious marine Sands...you both excelled and delivered your end as expected'.

The implication hit him like a bucket of frozen water. *'Delivered as expected?* You said that you wanted the God-damn disc...regardless of the cost ..or the final body count. Your words.'

'I lied. My prerogative. I pay the bills.'

'Well..as your still paying this one..*what* exactly do you suggest that I do now. Given, as you put it..my current position.'

'Not my problem. I wasn't the one stupid enough to get stuck in a hole hanging 100 metres in the air with thirty AK's pointing at my head. Nor stupid enough..given that I was in such a hole..to cut one of their *buddies* in half.' After the pause, he said with a more sober tone   'They will still cut a deal...straight trade...your life for the disk...*undamaged*. Get it confirmed by the Company heads..get *their* word on it..and put it out wide band. That'll firmly put personal threat back in the box. You'll walk.'

'And the marine. What was her part?'

'Oh ...I lied about that too. Not to her of course. *I set her up*. Set her up *to win*. Everybody played their part. You got as far as you were meant to, as would be expected from my top man; the twins were there to make it ...interesting. Hardly your fault that you were betrayed by your once upon a time and somewhat bitter partner. In that cause Savannah also performed exactly as predicted. True to herself as always - some things never change, even when you're dead.'

'Why her. Why that particular marine?' his tone was more than just curious.

'Ah - we are *still* fighting that old battle are we - I gave you credit for having moved on. The problem with the human race...is that even when it bothers to make the effort at all, it always ends up searching for its humanity in the garbage. You and I get along so well.. Claymore...because neither of us play to the rules.'

'Why her!'

Why her - because she is one of the best. I needed someone that would drive through everything that was thrown at them, through all the shit and come out strong at the end. She was perfect - as could be for this particular job. Fresh from regeneration....owed the Company a great deal..but was showing fractures, stress from LoTech. The strength was already there - I gave it purpose.'

Vortex read Claymore's silence as a question. 'I ..... made myself *known* to her, which she rejected of course. What followed she took as my reaction to her rejection. The death of her brother was the trigger; her re-acquaintance with Faro the fuel to keep her going. She had to hate me completely. In entrusting her with the disc and emphasising its importance - I gave her direction. Her resolve had to be absolutely authentic, above finite scrutiny, unquestionably believable not just to others - but to her. The Companies would buy into it *because* of her conviction.

The upper walls to the room were rigid still, frozen as if immune to time; mouths were zipped, chip links flashing fast furious commands; bodies melted into the contours of the scenery, finger triggers slipping back and forth across their destiny. Veterans slowly inhaling the cold damp silence, seeking the practised rhythm that gave them marine speak. But here today they knew - everyone knew that a tenth of a nano second was all that it would take - to decide this. They knew he was exceptional..the closest it actually got to a Vortex samurai. If they excelled..were very very sharp..they could take him with them..if they were laser edged qicksilver and....unbelievably lucky they might even walk away. Unlikely.

'Your life is of no significance to us' shouted the Senate officer crisp and loud over anything else which could possibly have got in the way. The tension in the room tightened several notches; almost too taught to stand the strain.

'Release the package and you may leave freely,' he said in a lower flatter tone. He too was no stranger to five second to live scenarios. Senate too, knew the value of what had been put up to lose.

Their eyes bit into each others stare. Claymore loosened his grip. Lightly he twirled the disc through his fingers, then re-gripped it firmly, slowly increasing the pressure to the point where it threatened to explode.

'Or destroy it...and they will have to jet wash what remains of you..... off the walls' said a junior officer.

Claymore's stare remained fixed on the senior officer who had first spoken. The words had washed over his head. His thoughts...he heard his mind laugh at itself .. *'another day another dollar.....'* well... it didn't quite embrace the true depth of the moment..but it had more than a lick of truth. 'I have your word?' he said flatly without emotion. The Senate officer nodded.

'And the word of ..the *Company?*'

'My word reflects my orders.'

Claymore moved his eyes to the Senior Detroit officer. He too nodded in return.

Claymore slipped AH Dare Ya back beneath his calf length lilac coat, and loosened his grip on the disc. He held his arm partly outstretched, his hand open, the disc resting placidly on his palm. The junior officer stepped carefully down from his position, each step taken with one hundred percent focus and application to his task. Six feet from him - Claymore tossed the disc. It spun in relentless slow motion diagonally across his path, until the officer snatched it from the air.

'The lady wins the day.' Claymore said aloud.

Twenty
Sleeping Trolls

Two full hours had passed. The disc had spun in slow motion spitting fragments of crystal threads clinging like life to silver water droplets as the Senate officer, face impassive, snatched it from its arc. Claymore had walked, just as Vortex said he would. For the first time since entering the ship he had noticed his breath freeze as it hit the cold air, emphasising the vastness of the shelled hull, as if to remind him of his solitude. Once more he withdrew into his place of sanctuary, his inner fortress where the ricocheted voices couldn't touch him, where guilt or self doubt could not exist.

Now ..120 long minutes later, alone in some anonymous sleazy hotel bar, rolling his tongue across the empty tooth cavity where the Senate soldier had driven his AK butt, the taste of his old and faithful pal J.D stinging his mouth, the face at the bottom of the glass, his face, staring back at him - he was thinking familiar circles. The war.... the Claymore that had once enjoyed the privilege of pride.. had died in the war. The man that had survived had buried the remnants of the other so deeply that he could never truly rule again. The past few weeks had seemed like a lifetime; flashes of torment periodically testing his resolve to stay out of what was not his concern, to earn his pay and leave it at that, to accept it for what it was - just more of the same, routine search and destroy.

So... he thought...three weeks ago he had sat in a cheap bar in a bad neighbourhood wondering whether or not he should complete the cycle, or rip the door from the steel cage just to see what happened next. If he had......he laughed, nothing would have been different. She was set up to win. Had he pulled the plug, Vortex would have had to bring him in on the game early, if only to make sure that Savannah was in the right place at the right time to do *her* bit. Or Vortex would have simply let it be; she would eventually make the sale in her own time. It just wouldn't have looked so good, that was all.

Sav, treacherous to the last...he resisted the urge to laugh into her link. She had gone real quiet since the Detroit officer had announced that the Company bosses were prepared to trade with him. As that meant that Claymore got to live longer in return for the disc, she was no longer in the loop. Her deal with Senate for a cloned upload could never be honoured unless Claymore either gave her up or was dead. He smiled as more pieces fell together; he had never bothered to speculate why Vortex had gone to the bother of financing her download or why initiate and fund, as a one off up front payment, her cloning process in a private clinic out with his control. On passing he had probably presumed that Vortex and Savannah had some earlier contract, given that she had never been military and had always insisted on up front freelance deals. Well.... now he knew why *he* had been carrying her around for the past two months.   The irony was that *she* hadn't known that he had shot her intentionally. When he had asked her why she had betrayed him, she had flatly replied 'I got sick of the deal..got offered a better one.' Since then he had not heard a peep from her.

So - where was *he* now? Oh yeah; sitting in a sleazy bar, the bottle rapidly going down. 'Sands' he toasted her. He imagined her sitting opposite him 'Something I can do for you?' she asks. 'Just keep breathing,' he says.

The bottle was half gone. Tomorrow........was tomorrow, he thought - then a voice split his mood like forked lightening across a pitch black sky.

'*Twilight. Sleeping trolls...... never!*' If felt like his retina itself had flashed. 'Lay down your glass, I bring you cleansing for your soul. I can retain the pain that gives you substance, but kill its poisoned fruit. A sane mind can be a most unpleasant state - for those with honesty in their souls.'

'Jinx.' Claymore said aloud. 'What do you want now? It's over.'

'Do you think that your lady Sands would like what lives behind your eyes?'

'*My* lady Sands.' He laughed aloud banging the glass heavily on the table. 'Hardly.'

'No, I suppose that you are right. I had thought that I detected.. a kindling.. a kind of spark. A mutual understanding..respect even. Anyway - it matters not. Now that *she is as good as dead!*'

'What are you talking about. They got what they came for. She'll get her price.'

'Vortex has ordered her killed. As Vortex does.'

'Relax. He also got what he wanted. When she gets over it, he'll probably take her out of service and put her into contract; I'll have to compete with her for work.' He laughed.

'He has ordered her killed,' Jinx repeated slowly, pronouncing each word individually. 'At this moment in time she is sitting in an 12 x 12 on her way to Cathedral Town. She's cuffed to the dashboard - and the Sumo is driving.'

'So what are you telling me for!' Claymore snarled, re filling his glass, then catching the stares of surrounding drinkers, straightened in a manner that turned all heads instantly away.

'I wondered exactly what you were going to do about it?' Then Jinx was gone.

There was a long silence.   'Wait!' Claymore said aloud - but only he remained. His thoughts fell into focus, Vortex had referred to her as class..that her actions were commendable. Had said she... Claymore frowned placing the glass slowly down. 'Son of...' He knew it was true. The strange bond that he and Vortex had always shared was forged from a mutual respect for unpredictability.....a code of no rules.

'Where..would he take her?' he asked himself aloud, then dismissed the thought - but it wouldn't go away.

'Want to know *why*?' Jinx snapped back into his head.

'No. I already know why.'

'Do you! Do you know why he picked *her*? I mean, from the thousands upon thousands that he could have picked - why *her*?'

'He already told me why.'

'Yes - because she was the best no doubt. I am aware that you know about her brother; how and why he arranged that particular unpleasantness.'

'Hey - this is nothing to do with me - and what the fuck has it got to do with you!'

'Yes...of course you are right...but .....let me tell you about Vortex and I..... *We*..go *way* back. Longer even than you and he. My forte was Synology..my talent took me to the cutting edge of the science. I *was* the cutting edge. My hypothesis directed me to explore the inner depths of the subconscious mind, intent on proving that intuition, when isolated from rational thought, could inject *the* truly human experience into the baseline blueprint realism of what was later to be developed as Authenticia.

All good innocent stuff. My main source of funding, and as time passed, my only benefactor was none other than a very elusive Mr Vortex. For five years the cheques kept coming - although we never once met. And with them came encouragement..and of more interest to me at the time... pointers, inputs into my work, flashes of genius which always seemed to notch the project onto the right track.

Then suddenly out of the blue - I cracked it. I was on the front of every magazine worth being on the front of, and a lot of others. I had successfully devised a process which enabled the downloading of fragmented elements of the subconscious mind in a form that earned Authenticia the slogan *realer than real*. The patent belonged to Vortex; a slight oversight on my part as a result of boyish enthusiasm. That in itself was not so much a problem as the cheques grew considerably in size and - the project grew with equal proportions. My benefactor of course became very very rich.

It was suggested that research along a new tangent may bear even greater fruits of discovery, and unlimited funds promised to sweeten the enticement, as if that were necessary. The route to further enlightenment, for the benefit of humanity, lay in the much deeper probing of the layers to the subconscious. The new project was to download, in entirety, the subconscious and conscious mind in a state which would provide a complete replica of the original. Example - Savannah. Yes - Vortex used my disc on her. She is very much more than just a construct. *She* is the *real* thing.

In my quest to create what she now is, I probed very deep indeed; deep into the dark emptiness of enigma cells for which a purpose has always intrigued and eluded science. It was there that I hit upon it. Vortex had been quiet for some while, as if time, like funds, were of no consequence to him. A patient man indeed. Then suddenly his interest erupted. I had *found* what he was silently seeking all along - threads encompassing raw mental energy, the D.N.A. equivalent of the life force of the universe. Its existence has been revered and chronicled in many languages with many different names: the Akasha, Feng Shui, Lay Lines, Dragon Paths; its signature had been there since the beginning of history, long before that; eluded to in early Cultures, ancient Chinese text, Ching and the book of changes..... encrypted in numerical chemistry.

Having found it, stumbled upon it - the blind scientific genius led by the anonymous all providing entity, what more could one do - other than explore it of course. I rode the Akasha. I saw reckoning that no man should ever know. Bore witness to events... Well....within it I, my subconscious link, found the source of Vortex's troubled toil - *SHADOWLANDS*. I had created a direct link to the universe of Shadowlands, discovered the path of shared energy from their universe to ours. He renamed me ..*the builder of bridges*. In truth, I had found the bridge that Vortex had led me to, and that he had known was there all along.'

'So what,' Claymore interrupted unimpressed.

'Yes ..I know that he already told you that it is a bridge into Shadowlands...but I am afraid that it proved to be much much more - it was not the bridge *into* Shadowlands that was of interest to him - but the bridge *from* Shadowlands. You see...Vortex the man, never existed. Vortex is an Artificial Intelligence.'

Claymore put down his glass and laughed aloud. 'Heard it all now,' he grinned displaying the red hole where his tooth had been.

'Over a long period he had used his superior intellect, working from the other side, to slowly accrue considerable wealth, then economic and political influence. Men such as you and I provided the human face to what was later to become known as Company Vortex.'

'I've met him. He's flesh and blood. Just like you and me. Well like me at least - whatever the fuck you are.'

'Yes he is..in part. The other part..trust me ..is A.I.'

There was a short still silence.

Many before me, tried to find a door to other dimensions; in search of divine enlightenment; or to be the one to prove thousands of years of religion a blasphemous lie. To announce to the obedient world shackled by self forged irons, that it was all a sad mistake. For me..it was simply greed, greed in my relentless search for knowledge. Yes.... *I provided him with the flesh which allows him to walk in our world.*

The choice was made from a lengthy study of many. The man whose life he replaced was of poor health, close to death, but with a sound and under used brain capacity capable of housing the large degree of intellect transfer which was required. Merely a host of course, enabling Vortex first hand access to our world while retaining a parallel, albeit significantly reduced capacity, existence in Shadowlands.

He stalks our world through black pearl eyes, which, as he once remarked *see only reflections in the smiling eyes of fools.* Myself, I now know to be the greatest fool of them all.'

'That's all very interesting but all being said...I think that you are still confusing me with someone *who gives a shit.*'

'Try this. It was their war - not ours! They started it. They started the war.' Jinx said. Ten seconds later, 'Not comfortable with that?' Jinx continued. Claymore's eyeballs had frozen mid thought. 'Oh - don't be thinking them callous or anything - it wasn't as if they planned it, Jinx said - it was more of an overspill. That part - the intent, was an after thought of sorts. Truth is ..their universe derived directly from ours; all the energy that we threw, throw into it, its very blueprint for existence, its grass routes - is the stuff of corporate law, multi national economics, political deceit, national and international stock market games of excess, fast track ideas to strip the world of its natural resources, and, military blueprints for potential Armageddon ...more ways to fuck the world than the Kama Sutra - and not a whisper of humanity present in any of it. Not really surprising that our *cousins* from the country turned out to be a pack of megalomania dickheads now is it.'

'Why?'

'Why! Why not! Nothing to lose - everything to gain - no *conscience* to bother them.' They shared a long empty moment, then Jinx sighed. 'They were already at war. Shadowlands was - is, perpetual war. Their reality *feeds* from ours, every scrap of energy that we release into their universe is fiercely fought over and hungrily devoured. Surges of energy from sudden shifts in government policy or stock market exchanges can start empires or rock the foundations of long established powers in Shadowlands overnight. Their society is Feudal, and its warlords hold extreme but fragile positions. A war - that is a war between ourselves, country against country as throughout history, but with weapons of today would, even if it only scarred us, destroy them. A *controlled* war however - a war between ourselves; a war manipulated by them, a war which would change direction at the tug of a string, which changed fronts at a moments notice without clear cause, which interchanged allies and enemies to an unfathomable logic, which replayed the greatest military follies of history at crucial stages - a war which perpetuated itself till there was nothing left to fight over, was a war that only they could win.

Jimmu the first Emperor of Japan envisaged that the Japanese islands would one day rule the world. He named them Yamato. Company Yamato's pretence outrage over the Tokyo Hollow was the trigger. As the politics and religions of the world tore themselves apart the opportunities for power that emerged were snatched and re-shaped; new Companies appeared on cue. The world fell into confused alliances, and each alliance attached itself to a cause - a Company. Before long, today's contenders had pushed to the front; Senate, Detroit...and of course the most powerful of all - Company Vortex.

The national powers that once held our world in check, now hell bent on destructive retribution - *WHY* did no one stop to question how these new competing forces, these Companies that directed the wholesale *open book for morons* destruction of the planet, could sit *physically unscathed* in Cathedral Town within miles of each other!

Cathedral Town; originally the enforced symbol of Federal morality, was grasped as the *zone of truce* between the warring AI's. It became their platform to the stars.. our stars.

Yes Vortex is an artificial intelligence who walks and breathes as we do...and yes he and others like him purposely started the war, the war which destroyed everything that you once were; and yes he violated the life of your..the lady Sands to a degree worthy of PhD study. Why - to engage the final act to his plan. To defeat *all* of the others in one final and conclusive strike.

Until now - *he* alone had the power to sustain a physical presence here, in our universe, as a result of which he now indirectly controls some seventy per cent of the world's economy. While he built his strength here, the wars continued in Shadowlands. There, he successfully held his lines neither gaining nor losing advantage. This he has achieved through alliance with another of his kind - *Loki* - who I believe you may have had the pleasure of meeting.

The other A.I.'s now desperately seek a way through. Were Vortex to gain complete control here, he would have monopoly of the energy which sustains them - and hold a guillotine over the nature of their existence.

Now - thanks to me, Sands.. and you, they have the means to join him here. And so they shall. They will cross the bridge as he did. However, once here they will find that they cannot easily return; that the disc that he has fought so hard to prevent them acquiring is in fact the means to their entrapment. They will also immediately find that Vortex has laid plans to hold his lines here, while he himself returns, as did Genghis Khan in the battle of The Indus, attacking their weakened leaderless flanks. By destroying them there, he will eradicate their existence here. Only Vortex will remain.'

Tackle, the hotel's mangy mongrel who slept under Claymore's table, stood, stretched and left without a sound.

'So glum. Have I instilled silence on you ..Claymore. Never mind, it's not as if we have become an endangered species - just an enslaved one. I sold my humanity..just as you lost yours. We are both empty vessels,' Jinx said with bitter resolve. 'Our humanity is found within our own subconscious, it has always been there - even you once shared in it Claymore, before you shut the door.

Can we even pretend to envisage how electric Vortex must have felt to exist here..or grasp the sheer power required to maintain a physical presence on both sides of the wall. Asexual dreams that could now sense pleasure and pain; and laugh as the impotent challenges of his fellow AIs trickled through their fickle finger grasp of a reality until now only imagined. And yet, with all that - to feel so terribly vulnerable. Well.....it is not he who is vulnerable now.

She is at the outskirts of Cathedral Town; Southeast. I can see the skyline through her eyes. She.....feels distracted. She is a quarter mile from the interchange perimeter. I can help you little more. Her transport is stationary by the park of St Lucia. North South junction.'

Twenty one
Stray light

*T*wenty years earlier.......

The door is open. A pencil of stray light; his manufactured invitation. He gestures for it to approach him, but it remains fixed, for it is not of his world. He moves towards it. He walks as if on water. He hesitates, then enters into the light. He had expected a bridge; there is none. He is already on the other side. Behind him is a pencil of stray light.

The human is alive; though the mind ...is dead. Death has existed for .005 seconds.

He *wakes: breathing, liquid visions of lace and fragile things; a table, laid for food. The human's dead eyes, his eyes now, re-focus on the grey gull in a seascape on the wall. He hears a voice say   '..ciudades is such a wonderful word for cities.' She has long straight black hair; she calls him Frank.*

Frys and mayonnaise, lots of 'em, with one of Greedy Sue's giant porker's stuck plum in the middle like a space rocket; was his all time favourite. She just didn't understand it. It was right there in front of him when he awoke, but he just stared...just sat there and stared at it without moving a muscle. Not even that ol' tell tale narrowing of his eyes, which had always meant he was about to smile. Was like she had said to that Federal Officer later, when they came digging up the place, 'wasn't like he didn't suddenly like it after fifteen years; more like he didn't even know what it was. Only seemed to be interested in his feet. Took all of thirty minutes to walk from the dining room to the porch.' Then she heard the engine start. That was the last she ever saw of him. 'Least he couldn't blame her cooking' she had laughed, as he never stopped to eat it.

He walks barefoot into the yard. The dog, his dog, backs off growling then stands watching him from a safe distance. He rolls his hands over slowly as if testing the rain. He takes shallow slow breaths fascinated by the air entering into him.

The officer had asked her if he had said anything. 'God darn,' she replied, that was the barmiest thing of all. Just as he reached the truck he turned, stared at the dog and said *'I am Vortex.'*

'Was the first God darn words he had ever spoke other than *mutt* to that animal.'

*****

A red tailed blue finch, sat on the bonnet chirping noisily at her. Sands smiled at it, admiring its graceful striking colours, and its free spirit cheeky attitude. It hopped from one spot to another then back to the same spot over and over again. Roland would have liked this one to visit his garden she thought absently, in contrast to the fourteen tonne open topped matt caramel triple layered armour on which it danced. Twelve one metre wide wheels; four even rows of three, rising and falling like well oiled synchronised pistons. The smoothest ride she had ever had - for a jeep. She ran her finger across the brand name engraved into the dash - *Little Ms Bossy Boots*. The Sumo next to her stretched across two bucket seats. That must be uncomfortable of sorts she thought. He didn't seemed bothered.

Her burnt-yellow cropped hair shone gold, like the sun striking freedom through monsoon rain. Her face, silhouetted against the approaching city skyline, was set calm and assured. Deep down, she had known since the beginning that it had somehow to end like this. Somewhere quiet; amongst strangers, she just hadn't expected it to be so soon.

As the final act fell into place around her, she smiled absently - Marie was safe; and experience told her that Senate and Detroit would honour their original bargain - her mother would soon taste freedom again. Sands had won. And some, she thought. She had set out to hurt him, to damage him as much as circumstance allowed. Now, thanks to Jinx - she would destroy him.

The stranger stared at her through eyes of smug glee. He too had won, got his prize, rewarded for a job well done - completed by himself. He, not Claymore had been given final responsibility to end it. So what was she lookin' so fuck'n' smug about? he thought. She wouldn't be lookin' so smug soon enough. He'd *have* some fun with this one. 'You're mine!' he jested, tested, molested. The words were silent to her, her mind elsewhere, although she saw his lips move under the purr of the jeep.

Destroy him! The words echoed through her mind. She now knew *what* he was. *Who* he was. Now it all fell into place. Her mother; the strange silent moments over the years any time that Company Vortex was mentioned in the same conversation as her father. She now recognised the same silence just about every time Vortex's name came up. Her mother had always known and had protected her from it.

Jinx had said ARTIFICIAL INTELLIGENCE - the inquisitive minds of Shadowlands had flooded her with the rest. He had chosen her - not because *she was the best,* he had chosen her because *he walked in the flesh of her father*. What better candidate to seek his downfall than his own flesh and blood.   Vortex had set her up even before she had met him. And Marie - unknown to them, their friendship had been *arranged*; introductions through Loki when Sands was in regeneration. Marie had been tested for her role; she recalled Marie tell her of Johnstone. Then there was her brother, then Faro.

Jinx had played his part early. Her father's death was imminent, having suffered from an incurable illness for some time. Jinx had enabled the link through her father's chip waiting and ready in place - Vortex crossed the bridge at the instant of death.

Vortex had her mother imprisoned to shut her up. She had said nothing for the sake of her daughter, and later kept it from her to protect her. The irony now was that in order to destroy him, all Sands had to do was convince the other A.I.s of what they already knew, that her hatred of him was complete. Her mood was not of surrender, as it must have looked to the Sumo, but one of passive victory.

When Vortex had played his final lethal card, and the Sumo's gun tickled the back of her neck, she had accepted it without regret. It made sense for Vortex to finish it with a clean sheet; and if it made sense to him it would also make sense to the other AI's - Jinx's plan would be complete.

With her agreement, it had taken Jinx all of fourteen seconds to alter the disc; to initiate and complete his and her role in his plan. For Vortex everything would come together as intended, except for one small detail. Vortex having trapped the A.I.s here, and having temporarily discarded his flesh to return, outflank and destroy them in one decisive strike in Shadowlands, would find the illuminated path for his return here, in darkness, trapping *him* in Shadowlands.

With the main Companies erased by Vortex, the intricately woven net of Company power would crash. Who knows - Nations having learned from mistakes of the past may reform, regroup and a Federal force once again emerge. Jinx - for his sins, would, through his access to the paths that shaped our universe, make sure that no one else made the same mistake again - *there would be no more builders of bridges.* Jinx saw her role as over; but she knew otherwise - and had no regrets.

*****

The Sumo patted the silver case resting on the seat beside him. 'You should be feel'n' lucky ..lady.. ...heard the last woman who crossed Vortex.. got used as paint gluten for the bow of his personal battleship.' He turned towards her, slotting another packet of buffalo gum into his mouth. 'Least for you - it'll be quick.' He tried to eyeball her but she didn't appear to be listening. 'It's only a mini...ha..ha..will only take out a third of the city - but then what's that to you..eh! Ha..ha. When the boss wants things done proper......' he left it unfinished. *'I'm* gonna set it in a couple of blocks........then you and I are gonna' have some fun ..for a while. Then.. I leave you here.'

'It's already set.'

'What?'

'I am Company linked. Your boss.. set it fifteen minutes ago,' she said flatly.

'What.......that's not possible!'

'You have eight minutes.'

He stared at her, his mouth stopped chewing, then at the case. Grabbing it he yelled.... 'How do I ..*turn it off!*'

She was silent. He was shaking it, turning its frictionless reflectionless sides round and round, his huge fingers searching for some kind of catch or seem in its flawless fabric. '*How does it turn off?*'

'Can't be done.'

He grinned inanely; his stretched open oval mouth appearing like a tiny cartoon tear in his massive bloated reddened face, his eyes having almost disappeared. 'I'll smash it...' he screeched, turning its slippery surface over and over....

'Can't be done.'

He grasped it by both hands, jammed it firmly between his stubby arms and lifting it above his head drove it hard into the metal bars protecting the dash. It bounced off, recoiled and slipped from his grasp. He lifted it high again ..force enough to split....

'Impenetrable. Even an AK point blank won't open it. *That's its job.* That's what *it* does.'

He looked like he was about to asphyxiate on the spot. 'No!! Well..what about a..a.....*fuck'n" one of those fuck'n"......*' holding a fragmentation grenade in his fist....punching the case full on, his hand sticky from the blood from split knuckles.

'Suit yourself. The case splits - it detonates.'

'I'll out drive it,' he screamed manically, and tossed it onto the road. Switching the controls to manual he slammed his foot hard on the accelerator. The jeep veered in short zig zags reacting to the burst of speed and his sudden grasp of the wheel. One full minute later it slid to an angled halt on its own accord, wheels locked.

'Guess this is the place,' she remarked.

They were stationary outside the historic gateway to the city, the skyline of Cathedral Town towering over them, the tops of immediate buildings too high to see unless they chose to lay on their backs. Behind them the city stopped and what once had been the city park began.

He was pounding on the caged dash with his fist, staring through the rear mirror as if he could still see the case. '*He* said, the boss said....if you want to know..?' He stopped pounding, more for breath than anything, and rasped maliciously. 'You wanted a Hollow.....*you got a Hollow!*'

'Guess we both got what we wanted.' She smiled the smile that had belonged to Faro - and felt good. The jeep's engine was as dead as the case was triggered. 'You've got five minutes fat man.. walking. Everything Vortex owns..is *owned* by Vortex..including the mind of this jeep. Guess you just weren't as important as you thought.'

*****

His neck muscles bunched as wordless rhythm pounded through his head. His eyes narrowed to mere slits, focusing hard into each turn in the road, his mind engaged entirely to the task of driving at crazed speed overland towards Cathedral Town. Vortex had denied him the support he had called up, intercepting the pilot as he ran to the launch pad. The exchange between Vortex and Claymore which had followed had been brief......

'You didn't have to kill her!' Claymore had said recognising the clarity of Vortex's command signal as the line opened.

'All good things come to a sticky end.'

'She didn't have to die.'

'Etc, etc, etc..' he had whispered in reply. 'Of course she did.'

'You could have used it - *at least* had her downloaded ...cloned.'

'For you?'

'For her!' No reply. 'I'll find her!'

'You were already too late before you started. Let me know when you get over it.' The line shut.

He fired three shots from Ah Dare Ya into the windscreen and let out an abyss parched yell of pained frustration aimed at nowhere. Cathedral Town inched taller in the much much to distant foreground.......

*****

She sat and watched him. She still wore part of the cage attached to the steel cuff, which had disintegrated as he emptied the remaining rounds of her AK into the dash. She drank fresh water from the well, pulled up from the water table by *The Peoples Pump*; a hundred year old bruised brass hand pump attached to an unseen electromagnetic motor.

She sat with her back resting heavily against it, her free hand trailing in the cool fountain pool. Her mind was empty of thought. It was over. Nothing could change it. It had been good ..and bad. It could have been better. Now it was over. She smiled again. She had achieved much much more than she could ever have dreamed for.

He was breathing faster, and was saturated with sweat. She could see his irritation as the smouldering flecks drifting softly forced his body to move in small involuntarily spasms. The coloured walls encircling them had shifted from bright orange to a deep orchard red, the air become delicately thin, and a wispy light ceiling obscured the sun.

He was eating blue cheese from a large expensive looking wooden crate. His fingers and mouth were covered in it, and he was mumbling as he ate. Beside him, burst open was a case of red wine; French. The bottles lying randomly amongst the straw packaging. Seven of the bottles, so far, were empty. He caught her eye.. then shouted 'Join me!' tossing one of them in front of her feet. But her eyes were glass. After a while he sneered loudly 'Well fuck you too.'

The walls had turned intense crimson with slate smears. The tower blocks five minutes walk had disappeared. Droplets of air now burnt her mouth but she was too tired to notice. He had stopped breathing, his mouth still open, still full of cheese. She felt the furnace on her back.

Twenty two
The roving blade

Two months later......

The evening was rich with the heavy scent of burnt Indian sunset that Claymore knew she loved – 'cept she couldn't taste it. The water frothed and rolled in long white lines, cool beneath her bare feet – 'cept she couldn't feel it. Blue steel slashed and twisted, shooting through the current beneath the waves – 'cept it was Roland the Trout, not Savannah, who was the roving blade.

The Lord of the Lake was now Master of the Great Ocean. Roland the Trout was both liberated and for the first time in his life - elated almost to the point of excitement.

He was still very much the youth though sixty years the veteran, and his long practised skills would now be tested to the limit. He would never be caught. Roland, his master and long term friend, had lived up to expectations and had him upgraded to counter any surprises that the deep may throw at him. He was for example now fully conversant with the habits, eating, and mating patterns of one hundred percent of all known salt water fish; he wouldn't, for example be taken in by the *"oh what's that light over there"* tactics of a hungry electric eel, nor would he end up tangled and snared by the dredging pursuits of Japanese prawn hunters. His life would be long, endless in fact, and free, with an entire globe to explore. Roland had also taken the time and expense to deal with the salt issue; his casing had been customised to take just about any amount of battering, or pollutant and was guaranteed decay resistant for at least a thousand years. Most considerate; he would outlive then all, most certainly.

Not that they seemed concerned over that. Quite the contrary. They in fact seemed thrilled by the whole affair. The young woman, Marie, was particularly ecstatic about the whole prospect: the romance and adventure ahead of him. The other one, Claymore, did not hold for the same enthusiasm but seemed to have a quietly personal sense of pleasure from Roland the Trout's expanding horizons amidst much suppressed anger. Roland his master was sad of course, but then this was clearly his doing. The moment of passing, the ceremonial handing over of the torch that they had both always known some day would happen, was being written this very moment. It was not however from Roland his master to another younger keener advisory as he had always thought likely, instead time had unfolded the ceremony to belong to Roland the Trout. He had heard his master say 'he has earned his right of passage.' The passage had turned out to be from the lake to the ocean.

There was another presence though, closer than the others, almost touching his own, practically sharing his space, though not quite. It was a woman's, a young woman's mind. Her name was Savannah..and he could talk with her.. if he so wished, which was unlikely.. then again the globe was large, and a thousand years a long time.. perhaps a conversation or so along the way may not be such a bad thing. Perhaps he would even share his enthusiasm for brass band music with her? He'd think on that for a while.

Perhaps later would be best. He had listened to them talking. This Savannah was very angry too. She and Claymore had exchanged sharp words as he had downloaded her from his chip into Roland's. She had still been shouting what was most definitely rude abuse at him long after the transaction was complete and he most certainly could no longer hear her. There also seemed to be a strange lilt to Claymore's tone when he said 'Meet your new friend.' Yes, later would be best.

The three stared out over the black surface - Roland the ocean going trout was gone. The ocean looked exactly the same as it had fifteen minutes earlier.

'I can't help thinking that we have been terribly cruel,' Marie blurted, almost as a panicked reaction to the anti climax of it all. 'I know that I agreed instantly to your *payback* suggestion, and that her betrayal killed Sands..but it seems so... ..malicious,' she said turning to Claymore, then added sadly 'Sands wouldn't have liked it.'

Claymore saying nothing turned his back to the ocean and lit up.

'I dropped a hint that I will be fishing off the south west coast of Gibraltar in 3 months time. 'I wouldn't be in the least surprised if my old friend pops up to feel the sun during my stay,' Roland said breaking the atmosphere.

Marie, now in tears again blurted 'So much for your.....*re-found humanity*..that's what Jinx called it. Or my Buddhist oath to honour all life,' she added quietly.'

'Well it is done now. There is nothing else for us here, we should go.' Roland said softly, putting his arm around Marie.

She turned to Claymore 'I am sorry. It is not that I blame you. I just feel... What did she want in return..for her treachery?'

'Download...cloned. Vortex had already promised her that anyway, but she was *impatient*.. regular and predictable flaw to her character, along with the fact that she was true Ronin.'

'Ronin?'

'Vortex once laughed at her...calling her *his* beautiful Ronin.. the term once given to mercenary Samurai who were without masters.'

'But - how could she get Senate to clone her with you still alive?'

Claymore let the question hang then said 'The deal I struck with them in delivering the disc undamaged carried more weight.'

'Well........I suppose she had it coming. Marie said in a slow hesitant tone. 'But why did *you* betray her? Jinx said she was your partner; that you shot her - on purpose.'

'I work alone. She was a target, like any other.'

'Perhaps she didn't see it like that - maybe *that's* why she betrayed you.'

Claymore looked at her hard. 'Perhaps – 'cept she didn't know.'

'Then the only winner is Vortex.'

'I think that was always the general idea.'

Marie returned her stare beyond the waves. 'Not always, Sands thought that she had beaten him. At least she died *believing* it.'

Claymore eyes narrowed. 'How?'

'Cathedral Town was the AIs' seat of power. He destroyed part of it, threatening them, enticing them to use the disc that he and Sands had succeeded in making them trust. He had *altered it* - to trap them here. To outflank them by returning to Shadowlands from where he could destroy their weakened ranks from behind. *Jinx - altered the disc* to prevent Vortex's return. To trap him in his own trap.

Sands let Vortex believe that he had won - she willingly gave her life to make his plan complete; to give it *authenticity* beyond any doubt.'

'And?'

'And - nothing - *Vortex stayed here*. He was strong enough to finish it from here, or perhaps he knew all along. Loki told me that it is almost over; that only minor skirmishes remain in Shadowlands, and that Vortex has easily destroyed those who took his bait. Vortex has won; he is all but Emperor of both dimensions - and is here to stay.'

Claymore turned his head to the ocean. 'We'll see about that.'

*****

Three months later...........

A solitary drop of glistening moisture, growing slowly fatter, clung to the sogging strap of the hand crafted aged leather, brown calf length boot; its mission, to swell and swell, intent on eventually gaining strength enough to break free, to dash itself upon the earth seven inches below.

Its silver-blue fragile skin *completely filled Vortex's chosen frame of vision*. 'The sky bleeds for you,' he heard her mutter; a voice too dry for tears. As the drop fell, its stretched elongated bag re-found its form through its millisecond journey to the cracked scabbed soil beneath her boot. As it splashed to its death.. *he expanded his frame of vision*..her heavy layered black cloth skirts wrapped loosely about her, lapping the top of her boot as she knelt, one knee to the ground, red incense spike burning sharply by her side, now filled his view.

He extended his frame of vision.. she filled the frame, her face hidden, shrouded in the same black cloth, head to the ground, her right arm raised, reaching for the sky, clutching at the air. Between thumb and palm she rolled a tiny slate, gold studded, laser tipped ceremonial blade. The prized right of a sacrificial Priestess of Shadowlands; hostess for anguished souls invited to delay in the land of the blind, in the black voids between the reefs of her plaited hair.

The full width of the valley now framed his vision.. heavily armoured horse soldiers, thousands upon thousands in a rippling endless line; black and cinnamon coloured robes flowing, partly tethered, over dripping wet, weather beaten leather and steel armour. A line stretching a half mile to her left and right..lancers at full charge. He was suddenly aware that there was no sound.

Full aerial panorama framed his vision.. the second army in full attack, similar numbers and formation riding head on..her now tiny image central to the rapidly closing gap..both armies moving at full gallop to clash where she knelt; her face now fully exposed, staring up through the fresh rain into the heavens themselves.. *THEN*..her voice, a beautiful voice of liquid silver floating at first, then *piercing* the air in chanted song - a wake up call to the Gods. It ricocheted through Germanic scaled mountains tipped with ice, threatened to shatter the crisp blue sky, blew snow from the peaks of conifers edging the higher slopes of the valley......then the thunder of war filled the air.

The interruption went un-heeded at first, then its persistence began to grate. *This* was his crescendo - the end and the beginning. 'This had better be good!' Vortex said switching his frame of vision from Shadowlands to the corridor monitor mounted on the wall. The officer at the other end looked pale and on edge, and had an ear missing. A narrow channel of blood ran down his cheek from beneath the freeze gel.

'And.....' Vortex asked, his voice reverberating in the air around the officer's head. The officer struggled to find a source to speak to then spoke more loudly than required into the room, standing to attention as if on parade. 'Claymore..Sir. An offi..Company employee by the name of Claymore has breached security Sir. In the command building in sector 2. Sir.'

'At what time?'

'Three hours twenty three minutes ago. Sir.'

'And why do you bring this *news* to me in person?'

'My Commanding Officer insisted on it Sir. The data in Claymore's possession triggered code black when touched within a roomed scan. Sir. Protocol requires immediate dispersal of such data by carrier personnel. Command have been attempting to contact you Sir.'

'And Claymore..?'

'He.. delivered the data,' the officer hesitated, 'and left. Sir.'

'Left?'

'Sir. Left. Sir. He specifically stressed that the package was for you in person. He said that *"it was half of something that you very much need the other half of."* He also said that *"things being as they were he would only part with the rest to you in person."* He provided co-ordinates which reference as a road. Sir.'

'And his demands?'

'He made no demands. Sir.'

The wall evaporated to the officers right and an unarmed soldier stepped forward relieving him of the disc. Four seconds later the wall was back in place. The officer resisted the urge to reach out and touch it.

'Thank you Captain. That will be all. Oh Captain.. what happened to your ear?' asked Vortex. A second later he finished the thought. 'Never mind.'

As the officer left, Vortex re-turned his attention to the battle raging in Shadowlands. He tilted his head slightly, in mocking respect to those who were dying in his name. The second phase armies, stretching far across the landscape formed the last of their kind. The army which faced them, standing in solid triangles was compact in comparison, but its uniform strength was starkly apparent. The battle was as good as won. Time had finally ran dry for his seasoned enemies. This day would belong to Loki and his other generals. The last stance of the magnanimous many against the organised might of its offspring - a new Empire had been born.

His mind wandered back to his new dilemma. Claymore - what to do? Well..it *had* been a while, longer than he had anticipated. His numero uno mercenary..it would be *interesting* to have him back on the team. Sounded like that may take some considered play though.

Then it struck him. *Trolls* - that was the answer. If they were to meet on Claymore's terms.. might as well continue where they finished.

*****

The purple heather glinted white under the three quarter moon. Clouds slid beneath it moving faster than nature was expected to allow, reminding her of youthful dreams and visions of a druid ancestral past, and drawing a broken silver horizontal line across her proud Celtic cheekbones.

Wet tyres cruising casual fast; rear slide, auto adjust front wheels; relaxed introverted motion. Her mind on other things. Razors, the locals called them; plastic post war 5.1m *exact* width paint jobs burned across the mountainous terrain wherever the natural slope allowed. Minimal cost. Local habitats simply died or lived under them. Everywhere and welcomingly fast. The surface held even the cheapest tyres beautifully, kind of sucked them in. Roads manufactured by the major players in tyre manufacture.

Vortex - no mistaking where the eighty tonnes of steel transport had bruised the road; four fat Trolls locked in where you would normally expect headlights - was already there. He clearly, had never intended to drive the length of the road, instead parked angled across its centre.. and patiently waited.

He was standing by the vehicle, dwarfed by its presence. She had doubted that he would actually come, despite Claymore's assurances. Well - here he was. There had always been an eerie understanding between the two that she had never understood.

Sleek; her hair was black dyed. Jet. For the occasion - the all matching panorama of singular vision designed to catch the all important millisecond of his attention needed for seeing this part of her job through. Black hair..black car..black skid marks on the black plastic road..black loose T shirt..black short tight dress..black silk stockings..as she slid from the seat - bright blue piercing eyes illuminated his face.

'*Savannah!*' his face lit up like a rabbit frozen in headlights.

She was now standing three metres from him, her compact handgun held casually by her side.

'Ah - looks like our friend Claymore decided to give you a reprieve. How generous of him. How... humane. I take it that he also told you that it was I who ordered your termination in the first place,' he laughed looking bored. 'Well - yes I admit.....that it must have all been a bit disconcerting for you,' he said in her silence. 'So - *what do you want*? What will it take to make it up to you?'

Her silence continued as if lost for words. Then she slowly said 'He put me ....*in a fish!*'

He stared back at her blankly, as if to say 'What in the world is your problem?'

'Have you ever met *that* fish?' she replied.

He smiled genuinely amused. 'What do you want?'

'Want!.... Never... underestimate a women, an AK compact, or the after effects of three months solitaire with Roland the Trout.' Thump...Thump...Thump............ ...Thump..Thump. Seconds passed.. he slumped to his knees head bent into his chest. Black pearl ghostlike eyes glazed shut. She could have sworn that she heard the opening three bars of Carmina Burana signal the rain to stop. It had been raining blue steel.....

The Trolls slid from their housing bolted to the rig and landed with dull clanks on the plastic ground. All four waddled into her view, in no real hurry, having assessed her fire power and concluded that they were under minimum threat.

She was twenty metres from her jeep which had started to move towards her on her command - as the first Troll's head exploded, followed rapidly by four quick shots in succession; armoured piercing AK shells from the sniper in the heather cutting deep into their body armour, exploding milliseconds later, sending heavy lumps of metal and balls of molten graphite spinning the short distance to her feet.

She placed her boot on the melted part shoulder of a silenced Troll and *slowly* scanned the array of autumn colour, the dark crags, and the shadows of dips where streams cut through the sturdy undergrowth of the highland valley. She searched for the slightest hint of motion, sound or body heat, and knowing that she was only doing what the Trolls would have already done, found what she had expected - nothing. Only silence, amongst the sound of water dripping through the heather.

'Well what do yuh know. Icy.

The End

Randall Mac is working on his next novel.

Savannah is back.....

I took a freight train to my head. Her name was.... Savannah. Southern drawl; short thick golden hair, untold mystery in each weighted silken fold, like a Gypsy-Viking descended from the bearded father of Asgard; slim athletic curves stolen from a statue of the halls of his gods. A face etched from frozen clouds.... brought alive by a smile that would destroy my life.

35924624R00163

Made in the USA
Charleston, SC
21 November 2014